She was overmatched. Seduction was a game whose rules she did not understand— a game of which she had neither experience nor understanding. A game she should not have rushed to play. Not with him.

Now she watched his hands wrap the twine about her wrists over and over, wishing she could go back in time. She wanted to feel his arms engulfing her again. She wished to drink again from those strong, capable hands and to kiss each of his fingers a dozen times.

Seth's blood, she was a fool. She could not accept her desire for him. Her body had acted against direct orders from her mind. But it had been more than that. It had been as if the moment he had embraced her all the disordered parts of herself had fallen neatly into line, and she'd wanted to stay with him like that forever.

Or maybe the Red Land had finally driven her mad.

Author Note

Five thousand years ago a civilization emerged in the Nile River valley to become one of the most enduring the world has ever known. For three thousand years it thrived, isolated by desert and sea and sustained by the river Nile itself.

We know it as ancient Egypt—though the Egyptians themselves called their kingdom Khemet, or Black Land, after the rich black silt deposited by the Nile's annual flood. The silt nourished crops, feeding one million souls and filling the coffers of Khemetian god kings—not called pharaohs until circa 1400 BCE—who used their wealth to build spectacular tombs.

Perhaps the greatest such tomb, King Khufu's Great Pyramid, inspired this story. For centuries the Great Pyramid has been the subject of intense scrutiny, yet many of its mysteries remain unsolved. Recently some researchers have argued that the Great Pyramid hides chambers containing King Khufu's funeral cache. If found, such an undisturbed hoard of wealth would rival King Tutankhamun's tomb as one of the greatest archaeological discoveries ever.

We might never know all the Great Pyramid's secrets, but we can dream. And we can imagine the people who labored to build and raid it. Their lives might not have been so different from ours after all. Like us, they lived in a time of climatic uncertainties and vexing social inequalities, but also a time of amazing discoveries and miraculous feats. And like us, they shared that most enduring wonder of all—love.

I hope you enjoy their story!

GRETA GILBERT

Enslaved by
the Desert Trader

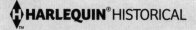

Recycling programs
for this product may
not exist in your area.

ISBN-13: 978-0-373-29894-5

Enslaved by the Desert Trader

Copyright © 2016 by Greta Gilbert

Printed in U.S.A.

www.Harlequin.com

Greta Gilbert's passion for ancient history began with a teenage crush on Indiana Jones. As an adult, she landed a dream job at National Geographic Learning, where her colleagues—former archaeologists—helped her learn to keep her facts straight. Now she lives in South Baja, Mexico, where she continues to study the ancients. She is especially intrigued by ancient mysteries, and always keeps a little Indiana Jones inside her heart.

Books by Greta Gilbert

Harlequin Historical

Enslaved by the Desert Trader

Harlequin Historical *Undone!* ebook

Mastered by Her Slave

Visit the Author Profile page at Harlequin.com.

For Diane Noble and Paul Gilbert
(aka Mom and Dad)

Chapter One

Memphis, Khemet, year twenty-three in the Reign of King Khufu, 2566 BCE

The serpent's tongue tickled her toes. It glided over her foot without fear, as if daring her to move. Its horns were large enough for her to see them clearly, even in the low morning light. Kiya sucked in a breath. Of the hundreds of men standing in the grain line, the horned viper had chosen her—the one man who was no man at all. It was just her ill fortune. After a full season of labouring undiscovered upon the Great Pyramid of Stone her life was now threatened by a creature the size of a chisel.

The men in the line near her had not noticed. Not yet. They continued to chatter, folding and unfolding the empty grain sacks they carried, their bare feet shuffling in the sand. They had all gathered—the quarrymen, the masons, the haulers—hundreds upon hundreds of pyramid conscripts, all awaiting their promised allotment of grain. They stood in a single sprawling line that encircled the Great Pyramid like a snare.

'Move on, brother,' urged a voice behind Kiya, but

she pretended not to hear. If she lifted her foot the viper would surely bite her, and she would have to stifle her scream—the scream of a woman.

She opened her palms to the sky and lifted her eyes heavenward, for no one could lawfully disrupt an act of prayer. *Blessed Wadjet, Serpent Goddess,* she beseeched in silence, *let the viper pass.* Still the viper did not move. It was as if the giant pyramid at her side were blocking her plea.

King Khufu's House of Eternity was not just a pyramid—it was a mountain splitting the sky. Now almost complete, the giant tomb would be ready to receive King Khufu when his time came. It would conduct the great King to the heavens, where he would secure the safety and abundance of Khemet for all time.

Or so said the priests.

The holy men who oversaw the construction of the tomb wore fine linens. They walked with their arms folded across their chests, self-satisfied and proud. But their priestly posture belied an insidious truth: it had been twenty-four full moons since the last flood—two terribly trying years. The Great River was but a stream—no longer navigable by the large imperial barges. Its life-giving waters had ceased to teem with the silvery perch and tilapia that normally filled Khemetian bellies. The riverside plantations of flax, barley and wheat—once green with growth—now stood barren and cracked.

The people of Khemet, too, were cracking. Their sacred Black Land—named for the colour of the rich, life-giving earth of the Great River's floodplain—had become brown and lifeless. Every day Khemetians grew thinner and hungrier. The priests assured them that the fate of Khemet would change once the Great Pyramid was complete.

But the tomb workers, whose food rations grew sparser each day, wondered if Khemet wasn't instead being punished. As they pulled their stone-laden carts up the dark, twisting inner tunnel they whispered among themselves: *What if King Khufu's ambition has grown too great? What if this tomb displeases the King's heavenly father, Osiris, God of Death and Rebirth? What if, with the stacking of each stone, we are not exalting the land of Khemet but dooming it to death?*

Kiya always kept her head down in the tunnel—and held her mouth shut. 'Mute Boy' she was called among her gang, and her strange infirmity cloaked her with an air of mystery that distracted them from her concealed gender. It was a useful part of her ruse, and necessary. A woman labouring upon the Great Pyramid of Stone was a sin against the King himself. If she were found out she would be punished. Under King Khufu, that punishment would likely be death.

Now the viper coiled itself more tightly around Kiya's ankle. She could feel its muscles squeezing her, its tongue gently caressing her skin. It was preparing to bite. When it did, the poison would quickly paralyse her, and death would come on swift feet. She opened her hands and mouthed the words: *Wadjet, I beseech you.*

'There will be time to pray later,' insisted the man behind her. 'Close the gap.'

He had spoken verily: she had allowed a gap to form in the line ahead of her. She needed to distract him. Impulsively, she pointed her finger eastward, towards the Great River, as if there were some significant sight to observe there. But something *was* there—or someone, rather. It was a man—a rider. His mounted silhouette made a sharp shadow against the paleness of the dawn.

'Who is that?' asked the man behind her.

Kiya shook her head. The rider was unusually large and broad-shouldered, as if he spent his days ploughing fields or hauling stones. He rode a strange hoofed beast whose long legs and thick, luxuriant tail set it apart from a familiar donkey. His flowing dark robes marked him as a Libu, an enemy of Khemet, yet his stature and carriage indicated other origins. He unwrapped his headdress and began waving it in the air above him vigorously, as if in warning. Then his figure dissolved instantly—obscured in the eruption of the Sun God's light.

Kiya shielded her eyes and glanced downward. To her surprise, her tiny foe was gone—disappeared, just like the rider. But there was little time to celebrate for she felt the ground beneath her begin to tremble. In the place where the rider had been there was now a cloud of dust. Then they materialised—an army of men, advancing towards the pyramid at great speed.

'Libu!' someone shouted.

The men in line scattered, but Kiya could not bring herself to move. There must have been a thousand of them—rugged, robed raiders whose shrill battle cries invaded Kiya's ears and filled her with terror. Some rode atop donkeys, but most came on relentless feet. As they approached they unleashed their arrows upon the tomb workers. A dozen of Kiya's fellow workers were struck instantly, collapsing where they stood. The rest ran. Some sought refuge inside the Great Pyramid itself. Others escaped into the desert.

Kiya dropped to the ground, playing dead. She counted her breaths. One. Two. Three. Slowly the rain of arrows abated. Kiya opened her eyes to find the Libu raiders gathering around the grain tent. It was as Kiya suspected: the Libu had not come for war. They had come to the plain of Giza for the same reason she had—for that thing that had become, after two years of drought, more precious than gold: grain.

This could not be. Kiya needed her grain. She had earned her allotment of it. And she had been so close, so very close to receiving it.

'Run!' a man yelled from far away, but Kiya did not heed him. She had no family, and not a single *aroura* of land to her name. Without her ration of grain she would have to return to a life on the streets of Memphis—to the life of a beggar.

And that she simply refused to do.

Slowly, she stood. She gripped her grain sack and, in the confusion of Khemetians running away from the grain tent, began to run towards it.

She wrapped the empty sack around her head like a turban. She was a Libu now, a new kind of imposter. On swift legs she darted among the Libu donkeys, and the animals' large bodies concealed her and protected her from the chaos.

Outside the grain tent few Khemetian guards remained alive. Their wooden shields had not been able to protect them. Like sacred bulls on feasting day the soldiers were being pierced, one by one, by Libu spears and arrows.

It was a grisly slaughter. So much Khemetian blood was spilt upon the sands. But Kiya could not afford to panic or to mourn. She rushed past the battling men and rolled under the tent's loose hide. Inside, a pile of grain the size of a temple rose before her. She did not stop to gaze or even to think. She just took off her sack and started stuffing it, until it was so heavy with grain she could barely lift it. She did not even hear the ripping sound of her shirt as she rolled over the rough ground back out into the fray.

She could hardly see for the storm of dust outside the tent. She crouched low and kept the sack close to her body. The acrid smell of blood thickened the air and she choked for breath as she dashed eastward, towards the Great River.

As she ran she noticed that her shirt was gone, and that the wraps she had bound so tightly about her chest had been ripped. The tattered strips of fabric hung from her waist like a tailor's loose strands and she felt the warm air upon her naked breasts. Her sex was exposed, but it did not matter for her sack was filled.

In fact it overflowed. She carried a windfall of grain— vastly more than she would have been allotted by the priests. And it was all hers. She hoisted it onto her back and felt her spirit grow large. It would be more than enough grain to sustain her through a full cycle of the sun. If she travelled far enough upriver she might even be able to find a plot of land to till and plant. She could trade some grain for her rent and await the flood, as farmers did.

She adjusted her course towards the southeast and be- came resolved: she would not be returning to the capi- tal city. Never again would she skulk around its docks searching for fish heads, or roam the central market hop- ing to discover an onion peel or a half-eaten radish. With her boon of grain she would finally be free of want, fi- nally merit her countrymen's respect.

She heaved the bag onto the ground and shook her fist

at the sky. 'Is that all you have for me, evil Seth, God of Chaos?' she shouted. 'For that is nothing!'

Suddenly an arrow flew past her. Then another. She ducked her head, afraid to turn around. She heard the thunder of heavy hooves behind her—not a donkey, something larger. They pounded the ground like drum-beats. They were getting louder, closer. She hoisted the sack upon her back once again and coaxed her legs to run, but soon the large donkey-like creature was upon her. Its rider's large, muscular arm reached down and wrapped itself around her body, and she and her sack were being lifted off the ground and into the air.

'Do not fight,' whispered a thick, husky voice into her ear. 'Now you are mine.'

Chapter Two

If it had not been for their mindless blood sport he never would have spotted her. Sickened by the massacre—the senseless loss of life—Tahar had let his eyes seek refuge upon the horizon. That was when he'd noticed her distant figure. She'd been running towards the Great River with a bag so full of grain that she'd scarcely been able to keep it off the ground. But it was not the bag that had caught his eye. It was the way her body had moved across the plain. Her small exposed breasts had swung to and fro in an awkward, seductive way—the way of a woman.

What was she doing there at all? It was well known that Khemetians did not allow women to labour directly upon the King's tomb. Women were thought to be too closely tied to the beginning of earthly life to be associated with the passage at its end.

And yet there she'd been—a woman to be sure. If she had been wearing a shirt or tunic he might have missed her completely, for in all other ways she was like a man: tall, thin, with taut, muscular limbs that gave no hint of feminine softness. She wore no wig, and her worker's perfectly shaven head shone like burnished copper in the morning sun.

She had the spirit of a man as well—or so he had discovered as she'd kicked and flailed atop his horse. So energetic had been her rebellion that she had given him no choice but to stop at the first oasis he could find to secure her bonds.

He stood above her now, admiring his work. She was seated against the trunk of a date palm, her ankles and wrists wrapped with twine he had wound three fingers thick. The palm gave little shade, and he smiled with satisfaction as he watched the hot sun melt away any remaining notions she might have of escape.

'I know that you are thirsty,' Tahar said at last. He squatted on the ground beside her and placed his water bag at her lips. 'Drink now, for we cannot linger here.'

The stubborn woman refused to drink. Instead, she pursed her lips together and shook her head.

He studied her angry face. She was no goddess—not yet. But she had potential. Her bones were fine and displayed excellent symmetry. Even in her emaciated state her lips were red and plump, and long, arched eyebrows hung high above her big dark eyes, giving her an air of readiness and making her scowl appear almost charming.

Tahar took a draught from the water bag himself. 'Do you see?' he asked. 'It is just water. You must drink. Quickly.'

The Libu raiders would be swarming every oasis from the Great River to the Big Sandy soon, celebrating their success. If they discovered Tahar and the woman they would insist that she be sold into marriage and would demand their share of her bride price. That was the rule amongst the desert tribes—spoils were divided equally.

But Tahar knew that, with any likely suitor absent, the raiders would demand their fair share of the woman herself—a possibility he simply could not tolerate.

He held out the bag again. 'Drink,' he commanded, 'for we must keep moving.'

'Why do you speak the Khemetian tongue?' she asked, and gave a small jump, as if surprised by the sound of her own voice.

'I am a trader. I speak many tongues.'

'You are a Libu raider. A murderer.' Her brown eyes flashed and her cheeks flushed with a fetching shade of crimson.

'I am neither a raider nor a Libu—not any more.'

'But you bear the Libu scar,' she said, her eyes fixing on the purple crescent framing the side of his eye.

'And *you* bear the callused hands of a man,' Tahar replied coolly. 'That does not make you one.' He placed his water bag near her hands, in case she might accept it.

'Just because you have tied me in bonds it does not make me a slave.'

'Then we are both imposters.'

'Hem!' she snarled, then batted the water bag out of his hands.

'Foolish woman!' Tahar shouted, watching the bag's precious contents spill onto the sand. 'Now I shall have to draw water from the oasis pool and boil it. It will be many hours before we drink again.'

He grabbed her arm in anger and an invisible spark seemed to ignite the air between them. He released her arm and she returned her remorseless gaze to the sun-baked desert.

'You are a Libu monster,' she muttered.

'And you are a Khemetian to the bone,' he said.

'*How* am I "a Khemetian to the bone"?'

'You are spoiled and superior, as if the Gods themselves sanction your decadence.'

'If you think ordinary Khemetians to be decadent, then you truly are dull,' she said, and a small tear pooled in the corner of her eye.

Tahar stood and placed the empty water bottle in his saddlebag. Better to wait for her to beg for it—something she would do quite soon, he was sure. Thirst was a powerful motivator.

As is hunger, he thought, stealing a glance at her small white breasts.

No—he would not conquer her body. He would not even think of it, though he admitted that he wished to. Taking her would be like drinking wine from the *amphora* you meant to trade.

He removed his headdress and draped the garment over her shining head. 'You must shield your skin from the sun,' he told her, laughing as her head disappeared beneath the fabric. 'What do you call it? La?' he mocked.

'The Sun God is Ra—blessed Ra. May he punish you severely,' she stated, but her voice was muffled by the thick fabric, making Tahar laugh.

'Gods do not care about *us*, silly woman. I have seen enough of the world now to know that it is so.'

'What can you possibly have seen to give you knowledge of the Gods?' she mumbled from beneath the fabric.

'I have seen the beds of ancient rivers that once flowed over this very oasis, and the bones of creatures unimaginable to us. I have seen paintings on rocks deep in the desert. They show people swimming like fish. Swimming! The Gods may be mighty, but they care little about us. We are temporary.' Tahar paused. 'We are…whispers in the grass.'

The woman was quiet for some time, as if trying to picture all the things he had described. At length, she spoke. 'Are you going to violate me, then? I am…'

'A virgin? I could tell that just by looking at you,' he said. It was a welcome confirmation of his belief, for it would raise her bride price significantly.

'Are you going to kill me?'

'Of course not.' *You are more valuable than all the salt in the Fezzan.*

The woman exhaled. Moving her bound hands with agility, she pulled the headdress off her head and gathered it around her lithe, muscular body.

He would have to fatten her up, of course. No rich Minoan sea captain or powerful Nubian chief would trade anything of value for such a scrawny, sinuous bride. Proper Khemetian clothing and adornments would need to be procured, as well. And her eyes would need to be kohled, and her lips hennaed in the fashionable manner. Finally, her hair must be allowed to grow. Though most wellborn Khemetian women wore wigs upon their shaved heads, Tahar knew that foreign traders preferred the real thing.

He would have to train her—just as he had done with his father's horse: tame her and give her time to swallow her fate. He would need to be wary, for Khemetian women were accustomed to more freedoms than women of the desert tribes. Given the opportunity, a Khemetian woman would take her advantage—or so he had discovered at the Houses of Women he frequented along the caravan routes. A Khemetian woman would rub your back while unclasping your necklace. She would nibble your earlobes while pillaging your saddlebags.

Still, after he had quieted her will and thickened her flanks there would be no trader able to resist the healthy young bride. She was Khemetian, after all—a goddess from the land blessed by the Gods—and she was going to make Tahar rich.

The woman cocked her head and looked up at him, her expression drained of pride. 'Please, let me go,' she begged. She lifted her bound hands beseechingly. 'I must return to my home. My mother and sister will not survive without the grain I carry...carried.' She blinked, and a lone tear traced a path down her dusty face.

Tahar felt his stomach twist into a knot. Her intentions seemed laudable. She apparently wished to save her family, to relieve their hunger. *Careful, man. A Khemetian woman will say whatever she needs to say.*

'The Great River will swell in only three more cycles of the moon,' he assured her. 'The flood will be late, but it will come. Your family will survive. Do not fear for them.'

'But how can you know when the Great River will flood? You are not a priest or a seer. You cannot know the future. You are a liar, a trader—'

'That is all!' Tahar snapped. He would not abide her disparagement of his profession, lowly though it was. It had kept him alive all these years, and in the good favour of his tribe and the merchants he served. 'You should give thanks for your life.'

'And what do you intend to *do* with that life?' she asked sharply, her lip betraying a tremble. Her eyes were so large and luminous. They challenged and begged all at once.

'I—' Tahar searched his mind, trying to remember his intentions. 'You will make an excellent bride. I intend to trade you.'

'Trade me? In exchange for what?'

'For a boat.'

'A boat? What will you do with a boat? Carry your sheep in it?' Boldness swelled in her bosom. 'You are Libu—a desert-dweller. Are you not?'

'Not any more. Now I am only Tahar. Tahar the Trader.' *Tahar the soon-to-be sailor, thanks to you, my lovely.*

He smiled to himself. He would find this fiery little viper a rich merchant husband, use the proceeds to get himself a boat, and they would all be the better for it.

'I am taking my horse to drink at the pool,' he announced, untethering the steed. 'We shall depart as soon as I return.' He walked several paces towards the pool, then mustered his most menacing voice: 'Do not even think about trying to escape.'

Chapter Three

There is nothing eternal but the Gods, Kiya told herself, watching the trader disappear into the thick willow and tamarisk foliage surrounding the oasis pool. She pressed her bonds across the jagged ribs of the date palm. *Everything else is temporary.*

The twine was made of unusual green fibres—not papyrus, something finer. Hemp, perhaps. It was exceptionally strong, but Kiya knew that even the strongest bonds could be broken. She had seen captive crocodiles do it with ease. If they could do it, why not Kiya?

What she could *not* do was become a slave. She had seen them on the streets of Memphis. They followed their owners like dogs, their shoulders slumped, their eyes cloudy and lifeless. Nay—she would rather die and become lost in the corridors of the Underworld than serve someone else in this one.

Not that the trader cared a fig about what she thought or felt. He had not wavered, even when she had told him about her starving family, of the souls who stood to perish if she did not return.

It had been a lie, of course. She did not have a starving family. She did not have anyone at all, in fact. But it didn't matter: he had failed the test. He, like most of his profession, was soulless, completely without a *ka*. And his certainty of the coming flood was beyond arrogance. Only a seer or High Priest could ever know such a thing. Certainly not a *trader*.

She rubbed the twine against the rough palm ribs and soon tiny ribbons of smoke began to weave into the air. She intensified her effort, remembering his stinging words. *Foolish and decadent*, he had called her. *Spoiled and superior*. Was that what the Libu thought of the Khemetians? Was that how they justified their raids?

The trader had denied being a Libu, though he bore the Libu scar—a brutish, crescent-shaped gash beside his eye. And he wore the long purple robes of a Libu, though they did not suit him. His broad, deeply contoured chest stretched against the thin fabric, threatening to break the seams. And his strange, liquid blue eyes suggested unusual origins. He was quite attractive, in truth.

For a fiend.

Her hands burst apart. She quickly untied her feet and leapt into a run. The soft sand gave beneath her, revealing her footprints, but soon she spied a patch of hardpan. She headed towards it, not stopping until her footprints were no longer visible upon the naked ground. Then she stopped. She had an idea. Carefully, she began to walk backwards in the very same footprints she had made.

This he would not expect. He would follow her footprints east, towards the Great River. Meanwhile, she would be in hiding back at the oasis, where he would eventually return, defeated and exhausted, and quickly fall asleep. He would not even hear the gentle hoofbeats of his strange beast as she rode it off into the night.

By the Gods, she wished it were night already, and not so impossibly hot. The Sun God bored into her skull, melting her thoughts and sapping all that was left of her strength. As her head began to swim a memory flooded in... 'Stay awake, Mother,' young Kiya whispered, crouching by her mother's side in the shadowy chamber. 'We must try to escape.'

Evil men had breached the walls of the harem and invaded the concubines' chambers. The panicked women and children had been running barefoot past the doorway of her mother's chamber, seeking their escape beyond the harem walls.

'Come with me, little one,' a voice had urged.

It had been one of the escaping concubines. She had stopped in her mother's doorway and held her hand out to Kiya.

'Come now, we have little time.' The woman had glanced at the empty vials that littered the floor beneath the bedframe. 'You must leave your mother here. Already she has begun her journey.'

'My daughter will sssstay with me!' Kiya's mother had slurred, rousing herself from her stupor. 'Leave us to our fate!' Her eyes had rolled back in her head. 'Beware the three serpents, my daughter,' she'd told Kiya, gripping her small arm. 'Each will try to take your life.'

'She is not in her right mind, dear,' the woman in the doorway had said. 'Come quickly!'

'The third will succeed,' her mother had continued. 'Unless you become like—'

Her mother's grip had been too strong—Kiya hadn't been able to pull away. 'Mama, please. We must flee. The bad men are coming!'

'All men are bad, Kiya. Remember, they only wish to possess you, to enslave you.'

By the time Kiya's mother had finally released Kiya's arm the woman in the doorway had gone.

'Conceal yourself under the bed,' Kiya's mother had instructed. She'd reached for the largest of the vials, uncorked the bottle, and drunk down its cloudy contents. 'Do not fear, my beautiful little daughter. They will not find you. And they will not take me alive.'

Kiya had felt hot tears rolling down her cheeks. 'Please do not go, Mama! Do not leave me alone.'

But Kiya's mother had lain her head upon her wooden headrest for the last time and slipped soundlessly into her world of dreams.

'Beware the three serpents,' whispered her mother's voice again now.

Startled, Kiya looked all around her. There was not a single soul in sight.

'Each will try to take your life,' the voice resounded.

Kiya looked up at the sky, half expecting to see her mother's face staring down at her. There was nothing. She looked to the ground, as if at any moment a serpent might materialise upon her foot.

'The third will succeed, unless you become like...'
Like what?

Kiya slapped herself on the cheek. The skin on her head had begun to boil and her mouth was dry, as if full of fibres. She knew that if she did not get out of the sun soon she would quickly lose her will to do it. Abandoning her plan, she broke into a run, heading as fast as she could back to the oasis, where the trader was nowhere to be seen. Heedless of anything but her own smouldering skin and desperate thirst, she dived into the oasis pool and let the cool water caress her. She drank her fill, then disappeared into the depths.

When she finally emerged for a breath she heard men's voices, nearing the pool. They were speaking in a deep, guttural tongue that she recognised immediately. *Libu.*

Her heart hammered as she cowered into a shady stand of flute reeds growing in the water on the far bank. She found the longest of the reeds and snapped it in half, then sank down against the bank, breathing slowly through the natural straw.

In moments a group of men arrived at the pool's edge. Their blurred figures were difficult to see through the water, but Kiya noticed their purple headdresses and the long copper blades that hung from their belts. The men spoke excitedly—joyfully, even. As their donkeys bent to drink, Kiya could see the animals' saddlebags bulging with grain.

Khemetian grain.

Kiya felt her heart pinch with hatred. They were Libu raiders, for certain. Their joy was the Khemetians' doom. All the workers—the thousands of peaceful farmers whom Kiya had joined in service to the King—would now return to their homes empty-handed because of these evil men. Many of the Khemetian farmers would not return home at all.

Kiya struggled to keep her breaths even and swore she would have her revenge. The Sun God would soon be on his nightly voyage to the Underworld and the murderous villains would be to bed. The Moon God would rise, and Kiya would execute her escape plan anew.

Curses on the trader, for she no longer needed him.

She had a band of Libu to plunder from instead. Besides, if her captor were any kind of trader he would have quickly understood the threat they represented to his grain. He and his strange, oversized donkey were probably halfway across the Big Sandy by now.

Chapter Four

But she was mistaken.

He slid down noiselessly into the water next to Kiya. He might have been a stranger, for he wore nothing upon his head, nor any distinguishing clothing. His chest was bare, and strands of his long yellow-brown hair floated languidly around his face like threads of smoke. Kiya knew him only by the two cerulean eyes staring out at her. Their colour was incomprehensibly blue, their gaze so deep and steady they might have belonged to a statue of an ancient god.

His arm slipped behind her back and she felt his hand grip her waist. Gently, he floated her body in front of his and pulled her against him. She could feel the hard, rippling contours of his stomach against her back as he nestled them against the bank.

Kiya did not know what to do. If she fought him she would reveal them both. What had he told her? That he no longer claimed to be Libu. If that was so, then perhaps he was in as much danger as she.

She held her breath as he took the hollow reed from her fingers and pressed it to his own lips, drawing in a deep

breath then returning it to her mouth. They passed the
breathing reed back and forth in this manner as the Libu
men began to retreat from the bank one by one. His arm
surrounded her waist and kept her body pressed tightly
against his, making her feel oddly safe.

Soon she began to feel something else as well. A growing firmness where her backside pressed against his hips.
Neither his loose-fitting pants nor her voluminous wrap
could conceal it in their folds. *That.*

At the advanced age of twenty-three, Kiya would have
never guessed herself capable of stirring a man's desire.
Indeed, she had worked quite hard throughout her life to
achieve the opposite effect. Did this man who wished to
sell her in fact desire her? Or was this simply what happened when that part of a man came into contact with
a woman's body? Surely it was the latter, for Kiya was
not the kind of woman men desired. Fie—she was not
the kind of woman men could usually even detect *was*
a woman.

Kiya gazed up through the water. The Libu raiders
were dispersing. She counted only two lingering on the
far bank. A large insect glided across the surface of the
water above them and a water snake swam languidly
past. Meanwhile, the trader's growing desire had found
its resting place in the cleft of her backside.

It was the first time in her life that she had been this
close to a man. She might have moved to the side, but the
sensation was not altogether unpleasant. As a test, she
allowed herself to imagine what it would be like to feel
him *there*. That was what happened when a man took a
woman, was it not?

She pictured the act, for she had heard the tomb workers discuss it in detail, and had seen it depicted in the

reliefs carved upon the gates of Hathor's temple. In this case he would not be above her, as the reliefs often depicted. He might lift her by the waist, for example, and then settle her upon him, pushing himself into her. But how could that be? How could she possibly contain him? For a moment an unfamiliar pain akin to hunger shot through her, then it was gone.

No, there it was again.

To further the test, she pushed gently against his firmness, giving resistance, and thought she could feel him grow firmer still. Was this the power of a woman? Was this the fantastic faculty that the storytellers sang of in the taverns? And was this the beginning of the act that the young men sketched in the alleyways of Memphis, chuckling conspiratorially?

If it was, then she might be interested. Perhaps.

But not with a murderer. And *never* as a slave.

The trader's hands pulled her against him more tightly. She knew she needed to escape his grasp, for her body was starting to move against her will. But escape was impossible, for there was still one Libu raider left at the pool. He was standing motionless at the water's edge.

He appeared to be looking right at them.

Kiya froze. The man could not see them. They were underwater, in shadow, and concealed by a patch of reeds. Her heart pounded so hard that she imagined it creating a ripple. Tahar, too, seemed to have noticed, for he squeezed her gently. *Hold still*, his hands told her.

The Libu man walked to their side of the pool and stood above the stand of reeds. He pulled his long sword from its sheath and began poking it into the water. The sword probed to the left of Kiya, then to the right. Kiya held her breath.

Chapter Five

The sword's penetration into her arm was not deep, but Tahar watched as it shattered her senses. Pierced as the woman was, even the mightiest of warriors would not have been able to stifle a cry, and as they floated to the surface he knew he could not prevent her coming scream—the scream of a woman.

'Ah!' she cried in pain.

'Hazah!' Tahar yelled, covering her voice with his own.

He grabbed the Libu man's ankle and pulled him into the pool. Amidst the splash of water Tahar pulled her close. 'Swallow your agony,' he whispered frantically. 'And keep your mouth shut. He must not know that you are a woman.'

The Libu man surfaced. 'Villain!' he shouted at Tahar.

Tahar eased the woman behind him. 'You have discovered me, brother,' he said, splashing water at his tribesman playfully. 'You were the only one who even came close!' He could feel the warmth of the woman's blood draining into the water all around him. 'Dakka, you scoundrel,' Tahar continued lightly. 'You've damaged my slave.'

'I did not see him,' Dakka spluttered, casting a quick glance over Tahar's shoulder. 'And you've made me release my sword.' The young man scanned the surface of the pool.

'Well, go and fetch it, man,' chided Tahar, 'before the Khemetian Pool God consumes it!'

Dakka scowled, then drew a deep breath and plunged into the depths.

Tahar turned to the woman. 'You are my slave now. Do you hear? You are again a young man.' Tahar pulled at the part of her headdress that she had spooled over her head and wrapped it around her wound. 'Let the men see your bald head. Keep your eyes down and do not speak. Do everything I command.'

Dakka resurfaced, his gleaming copper sword held high. 'It needed a good cleaning anyway,' he stated. 'Khemetian blood makes an ugly stain.'

Ugly indeed, thought Tahar. The woman remained in the pool while the two men hoisted themselves up the bank and embraced. 'You ride with a large party?' asked Tahar.

'Nay, there are but a dozen or so. Some from the Libu tribes of Garamantia, the rest the Libu of the Sardana region, including the Chief. The only Libu from the Meshwesh region is myself—and now you, brother. But where is your...beast?' Dakka's eyes searched the perimeter of the pool.

'It is called a *horse*, Dakka,' Tahar said with feigned annoyance. 'How many times must I remind you? It is tethered in the shade of the acacia bushes yonder.' Tahar pointed vaguely beyond the pool, watching out of the corner of his eye as the woman strained to pull herself from the water.

'Since when do you own a slave?' Dakka pressed.

'Since this morning, of course.' *Now cease your questioning.*

Dakka's gaze settled upon the woman's sopping figure. Thankfully Tahar's ample headdress concealed her breasts and thighs well. At length, the young man smiled. 'Then well done, brother, for you are one of very few to obtain one.' Dakka unwrapped his headdress and his long dark hair fell around his shoulders.

'Oh?'

'We sought to collect slaves after we'd finished with the guards, but by then the tomb workers had all disappeared.' Dakka squeezed his hair and twisted it into a bun.

'They escaped into the tomb, doubtless,' said Tahar, shaking his own shoulder-length hair and placing it behind his ears. 'I have often wondered what lies within that mountain of stone.'

'Surely riches beyond our dreams,' said Dakka. 'But sealed in secret chambers we shall never know. Chief Bandir found the workers' entrance soon after the raid. It led to a tunnel that plunged beneath the earth, but we found nothing in it.'

The woman stationed herself in the shade just behind Tahar, concealing herself well.

'Neither gold nor slaves?'

Dakka shook his head. 'Chief Bandir was enraged. "Where did they go?" he yelled, but soon gave up. The tomb workers' settlement was also without reward—not one miserable soul to be found. But the raid wasn't completely fruitless. There was more grain than we could carry, and three large sacrificial bulls were discovered near the boat pit.' Dakka rubbed his engorged belly. 'Two hundred Libu feasted on food marked for the Khemetian Gods! You missed the banquet.'

'I had my prize. I wished to be on my way,' Tahar said, glancing back at the woman. The blood had already begun to soak through the fabric around her arm.

'Indeed,' said Dakka, 'though the boy appears rather... gaunt. Do you think he will endure the journey back to your tribe's camp?'

'We shall see. It is less likely now that his ability to survive has been greatly diminished by the sting of your blade.'

The veiled compliment had its desired effect, for Dakka finally took his eyes off of the woman. 'You should have seen how many Blacklanders I plucked today, brother—'

'Bah!' interrupted Tahar, for he could not bear more talk of bloodshed. 'Save the bragging for around the fire. Now, lead me to the others. Let us surprise them together.'

Soon Dakka was leading them back towards the same flat, sandy spot where Tahar had tied the woman less than an hour before. She walked without a sound behind the two men. If she was in pain she did not show it, and as they entered the bustling camp Tahar noticed that she had cleverly adjusted the headdress to further conceal the bumps of her breasts.

'Shame on you, brethren,' Tahar announced, hailing a dozen Libu warriors with a grin. 'I had hoped to test your hunting skills, but not one of you spotted me!' Tahar pointed at Dakka. 'It was this young jackal who finally sniffed me out.'

Tahar smacked Dakka gamely on the back and scanned the company. He recognised some of the men, but others were from distant tribes who had joined only for the raid. *In a few moons they will all be enemies again*, Tahar thought bitterly.

'And who is that?' asked a small, cadaverous man sitting against a rock. He pointed a long, knobby finger in Tahar's direction and opened his one good eye wide. 'That wretched urchin behind you.'

'Greetings, Chief Bandir,' Tahar said, bowing low. 'The boy is my slave. I acquired him at the raid, though as you can see he has been recently injured.' Tahar cast a scolding gaze at Dakka, then smiled forgivingly.

'I'd always thought you partial to women,' sneered the Chief, 'Tahar of No Tribe.' The Chief adjusted his leather eye patch and narrowed his good eye into a slit.

Tahar of No Tribe. The title stung worse than the cut of any blade. Tahar had been with the Libu of the Meshwesh region since he was twelve years old—over twenty cycles of the sun now. He had led countless trade missions and brought great wealth to the tribe. He was well known along the caravan routes, and by merchants from Napata to Uruk. They called him the Blue Serpent, for his rare blue eyes and quiet, watchful manner. The men of his own tribe didn't call him that, however. They had come to call him brother.

'If I am not a Meshwesh Libu by now, Chief Bandir, then let the Gods bury me in the sands,' Tahar said, meeting Dakka's supportive gaze. 'And I am partial to women, of course… But I am also partial to help!'

Tahar laughed lightly, but only Dakka laughed with him. Tahar stared out at the collection of men—herders, most of them—all taking their cue from the rich, unsmiling Chief.

Tahar turned to the woman. 'Go fetch the horse,' he commanded in Khemetian. 'Do it now, boy!'

The woman made an obedient bow, then disappeared across the oasis. He realised suddenly that he had no way of knowing if she would return. Meanwhile, the men eyed Tahar sceptically. His mind raced. He had to convince them of his loyalty, and somehow alleviate their suspicions.

'I was wrong to conceal myself in the pool,' Tahar began in a feigned confessional tone. 'In truth, I was being gluttonous. You see, I wished to consume all the wine myself.'

Tahar paused, letting the men absorb his statement. 'Wine?' repeated a barrel-chested man, his dark brows lifting. 'You carry wine?'

A low murmur rippled through the crowd.

'Not just wine, brother. *Khemetian* wine.' Tahar flashed the party a roguish grin. 'I procured two *amphorae* from the grain tent during the raid. I drained them into udder bags and hoped not be discovered.' Tahar looked around at the dozen men sheepishly. 'Will you forgive a greedy trader? There is certainly enough for everyone.'

Just then the sun vanished below the horizon and the heat loosened its grip on the land. One of the men let out a sigh. 'A few drops of Khemetian wine would be most welcome,' he said.

'Aye,' agreed another, his dust-reddened eyes brightening. 'I have not tasted Khemetian wine since before the drought.'

As the stars began to appear above them, Tahar was transformed from dubious outsider to honoured guest.

'Well, get the wine, then, Tahar,' said Dakka. 'Let us celebrate our success.'

Tahar turned to find that the woman had quickly and silently returned with his horse. She stood beside it holding the reins, her head bent in subservience, her legs spread and her toes pointing outward in a convincing male pose. She was a true imposter—a snake of many colours—and Tahar found himself admiring her.

'Tahar, why do you tarry?' said Dakka, coming to his side. 'And why do you wear the smile of a fool?'

'What?'

'The wine!'

'Oh, aye. The wine,' Tahar said, fumbling in his saddlebags.

'Yes, the wine,' someone called. 'Before we all perish.'

Tahar returned to the circle with two udder bags full of what was sure to be the most potent wine the men had ever tasted. Ceremoniously, he handed both of the bags to the Chief, aware that he had lied once again. Tahar had not stolen the wine from the grain tent, as he had claimed. Long ago he had discovered that wine could be a tool of his trade, and he carried it wherever he travelled.

The Chief placed both bags in his mouth and drank his fill. When he'd finished, a trail of red liquid dribbled down his chin. 'Blood of Khemet,' he said, and the men repeated it.

'Blood of Khemet!'

Tahar was glad the woman could not understand the Libu tongue, for the Chief's words would have surely destroyed her. The rich crimson liquid was indeed known as 'Khemet's blood', but drunk so cheerfully, and held by a hand that still bore the stains of actual Khemetian blood, it seemed poisoned. Tahar did not wish even a sip.

'The Khemetians are decadent,' the Chief said, passing the bags to the men. 'They deserved what we gave them this victorious day.'

'Aye! Aye!' the men cheered.

'The arrogance of their Great Pyramid of Stone!' continued the Chief. 'The Gods do not approve. That is why we have this drought, why the people of the Red Land starve.'

Bandir did not mention the fact that the Khemetians, too, were starving. What he did note was that the Siwa Oasis—which Bandir himself controlled—had seen less than half of the trade caravan traffic of two years ago. He described his empty toll houses, his idle wells, his vacant brothels.

'Today, the Libu tribes have taken back only a small part of what we are owed,' he concluded.

Tahar felt the hairs on the back of his neck stand on end. What was the purpose of this tirade? They had raided the Great Pyramid of Stone and taken hundreds of lives, along with a large haul of grain and three sacred bulls. Was that not enough?

The Libu raiders raved and howled, passing the wine bags between them as the full moon rose. When a bag was finally handed to Tahar he only feigned taking a draught. He had struggled his entire life to be accepted as Libu, but as he watched the men rally behind their bloodthirsty Chief he realised that he did not want to be. Nor did he have to be—thanks to the woman who stood silently in the shadows, pretending to watch the moon.

Chapter Six

It felt almost pleasurable, at first—that flick of a tongue across her thigh. That cool, soft skin pressing against her calf. She tried not to move, tried not to breathe. Perhaps this was only a dream.

Then she heard it—a soft, almost imperceptible hiss, like the sound of fire consuming grass. She worked to free her hands, but she could not. Tahar had tied them before she had fallen asleep. Nor could she jump up—he had bound her ankles too. She felt the movement of the creature's skin on her leg. This was no dream. This was the certainty of death, twisting up her body like a rope.

Another serpent.

Kiya lifted her head. There was Thoth, the Moon God, his face round and full. In his powerful light she could see all the men. They sprawled around the dying embers of the fire, sated with wine. Their cacophony of contented snores burned Kiya's ears and filled her body with hatred.

Thieves. They did not deserve to rest so well—not with so many innocent lives on their hands. Yet as she watched the serpent disappear under her wrap, it seemed that it was Kiya whom the Gods wished to be punished.

This was not an accident, as she had believed the viper to be. This was her mother's prophesy unfolding. *Beware the three serpents*, she had warned Kiya, so long ago.

If the viper had been the first serpent, then this asp was surely the second. Or was it? A water snake had swum by them in the oasis pool. It had veered towards her, then veered away, deterred by a brush of Tahar's hand. If the water snake had been the second serpent, then this asp was the third. Perhaps this was not the continuance of her mother's prophesy, but the fulfilment of it.

But why? Why did the Gods wish Kiya dead?

Suddenly it came to her. *The tomb.* She should have never heeded King Khufu's call to service. She should have never gone to labour upon his Great Pyramid of Stone. Instead she should have listened to the priests, whose message was clear: no female should ever set foot upon a tomb. She had broken the taboo. Now the Gods were merely exacting their punishment upon her.

Kiya resolved not to fight the asp. She would face her death bravely, for it was the Gods' will. She took the part of her headdress that she had placed under her head and stuffed it into her mouth. To cry out would mean to wake her captors, and she refused to give them the pleasure of witnessing her death. She slowed her breathing and braced herself for agony.

Then she felt it—the sting of two sharp fangs in the tenderest part of her thigh. The exquisite pain crackled through her body, followed by a kind of squeezing inside her that made her breath grow short. She studied Thoth's pocked white face, which seemed to grow larger, closer.

Her strength drained away and the needling pain in her thigh grew. She had failed her people, who asked only that she revere the Gods, that she heed their simple rules. Soon she would face Osiris, the King's heavenly father, in his Hall of Judgement—though she probably would not even make it that far. She had no papyrus to tell her the names of the doorkeepers, nor any priest to say the spells. She did not even have any gold with which to pay the boatman.

Not that any of it mattered. She had sinned against the Gods. She was doomed to wander for all eternity in the labyrinths of the Underworld, lost as she had always been, among strangers.

Now the serpent's figure slid into view, profiled against Thoth's blurring face. The creature had climbed the entire length of her. Its hood expanded, it hovered above her, as if considering her transgressions. She would go now, willingly. She let her eyelids close.

But behind her eyes she found only darkness. She did not hear the howls of the jackals, who guarded the gates of the Underworld. Instead, she heard the sound of footsteps in the sand.

She could no longer feel her limbs, and the world began to spin. She heard a sharp hiss, and the rough scuffing of feet upon the ground. Then something else— a soft, wet noise, like the suckling of a babe at its mother's breast. There was a strange tugging sensation at the site of the wound.

Was someone attempting to suck out the venom? Yes, it did feel as if there were a mouth tugging at her thigh. There was no time for reflection, for soon an acute pain ripped through the numbness in her leg. She had never felt such agony—not even when she had been pierced by the Libu blade. She opened her mouth to scream and felt a large hand over it.

'Stay silent,' the trader's voice growled.

She bit down hard on the cloth again. The feeling of suction at the site of the bite returned, then ceased.

'Tahar,' sneered the Chief. He muttered something in the Libu tongue, then bent over Kiya and switched to Khemetian. 'What is wrong, slave?' he asked.

Kiya felt the fabric of her headdress being arranged to cover her face.

'The boy will not answer you,' explained Tahar. 'He has suffered the bite of an asp. He is all but dead.'

'Are you alive, boy?' asked the Chief, ignoring Tahar. Kiya stayed silent. 'Let me see you.' Kiya could feel the fabric of her headdress being tugged.

'There is no need to look at the site,' the trader explained steadily. 'It is already too late to stop the poison.' His voice was like the edge of a blade.

'There is enough moonlight to at least see the mark,' said the Chief. 'Or would you deny my will?'

Kiya felt the cover come briskly off her face. She smelled the Chief's strong, sour breath. 'The boy still breathes,' the Chief said. 'If I can save him, Tahar, he is mine, for you have clearly forsaken him.'

Kiya felt her wrap being folded back, then a sudden sharp pain as the Chief's finger probed the tender site where the asp's fangs had penetrated her thigh. He pushed his hand further up, and she drew a breath when she felt Chief's bony fingers discover her woman's mound.

'What is *this*?' the Chief exclaimed. 'Not a boy at all!' The Chief yanked his arm from beneath Kiya's wrap. 'You have lied to us, Tahar.'

Kiya opened her eyes, but could see only shadows all around her. Her body was limp with exhaustion, but she felt a small tingling sensation returning to her legs, and the tightness in her chest had diminished. She saw the shapes of slumbering men stirring upon the ground. They growled and moaned, still heavy with the effects of the wine. The shadowy figures of two men stood above her, motionless.

'If you give her to me now I will forgive you,' whispered the smaller shadow—the Chief.

'Never. She is mine.'

'She is *ours*,' the Chief said, his voice growing louder. 'She is a spoil of the raid. She belongs to every man here.'

'Nay, she belongs to me and me alone.'

What happened next Kiya wasn't entirely sure. She felt her limp body being scooped into the trader's strong arms. She was placed atop the horse and felt the trader's large, warm body slide behind hers. He gripped her tightly by the waist.

'Do not fight me,' he whispered with hot breath. 'Not now.'

As they rode away she heard the frantic sound of the Chief's shouts. Though she did not speak the Libu tongue, she could imagine what he was saying.

'Why do you delay, you drunken fools? Get her! She is ours!'

Chapter Seven

'I am yours, My King. You may take me if you wish,' breathed the young woman. She had draped herself across King Khufu's lap, as she had been instructed, though she could not bring herself to relax her limbs.

'I wish you would get off my legs,' said the King. 'You are stiffer than a mummy.'

The woman scrambled to the floor and waited obediently upon her knees.

'Just rub my feet, woman,' the King bristled.

The King's newest concubine took his soft right foot in her hand and began to knead. 'You are the handsomest, most magnificent king who has ever lived,' she said as she worked, for concubines were trained to flatter the King in such ways.

'Indeed?' answered King Khufu, bemused. He plucked a grape from the fruit basket on the table and stared out at the brown rooftops of Memphis.

'And the most intelligent and the most powerful and…' The woman paused.

'And?' asked the King.

'And the most accomplished.'

'Ah! Accomplished. Did you hear that, Imhoter?' The King pointed a shrivelled date at his elderly advisor, who was kneeling at the foot of the King's divan.

'Yes, My King,' said Imhoter, keeping his head bowed.

Of course the holy man had heard it. He had been kneeling with his head bowed for some time, waiting for the King to release him from his obeisance.

'Do you think she refers to my ossuary, Imhoter?' asked the King. 'You know—that little building I made?'

'Yes, Majesty,' Imhoter intoned, studying the lapis tiles beneath his knees. 'That is the structure to which I believe she refers.'

'Is that it, coddled one?' the King asked his concubine. 'You refer to my heavenly catapult?'

The beautiful young woman ceased rubbing his foot, utterly confused. After several moments the King's lips narrowed into an angry line. He pointed his royal finger north.

'Oh!' the woman exclaimed. 'Yes, My Lord, the Great Pyramid of Stone. Yes, yes. That is the accomplishment to which I was referring. It is truly…awe-inspiring. Future generations will look upon it with…awe.'

The King wrenched his foot from the woman's hands. 'You bore me, young blossom.' He turned to the priest. 'Imhoter, remind me to send a teacher to the Royal Harem. A historian, and perhaps a scribe versed in the embellishments of language. These new concubines are as thick as palm trunks.'

'Yes, Majesty,' said Imhoter, keeping his gaze upon the floor.

'Well, get up, then, Imhoter!' the King said finally. 'Or am I surrounded by fools?'

Imhoter stood slowly, glancing sidelong at the young

woman. Her eyes had been kohled with an elegant, swirl-
ing design, but tears now threatened to smudge the lovely
black circles.

The King levelled an icy stare at the woman. 'And get
a special tutor for this one. This…' The King paused.
'Pray, what is your name?'

'Iset, My King,' said the woman.

The setting sun shot a golden ray across the terrace and
lit up her ochre-red lips, which trembled like a child's.

'Iset,' Khufu said. 'Even the name is dull.'

A single tear traced a path down the woman's pow-
dered cheek. Imhoter knew that the woman had been preparing her entire life for this—her first encounter with a
Living God. As his concubine she would share his bed,
would bear his bastards, yet up until this moment he had
not even bothered to learn her name.

Imhoter watched the woman wither beneath the King's
gaze. The King did not know her name, and neither would
any man, for the life of a concubine was foremost the
life of a loyal servant. She would live out her days in
the seclusion and isolation of the harem—available for
the King whenever he wanted her, alone and lonely when
he did not.

This was the fate of all concubines—glorious and terrible. Imhoter could not understand why women went
so eagerly towards it. In his fifty years of service to the
King, and the King's father before him, there had been
only one concubine who had resisted that fate. Imhoter's
heart squeezed and he pushed the memory from his mind.

Now Iset wiped her tear and gestured meekly towards
the King's foot. 'Shall I continue, My King?' she asked.

'Tsst!' the King hissed, brushing her away.

If only Imhoter could tell the poor woman that the

King no longer welcomed *any* woman's touch. Indeed, it was well known amongst King Khufu's priests and advisors that he hadn't taken either of his wives nor any of his concubines to his bedchamber in many, many moons.

'Leave me now,' the King spat at the woman. 'Go!'

She jumped up and rushed across the expanse of the terrace, the train of her long white tunic dragging behind her like a sail unable to catch the wind. Imhoter could hear her sobs as she disappeared behind a distant column.

It was another ill omen, for the mark of a king was his virility—his ability to fertilise the land of Khemet with his seed, which he was expected to plant in as many concubines as possible. In that particular function King Khufu had lately begun to falter. The younger priests were already scandalised by the King's behaviour. They whispered among themselves like harem girls. *Has Horus Incarnate lost his virility?* That was the question on their minds, for the King's body was Khemet's body, and for two years Khemet had been suffering a drought.

'Do not condemn me, priest,' the King growled, reading Imhoter's thoughts. 'Am I not the Living God? Can I not do what I please, my actions reflecting the will of Horus, God of Order and Protector of both Upper and Lower Khemet?'

The King lifted his empty goblet, and a slave boy holding a large pitcher emerged from the shadows and filled it.

'Of course, Majesty,' Imhoter said.

'Then open your mouth, eunuch,' the King commanded, reminding the former priest of his debased status, 'and tell me why you have come.'

A rush of shame pinched Imhoter's chest, but he did not show it. Instead he reminded himself of his duty to

Khemet. He had faithfully advised King Khufu's father, Sneferu, and now he served Khufu himself.

He took a deep breath and began. 'Keeper of Khemet, I had a most compelling vision as I slept this morning. It involved your House of Eternity, the Great Pyramid of Stone.'

Khufu nodded, squinting at the glowing white pyramid at the horizon's edge. To reach it required a day's journey from Memphis, but even at this great distance the building appeared powerful, impermeable, eternal.

Still, Imhoter could not help but feel a growing sense of dread. It had been two years now since Hapi, the life-giving flood, had blessed the land of Khemet with its waters. And now *akhet*, the season of the flood, was almost over. If Hapi did not arrive soon there would be no crops again this year. Without any reserves left, the people of Khemet would slowly begin to starve.

'Tell me, Imhoter. What did you see in your vision?' the King asked.

'I saw an army of men clad in violet and blue. They seemed to be bursting out of the sun itself. Some ran; others rode donkeys. They were running towards the Great Pyramid of Stone.'

'Libu?'

'Aye. It appeared to be a raid, though I did not see more than what I have said…' The priest paused.

'What else, Imhoter?'

'Nothing, Majesty.'

'I know there is something else,' Khufu said, and His Majesty was right. The King read Imhoter like a scroll. 'Tell me, Seer, for the Gods speak to me through you.'

'As you wish—but this part of the vision confuses me,' continued Imhoter. 'I also saw a woman. She was a beautiful woman, as splendid as the Goddess of Love and Abundance herself. Two black serpents hung from her temples. They touched her collarbone like strands of hair. You commanded that she be sacrificed.'

'Sacrificed? It is not since the time of Zoser and the Seven-Year Drought that a human has been sacrificed.'

'That is why I do not understand the vision. I know that Your Majesty would never return to that barbarous ancient practice.' Imhoter swallowed hard. In his haste to placate the King he had divulged too much of his vision. Now he could see Khufu turning the idea over in his mind.

'What did she wear, this sacrifice?'

'She wore golden serpents on each of her arms and legs.'

'Did you see anything more in your vision? Did you see Hapi, our precious flood? Is it coming at last?'

'No, I am afraid I saw nothing to do with Hapi.'

'Nothing at all?'

'Nothing at all. Just a legion of Libu...and a lady of serpents.'

Just then a King's Guardsman appeared at the far end of the terrace. The Royal Chamberlain announced the man's arrival as he strode the length of the space and prostrated himself at the foot of the King's divan.

'I bring urgent news for the ears of the Living God.'

'Speak,' commanded the King.

'Your Majesty, I was sent by Hemiunu, Chief Vizier and Overseer of the Great Pyramid, just before he perished.'

'Perished?' The King's goblet made a loud clang as it fell upon the tiles.

'Yes, My King, along with most of the King's Guard.

A Libu horde attacked the grain queue early this morning. Lord Hemiunu bade me tell you. It was his dying wish.'

'And the grain?'

'It is all gone—stolen by the Libu filth.'

The King cast an awestruck gaze at Imhoter, then sat back.

Imhoter could not believe the guardsman's words. The grain tent had contained the last of the royal grain stores. Now the tomb workers would have nothing to help them see their families through the drought.

'The lady of serpents,' muttered the King vacantly.

'Your Majesty?' said the guardsman.

'A woman wearing golden serpents upon her wrists,' the King said, 'did see her?'

'No, My King, I am sorry. There were no women at the raid.'

The King sank back into his cushions and it appeared to Imhoter as if he had shrunk to half his size. 'And Hapi, our magnificent flood?' the King muttered, the colour draining from his face. 'When will it arrive? *When?*'

Chapter Eight

There was and there was not. That was how Kiya began all her tales. It was the traditional way, the way of the entertainer. It was the way her mother had taught her, for concubines were expected to provide diversions for kings, and stories were one of them.

Kiya remembered few details from her mother's tales, but she remembered how her heart had swelled as her mother had described worlds beyond Kiya's wildest dreams—worlds in which animals talked and people did magic and everything came in threes, including wishes.

After she'd lost her mother and gone to live on the streets of Memphis, Kiya had often loitered outside the taverns, where men told tales for money and fame. Her aim had not merely been diversion: there had often been food to be had, as well. Kiya would huddle undetected under the kitchen windows behind the taverns, hoping to filch a half-eaten honey cake to fill her stomach and catch a story to sustain her.

There was and there was not, the storytellers would begin, and she would strain to hear their fantastic false-hoods—stories of giant crocodiles and shipwrecked sailors and men who lived for hundreds of years. The storytellers' words would transport her to places far beyond the dusty streets of Memphis, and for a short time she'd feel worldly. Not an orphan, but a traveller. Not a street beggar, but a princess. The storytellers carried harps and, for the right amount of beer they would sing and play. Kiya always smiled when they sang her favorite song, 'The Laundry Woman's Choice,' about a poor laundry woman who must choose between two suitors. 'I will wear the shirt I love best, no matter how it fits' went the chorus, and Kiya would quietly sing along.

She was fascinated by the bond the storytellers called love. She longed to feel it. She had searched the faces of the young men in the marketplaces, and as her womanhood had begun to bloom they had searched her face in return. But they had always looked away.

Slowly, Kiya had begun to realise that she was not desirable to young men. And why should she be? She had no family or property—not even a proper tunic or wig. She clad herself in rags and grew her own hair, which hung in tangled ropes that smelled vaguely of the docks.

One day Kiya had been digging for clams in the shallows of the Great River when an old man had approached her. His gait had been crooked, and Kiya had been able to smell the sour, vinegary aroma of wine upon his breath.

He'd grabbed her by the arm. 'You are mine now, little mouse,' he had slurred.

He had already torn away most of her ragged wrap by the time her teeth sank into his flesh.

She'd bitten down hard, unaware that it would be the first of many such bites. As she'd run away she had remembered her mother's words: *Stay away from men, Kiya! They only mean to possess you, to enslave you.*

How right her mother had been. As she'd got older the menace of men had only grown. She'd needed protection, and had been confronted with the choice all street girls faced: to sell herself into servitude or to sell her body in a House of Women.

Kiya had not wanted to choose. Each time she'd considered the options she had felt her *ka* begin to wither. She had meandered through the marketplace and splashed in the Great River, desperately clinging to her old life. She had lingered outside the taverns, listening to the storytellers' tales, remembering the urgency of her mother's words and trying to conceive of another way.

Finally, she had: shaving her head, concealing her curves and covering herself in rags, just like a character in a story.

Kiya had became Koi.

There was and there was not.

'Awake!' a deep, familiar voice commanded.

But when she opened her eyes darkness enveloped her still.

'I have arrived in the Underworld?' she stuttered.

There was a menacing chuckle. 'If you consider a cave in the banks of an ancient river the Underworld, then, yes, indeed. You have arrived.'

Kiya's head throbbed. 'I am...alive?'

'Yes, you are alive—though you have been sleeping the sleep of the dead for many days.'

The air around her was cool and still, and her eyes could discern nothing in the inky darkness. Layers of cloth swaddled her, but beneath them was a hard surface. She attempted to sit up, but a searing pain shot through her inner thigh and she collapsed back onto the ground with a curse.

'Don't forget that you have been bitten by a deadly asp,' said the voice from somewhere close. 'And pierced by a Libu blade.'

She touched the tender wound on her arm. Where had that come from? A confounding fog stifled Kiya's thoughts. Where was she? And what menace stalked her now? She needed to find a weapon—a stone, even a handful of dirt would suffice. A desperate thirst seized her and she coughed.

'Nor should you forget that you drank from an oasis pool,' the voice added. 'You have been vomiting for two days.'

'And still I am not dead?'

'Your Gods apparently wish you alive.'

'Nay. I am certain they wish me dead.'

'Well, you are fortunate to know me, then, for I have saved you from their will.'

'And who are *you* who would thwart the Gods?'

'You do not remember?'

'I scarcely remember who I am,' Kiya moaned, for she was no longer Koi, the stealthy street orphan, nor was she Mute Boy from Gang Twelve of the Haulers. She was someone else entirely—someone positively new. But who?

'In your fever you raved of serpents,' said the voice.

Kiya heard the sound of stones being placed upon the ground.

'Three serpents would try to take your life, you said. One would succeed, unless you become like…'

'Like what?' Kiya asked.

'That was all you said.'

'I heard a voice in the desert,' she remembered. 'A prophesy.'

'If you heard such a voice in the desert, then it was no prophesy. It was an illusion—a waking dream. Illusions occur in the Red Land when a person lingers too long in the sun.' A ray of sunlight flooded into the cavernous space. 'Now, let there be light.'

Kiya blinked and a large figure stepped into her view. The light was behind him, keeping his body in shadow, and she imagined him a demon. His dark silhouette towered above her, the expanse of his chest terminating in long, well-muscled arms that appeared strong enough to break her in two. She groped about desperately, her hand finally closing upon a loose stone.

The demon bent down and placed his large hand over her fist. His thick voice was at her ear. 'Do you really wish to bite the hand that feeds you, Little Asp?' He lifted her fingers, one by one, from the stone, then tossed it aside. 'Do not try to fight now,' he said gravely, 'for you will most certainly lose.'

He wrapped one arm around her shoulders and threaded the other under her knees. Without effort, he lifted her body. She could smell his scent—something rich, earthy and unmistakably male. He carried her across the cave to the wall farthest from the entrance. There, he gently set her down in a sitting position.

He remained in shadow, but as he walked back towards the mouth of the cave the light hit him and she could discern a loincloth wrapped neatly around his lower body. Below the cloth his legs bulged outward, as if the Gods had decided to allot him the strength of two men instead of one. Above the loincloth the great swathe of his back seemed to bloom from his round buttocks in an array of taut muscles.

The demon was well-made.

He was also enormous.

Kiya glanced at her own scrawny, swaddled figure and concluded that he had wrapped his own clothing around her many times.

'You were very hot for a time, then very cold,' he explained as he reached the mouth of the cave and bent to retrieve a water bag. 'You endured a terrible fever. The oasis water you drank was dirty and should not have been consumed.' He returned to her side, held the water bag out to her and paused. 'Please don't make this like the last time.'

'The last time?'

'You don't remember that either?'

Ah, but she *did* remember. It came all at once, in a flood of images: how she had punched the water bag from his hands; how she had tried—futilely—to outmanoeuvre him; how the blade had plunged through the water and through her arm. She touched the inside of her thigh and for a moment could feel the asp's sharp fangs puncturing her skin once again.

She remembered all of it—even the feel of his hands as he'd picked her up and hoisted her onto his strange beast. Even…even the pool. She felt a flush of heat in her cheeks. Those hands. They had been so confident upon her waist. It had been as if her body were a dune of sand they might traverse expertly, if only given the chance.

'Nay, I do not remember,' she lied.

She reached for the water bag and tilted it to her

mouth. The water was cool and fresh, and she drank until she had drained the entire bag.

'Don't be shy,' he said, flashing a shadowy smile. He lifted the empty bag from her grasp. 'Since you do not remember, I will have you know that you are my captive. I took you in a grain raid. I saved you from Libu raiders and nursed your wounds. I am Tahar, and you are mine.'

He put the water bag down and held up a bowl full of rich-smelling game.

'This is addax. I caught it last night in the wash below the cliffs. The meat is tender—like oryx, but lighter in flavour. I have cured it with smoke, so that we may consume it over the next few days. You may eat as much as you like, but first you must say my name.'

Kiya stared into the bowl of meat. *Meat?* How long had it been since she'd eaten meat? She could hardly remember. She reached for a piece of addax.

'Not so fast, my little imposter,' he said, pulling the bowl away. 'What is my name?'

'Tahar.'

'And what is your name?'

Her name? Was this a cave, or some earthly Hall of Judgement? His eyes were in shadow, but she could feel them studying her. Ah... She knew exactly what this was. This was her first lesson in submission.

'I'm sorry. I do not remember my name.'

'That's unlikely.'

'Please, Tahar, I do not remember,' she lied. She blinked her eyes and was able to produce several fine, false tears. *Oh, handsome trader, from beyond the Big Green, you are overmatched.*

Annoyed, he thrust the bowl out to her. She placed a piece of the fresh smoked addax into her mouth and every part of her body awakened to the act. The meat was so rich—almost sweet—as if the beast had lived a life of luxury and not scratched its lean existence from the desert sands.

She ate another piece, feeling the animal's spirit pass into hers, feeling strength return, feeling...gratitude.

She thought of the traditional Khemetian proverb: *If I shall die, I shall die in thanks, having tasted all of life.*

She stopped her chewing. 'It appears that I am in your debt.'

Tahar was as still as the shadows that concealed him. 'Indeed you are...'

She could not see his expression, but he seemed to be thinking.

'And you shall pay that debt soon.'

In a few brisk strides he had returned to the mouth of the cave, where he bent with his knife and began scraping what appeared to be the addax's hide.

'How? How will I pay that debt?'

'I shall sell you into marriage to the richest man I can find.'

His words burned through the last bit of fog that lingered in Kiya's mind and a familiar rage began to smoulder in her heart. 'You misunderstand me. I said that it *appears* that I am in your debt, but in fact I am not.' She had his attention now. 'For I would be halfway to Abydos by now if it weren't for you.'

'Is that where your family lives? Abydos?'

'Family—?' She stopped herself. The demon had almost caught her in her lie. 'Aye, it is where my family lives. Though I wouldn't call it living, for there is no food, and now I have been captured and cannot aid them, and they will continue to starve unless I am released, and—'

Kiya stopped when she discovered that she was talking to the walls.

Tahar had apparently exited the cave.

Chapter Nine

Wretched viper of a man. In the softness of her gratitude she had exposed herself to his fangs. By the Gods, where was her sense? This trader was no different from other men—always seeking to possess women and use them for profit. As soon as she had her strength back she would slip out of his grasp. There was naught she could do now while her injuries healed. She would eat his meat and bide her time, then simply disappear.

She regained her calm and looked around the cave. Slowly, a grand vision emerged before her eyes. Images—hundreds of images—upon the walls. Birds and beasts and plants—some familiar, some utterly strange.

'Remarkable, aren't they?'

Tahar's voice made Kiya jump. He had silently returned to the mouth of the cave. When had he done that? He was staring at Kiya, and in the shifting light she thought she could detect a wistful look in his eyes. 'So beautiful and mysterious.'

'What is this place?' asked Kiya. 'A kind of temple?'

'I suppose so, though only a blessed few know of it. Welcome to the Cave of Wanderers.' Tahar pointed to the wall across from Kiya. Upon it was drawn a family of river cows, basking in the shallows of a river. Above them the long, elegant bodies of several sacred ibis floated in the sky. Beneath them a great school of perch swam for all eternity.

'A Khemetian surely did this.'

'Very certain of that, are you?'

'I know the work of my people,' Kiya said. 'That is the Great River. And those are hippos—river cows. They bask in the water during the daytime. I have witnessed this scene many times on the banks of our sacred river.'

'Indeed? Well, in that case, you can tell me the name of the tall creature standing on the bank.'

'What tall creature?' Kiya asked. She studied the vegetation—papyrus, lotus, thistle. There were drawings of palms, acacias, tamarisks, and even a few fig trees, but there was not a single creature of any significant height. 'There is no tall creature standing upon the bank.'

'Then your eyes deceive you.' Tahar traced the trunk of a sycamore tree with his finger, then continued upwards to the ponderously long neck of a creature that in all other ways resembled an ass. 'It is called a giraffe.'

'A giraffe? What is that? What gods made this place?'

'No gods—' began Tahar, then stopped himself. 'Long ago, the desert was not the desert.'

Kiya was too entranced to ask his meaning. Though the animals were but dark outlines, they seemed alive somehow, as if they might jump from the walls and be reborn inside this secret womb of stone.

Animals weren't the only figures. There were humans carrying arrows and spears. Some rode atop beasts with long, serpentine snouts. Kiya drank in the images, letting them fill her with their secret messages, amazed as her world expanded before her eyes.

There was that feeling again—gratitude. *Think, Kiya. Remember he is your captor. He intends to sell you for his own gain.*

Soon Tahar was crouching at her side. He held a small linen packet. 'In order for the wound on your thigh to heal properly I must ensure the poison is completely extracted. Then I must apply this poultice to encourage healing. May I tend it now?'

'How do you know the flood is coming?'

Tahar eased her body into a more reclined position. 'I just know.' He gently pulled apart her legs.

'*How* do you know?'

'I am going to lift the headdress cloth to address the wound now. This is necessary.'

Kiya squeezed her legs together. 'First tell me how you know about the flood.'

Tahar sighed. He placed his hands upon the ground on either side of her, then moved up the length of her body, stopping with his mouth just inches from her face. 'Do you really want to know how I know?'

'Yes,' Kiya whispered, 'for you are not a god. You cannot see the future.'

'Nay, I cannot see the future,' he said.

His hot breath smelled of sycamore and smoke.

'But I can see what is right before my eyes.'

He gave a quick glance downward, into the small space of heated air between their two chests. She could feel the muscular hardness of his naked midriff as he rested it lightly against her stomach, realizing that she feared his weight, yet also yearned for it.

'The locusts, for example,' he said, finding her eyes.

'They swarm on the eastern sides of the dunes but they do not fly. And the acacia seeds that rest in the sands have lately begun to crack.'

Kiya gulped. 'That is all?' His lips were so close.

'That isn't even the beginning, dear woman.' He bent his lips to her ear and whispered. 'The wind has begun to waft its way northward in the deepest part of the night. Have you not noticed? And the wild aurochs have retreated to the inland mountains. They no longer graze with their cousins near the river. Songbirds from the south have begun to perch in the tamarisk branches. Have you not heard them singing just before dawn? If you Khemetians would simply observe the world around you, you would know that the flood is coming. Instead you pray to gods who do not listen. You do dances and sacrifice bulls. You are silly, frivolous people.'

He was hovering so very close. She tried to imagine the warble of songbirds, but all she could hear was the sound of her heart throbbing in her chest. 'You insult my people. You insult *me.*'

'Nay, I honour you.'

'How do you honour me?'

'By speaking what is in my heart.'

His eyes flashed. He moved back down her body and lifted the cloth that covered her thighs. On the inside of her left thigh an alarming red mound had appeared. It was punctuated by four tiny black holes: the mark of the bite that should have taken her life.

Tahar hovered over the wound, then encompassed it with his mouth and began to suck. Kiya gasped, powerless, as he drew out the remaining poison, his long, sandy-blond locks cascading around his shoulders as he worked. The thick hair appeared clean and soft, as if recently washed. Kiya wondered what it might be like to put her fingers through it.

Impulsively she opened her legs a bit wider, suddenly wishing that *all* the parts of her body had been bitten by a snake so that he might suck them each in turn. A low moan escaped her lips.

Tahar stopped his work on the wound. Without moving he peered up at her, and she felt a twinge of fear invade her body. *You say what is next*, his eyes told her. He appeared to be poised at the edge of some terrible divide, and she knew that if she wanted him she would only have to tell him. Nay—she would only have to touch his hair, to twist a long, shiny strand around her finger.

Ah, but she could not do it.

For if she did, who would she become? Certainly not the tough girl who had scratched her living from the streets of Memphis, who had won her right to survive every single day. And not the daughter of her mother, who had warned her against men and the danger they represented. And certainly not the clever woman who worked on a king's tombs and defeated men at their own silly games. Who would she become if she allowed this man to pleasure her, knowing that he was planning to trade her?

The answer to that question was easy: she'd become a slave.

Kiya stiffened and sat up. 'Are you not going to say a prayer?' she asked, quickly closing her legs.

A burst of air rushed through Tahar's nostrils. He shook his head angrily, then walked to the cave entrance and spat. He wiped his mouth with the side of his arm and stared out at the landscape. Then he returned to Kiya, scooped up another water bag and drank a long draught.

'Nay,' he responded. 'It is not necessary.'

'Of course it is necessary. A god can accelerate the healing of a wound. The Goddess Sekhmet, for example, or even—'

'I do not believe that gods can affect the healing of wounds,' interrupted Tahar. Avoiding her gaze, he bent down and trickled a stream of water onto the wound. Then he tied the poultice firmly into place upon it. 'Now, cover yourself, woman.'

Cover yourself.

She felt her insides twist in shame as she realised that she had been mistaken. Moments ago it had not been desire that she had read in his eyes, but derision. Now he couldn't even bear to look at her.

Kiya quickly pulled the headdress over her thighs. This was the second time she had mistaken his kindness for caring, and she scolded herself for the error.

'You said these drawings were made by the Gods of the Desert,' she muttered angrily, 'but you are wrong. Khemetians made these drawings.'

Tahar's cheeks flushed red. 'Of course you think Khemetians did these, for you are Khemetian and you believe all the universe revolves around you.'

'Well, it does. The Gods made the land of Khemet— the Black Land—and they made the Red Land—the desert. They made the lands separate and they stay separate. One defines the other. That is how the balance of *maat* is maintained. These drawings show the Great River as it was long ago. And it shows Khemetians—the guardians of the Great River. The chosen ones.'

Tahar grabbed his water bag and stood. 'If you believe that, then you probably also believe that your Great River begins in a cavern at the Isle of Abu.' He returned to the mouth of the cave.

'That is where it *does* begin.'

'Woman, I have travelled the length of the Great River, and I can assure you that it does not begin at the Isle of Abu. It is vastly longer.'

'It appears that life in the Red Land has driven you to madness, for even the lowest beggars on the streets of Memphis know that the Great River begins beneath the Isle of Abu. The God Khnum controls its waters. If you believe otherwise, you are perhaps experiencing a feverish dream.'

Tahar shook his head, rolling up the addax hide. 'I might be mistaken, but I believe it is you who has been recently stricken by a feverish dream.' He lifted the packet and stood. 'We leave at sunset.'

'Where are we going?'

'To find you a husband, of course. We are going to Nubia, where you don't have to be a king to have many wives. You just have to have plenty of gold.'

His words were like daggers in her heart. 'You are the worst kind of demon.'

'And on our way to Nubia we will stop at the Isle of Abu. To prove you wrong.'

Chapter Ten

'The Isle of Abu!' the King shouted. His voice carried across the rooftops of Memphis, sending a hundred pigeons into flight. 'We must go there now, Imhoter. It is the only way.'

Imhoter stood with his head bowed. 'You would leave Memphis without its King?' The long sleeves of Imhoter's robe concealed his hands, which he squeezed together nervously.

After the Libu raid on the grain tent the King had ordered the remaining members of the King's Guard into the desert. They were only a few dozen soldiers in search of hundreds of Redlanders who might as well have been ghosts. It had been a thoughtless decision, for it was well known that the desert tribes were highly dispersed. They came together only for raids, and could easily evade the Khemetian headhunters.

But such facts were meaningless to King Khufu. In his fury over the grain tent raid he had acted without thinking. He had sent the city's defenders on a fool's errand and left the city itself vulnerable to attack. And now he apparently wanted to abandon the city completely.

'Abu is the only answer,' the monarch ranted, thrusting his soft, thick finger at Imhoter's chest. 'I must go to Abu and appeal to Khnum, God of the Great River. If we do not have the flood soon, we all shall perish.'

Imhoter measured his response. 'I would merely suggest that you consider the idea more closely, Your Majesty.'

Imhoter knew of several wealthy priests who had accumulated enough grain to support small armies of followers. One priest in particular—a wretched old man named Menis—seemed poised to usurp Khufu's power. The King's departure would be just the opportunity Menis needed to install his army and take the throne.

'Abu is very far away. Let us think on the idea for a time.'

'But there *is* no more time, old eunuch!' The King barked. He paced across the shady terrace, his leather sandals slapping against the tiles. 'The royal grain is gone; the people of Khemet grow desperate. If the waters of Hapi do not come the citizens of Memphis will unseat me soon.'

If you leave the city, they will unseat you sooner! Imhoter thought, though knew he could not speak his mind.

Like his father before him, King Khufu was prone to flights of rage, so Imhoter spoke calmly, keeping to the facts. 'The upriver journey is long—four weeks at least, even with strong north winds. Your idea is brilliant, but I am sure you wish to think on it.'

'There is no thinking, eunuch, only listening to the Gods—and what I hear is mighty Horus, whispering to me. He is telling me to go to the Isle of Abu, to beg for Hapi.'

King Khufu paced incessantly, but Imhoter remained

still. He, too, yearned for Hapi, but not for the same reasons as the King. The farmers of Khemet suffered, and it tried the holy man's soul. Their limbs grew lifeless, their bellies ballooned with want. To watch them wither and die was a punishment Imhoter did not know if he could endure.

What gives a King's life more value than a farmer's, or even a beggar's? The question tickled the edges of Imhoter's mind like an itch he could not scratch. It had been a long time since he had considered it, though it was perhaps, the most important question of his life. A woman had asked it of him in innocence long ago, and he had been unable to answer her. She had been a forgotten concubine of King Sneferu, and she had studied him with eyes as deep and endless as the night.

Now Khufu lifted his hands to the sky. 'The Gods must verify that I am Khemet's rightful ruler—that my great tomb was not erected in vain. I must bring the flood.'

Imhoter nodded obediently, hoping that the King's reckless compulsion would pass. He closed his eyes and begged the Gods to send him a vision of the future— one of the river rising and the King seated safely on his throne. But no such vision came.

'Advise both my queens,' the King pronounced. 'If Hapi does not arrive by the Feast of Hathor, we make for the Isle of Abu.'

Chapter Eleven

Tahar had not planned on taking the woman to the Isle of Abu, so exceedingly far south. He had wanted to stay near the Big Green ports, where the boats were as plentiful as merchants in need of brides. He could have traded her for a fine vessel at some dock in Alexandria, for example, or at one of the marshland bazaars in Tanis.

Thanks to his own stubborn pride, however, they were headed for Abu, as far south as one could go in Khemet before passing into the tribal lands of Nubia. Instead of days, their journey would now take many weeks, travelling from oasis to oasis by night, paralleling the Great River as they moved ever southward through the desert.

Lands, he was a fool. It would be a long, difficult trek, made harder still by the fact that he was a wanted man. By now all of Khemet would have heard about the grain raid, and his Libu scar marked him as the enemy. It did not matter that he was Libu no more, that he had renounced the bloodthirsty thieves whom he had once called brothers. The Khemetians needed scapegoats as much as the Libu did, and Tahar made an easy target.

The morning sun lifted above the horizon, piercing

Tahar's eyes. They would arrive at the next oasis soon. He could see a small verdant patch in the distance, at the base of several low cliffs. Meanwhile, the woman had begun to doze in the saddle. He had not joined her there during the night's journey, choosing instead to walk. He did not trust himself so close to her, though he knew he would have to ride with her soon. They had a long, dangerous journey ahead.

If they survived, however, Tahar stood to reap a fine reward. Though much of Nubia's gold now lay buried in the tombs of Khemetian kings, the Nubians were no paupers. A wealthy Nubian chief would not pass up the opportunity to add a Khemetian bride to his harem, and he would pay well for her—in dozens of gold ingots.

The promise of a well-paying Nubian husband was not the only reason they journeyed south, however. Tahar's purpose was also philosophical. The Isle of Abu was just that—an island—and he was determined to prove it to the obstinate woman. The Great River did not begin at Abu, as she so passionately believed. And an imaginary god did not dwell beneath the island, considering when to release his torrent.

But he did not only wish to educate her—he wanted to astound her. What would she think the moment she saw her Great River from the top of the Theban peak? Finally she would understand that her gods did not simply conjure the Great River from under their robes!

Not that she would likely appreciate the geography lesson, or *any* of his knowledge of the desert. The woman had pricked his nerves with her talk of gods and *maat* and the eternal, infernal land of Khemet. If he could just get one single Khemetian to understand that Khemet was *not* the centre of the world, and that their precious river was *not* controlled by gods, he would die a happy man.

But why was it so important for him to convince her? Perhaps it was her incredible obstinacy that had baited him. What had she called her people? The 'chosen ones.' The nerve of that!

'We shall eat and take our rest at the oasis ahead,' Tahar explained, attempting to rouse her.

She opened her eyes and swatted the air, as if his very words were a nuisance. Then she resumed her sleep.

By the Gods, she was spoiled. She had no idea of the knife's edge of survival upon which they trod. She was the kind of Khemetian woman he loathed.

So why did she invade his thoughts like a swarm of locusts?

He stole another glance at her. She still wore his head-dress around her breasts and waist. He would ask for it back soon. In exchange he would gift her the sandals and addax-skin dress he had made for her. The soft amber-haired garment was now completely dry and ready for donning, and he looked forward to seeing her in it.

He led the horse to a cluster of large boulders at the base of the cliffs. 'Stay here while I see that the oasis is safe,' he explained to the woman, who appeared barely to be able to keep her eyes open. 'I will not be long.'

It took him no time to inspect the site. The pool was small, but it looked cool and inviting. There were no Libu raiders about, nor any men of the King's Guard. Tahar studied the ground and found no footprints of predators or any other kind of threat. But when he returned to the boulders there was no horse...and no woman.

He did not panic, though he cursed himself for not having foreseen it. Of *course* she would try to escape on his horse. Her drowsiness had been feigned: she had been waiting for this chance all night.

He rounded the boulders and spotted her, heading east at a full gallop. He swallowed hard—because she looked so beautiful and strong atop the horse, because her plan was both bold and clever, and because he knew exactly what he had to do next.

He placed his fingers to his lips and his high whistle split the morning. His horse slowed, then reared up, just as he had trained it to do. Its front legs swam in the air and the woman tumbled to the ground in a pile of purple cloth.

She was, thank the Gods, unharmed. She stood immediately. Her headdress had come unwrapped and one of her small delectable breasts had burst free. Tahar smiled as he watched her struggle to cover herself, cursing the Red Land and everything in it.

She was dusting herself off when the first arrow pierced the ground beside her. Another followed close behind, and if she had not had the awareness to get moving she would surely have been hit. Scanning the cliffs, he quickly found the arrows' source—two men clad in the unmistakable blue linen of the King's Guard.

Tahar's horse had now returned to his side, and he mounted it. 'Khemetian filth!' he yelled at the guards, and they momentarily ceased their shooting.

Tahar barrelled towards them on his stallion. Now the guards had two targets to shoot for, and soon the arrows were flying in Tahar's direction as well.

Tahar rode unflinchingly towards the archers, catching one of their arrows in his saddlebag. He plucked a second arrow right out of the air with his hand. He changed direction, moving as unpredictably as he could, buying himself time enough to fashion his long rope into a large loop.

The guards were dumbstruck when the rope encircled them. It yanked them to the ground like captured goats. Tahar swung out of the saddle and pulled the rope taut, so the men were pressed together, back to back. He wrenched their quivers and bows from their arms, broke one bow in half upon his knee, and placed the other on the ground beside him with the remaining arrows.

'Your beast is no donkey,' said a smooth, feminine voice from behind him. 'And *you* are not a simple trader.'

She was staring up at his horse in awe. How had he not noticed her there?

'Nay, it is no donkey,' Tahar said, keeping his eye on the guards.

'What is it, then? It runs like a gazelle.'

'The people of my tribe call it a horse.'

'Your tribe? What tribe is that?'

'The People of the Grass. From the lands beyond the Dark Sea.'

The Khemetian guards stared up at their captors in confusion, and Tahar read their thoughts. Who was this Libu man whose tribe was named for a cow's food? And who was this Libu woman who dressed like a man and spoke perfect Khemetian?

'Look there!' the woman exclaimed, pointing to a donkey lurking in the shade at the base of the cliffs.

In minutes she had returned with the beast, and Tahar inspected its saddlebags. Inside there was water, a hunting knife and two sleeping carpets, but not a bit of food. Tahar studied the men. They appeared quite thin.

'Your King has placed a reward on Libu heads, has he not?' Tahar demanded. 'That is why you hunt us?'

'Aye,' confessed the older of the two guards. 'Finish us quickly,' he urged, glancing at the dagger wedged in Tahar's belt.

The younger man's lips were trembling.

Tahar shook his head. He would not be a part of any more killing. He pulled out his dagger, but did not use it to cut any throat. Instead he cut off a large swathe of the woman's headdress, fashioned it into a kind of sack, and filled it with grain from his own saddlebag.

'I'm sorry that I cannot give you our heads,' Tahar said, tying the sack closed, 'but this purple cloth may be used as proof to collect your reward, and the grain it contains is worth its weight in copper.'

He held up the heavy sack and placed it in the donkey's saddlebag.

'This is smoked addax,' he explained to the men, retrieving a large palm leaf bundle from his horse's pack. He tucked the addax in beside the sack of grain. 'Together with the grain, the addax will be more than enough to sustain you on your journey back to Khemet,' Tahar said. 'Now, stand.'

The two men pushed themselves to stand and Tahar slowly undid the rope.

'You must go north before you go west,' Tahar explained. 'Keep to the oases and be wary of thieves.'

Shock and confusion spread across the men's sunken faces as Tahar bent to help them onto their beast. Securing them in their saddle, Tahar slapped the donkey on the rump.

'Now, go,' he said.

As the beast ambled away the older man turned. 'You have our thanks, Man of the Grass,' he told Tahar. 'Your kindness will not be forgotten.'

Chapter Twelve

'You gave them all our meat,' the woman said, her eyes as big as plates.

'That I did.'

'But…it was *meat*.'

'I took their arrows,' explained Tahar. 'I left them without the means to hunt.'

'But they were trying to *kill* us.'

'Ah, but they did not succeed. Come, let us take our rest at the pool.' He placed his hand against the small of her back.

Too exasperated to swat it away, she allowed him to guide her towards the oasis. 'But—'

'But what?'

'It was *meat*.'

Tahar spoke as cryptically as he could, for her growing frustration was proving quite entertaining. 'We will find more meat. Do not forget that I am now the owner of a fine bow.'

'And the horse?' she gasped, glancing back at the placid animal he led by the reins.

'What about the horse?' asked Tahar, hiding his grin.

'How on earth did you learn to command such a beast?'

Tahar closed his eyes, remembering his father's towering figure. 'My father taught me.'

Tahar's father had learned to command horses from Tahar's grandfather, who had ridden the fleet-footed beasts across the steppes of their homeland, battling rival tribes and ransacking villages near the Dark Sea. When his grandfather had died, Tahar's father had inherited both the old man's battle axe and his restlessness—but not his lust for blood. Instead Tahar's father had the 'seeking sickness'—which was what Tahar's mother had called her husband's relentless curiosity about the world.

'There's so much more beyond this sea of grass, son,' he had told Tahar. 'We must see it for ourselves!'

Tahar's father had been fascinated by a land called Khemet, which he had heard lay beyond the Dark and Big Green Seas. 'The Land of the Date-Eaters', he had called the fabled kingdom. He'd told Tahar that the sun always shone in the Land of Khemet, and giant stone pyramids poked into the sky. At the kingdom's heart was a city in which thirty thousand souls were said to reside. *Thirty thousand souls!* It was a land of untold wealth and prosperity—an earthly paradise where nobody ever went hungry and nobody ever died, or so his father had heard. His father had wished to journey to Khemet, and he'd wanted Tahar to join him.

'The boy has scarcely seen a dozen years,' Tahar's mother had argued. 'He may not go.'

But Tahar's father had insisted, explaining that the journey would make Tahar a man.

Tahar remembered the soft, fragile sound of his mother's voice when she had finally acquiesced. 'Bring him back to me,' was all she had said.

'Aye, and a dozen gold coins to boot,' Tahar's father had pronounced, wrapping his shining copper battle axe in cloth. 'We shall have no need of this but for trade,' he explained, and it had occurred to Tahar that his father was bold indeed, and that he loved the man more than all the stars in the sky.

It was his father's boldness, in the end, that had been his demise. They had sailed across the Dark Sea without incident, but his father had underestimated the moods of the Big Green. Or perhaps he'd wished to be tested, for as the storm had approached he'd refused to guide their old wooden sailing boat to land.

'Let us see what the Khemetian Gods can conjure for the Men of the Grass,' he had told Tahar. And he'd held his battle axe high in the air as the storm approached, as if the shiny copper weapon could somehow vanquish the immense waves.

When they'd washed up on the shore the next day there had been no more boat—just Tahar, his father, and his father's horse. Before them a sea of green-blue water had stretched into the distance; behind them a sea of sand. His father had told him that he was going to find help, that he wouldn't be long.

'Will you not take the horse?' Tahar had asked, but his father had refused.

'If I am not back in two days, come and find me,' he'd said.

But as Tahar had watched his father's grand figure grow blurry in the heat haze he'd feared it was the last time he would ever see the beloved man...or his mother... or the distant grassy plains he called home.

Now, with the boon of this woman, he would finally have the means to return to his homeland. All they had to do was survive the journey to Nubia. And survive they would—for, unlike his father, Tahar had been humbled by the Red Land, and his humility had gifted him the patience to learn its secrets.

'There is our food,' he remarked now, pointing to a large acacia bush. 'Do you see it?'

They had reached the area at the base of the cliffs where they had earlier tethered the horse. Confused, the woman bent beneath the bush and pushed her fingers into the sand, seizing upon a single seed.

'There is but one—not enough to eat,' she said, showing him the seed and then stuffing it into the folds of her wrap.

'I refer not to what is beneath the bush, but what is balanced upon it.' Tahar pointed to a single white hair, balancing on a branch near her head.

She plucked it free and handed it to Tahar. Her touch was light, yet it seemed to leave a deep mark upon his skin.

'The sign is new. The ewe is near,' he said.

'How do you know it is near?'

Tahar considered whether to explain that the wild desert sheep travelled in the cool of morning, that in the afternoon the winds whipped the sands and left no bush unshaken. The sheep had to have passed that morning, because by the afternoon its hair would have been blown to the ground.

'I know this because I have lived in the desert for most of my life,' he told her coolly. 'I know how to find water and I know how to find food. You must listen to me and follow my commands if you wish to survive.'

A rush of air escaped through her nostrils, but she held her tongue.

They discovered the sheep grazing on a stand of salt-bush—a large female with its udder full. It lifted its horned head and stared at Tahar, its big eyes unblinking. Meanwhile, the woman slipped behind the bushes.

'Bah!' she shouted suddenly, rushing at the animal from behind.

With a quick lunge, Tahar trapped the ewe in his arms.

'Well done,' Tahar said, keeping firm hold as the animal struggled to wrestle free of his grasp. 'Get the water bag from my saddle,' he explained. 'I shall hold her steady while you milk.'

The woman nodded, quickly returning with the empty water bag. Instead of kneeling to milk, however, she stared at the ewe's bulging udder with alarm.

'Get on with it,' urged Tahar, but still she hesitated. Could it be that she had never milked an animal? Impossible. It was well known that in the land of Khemet there were more cows than Khemetians.

Tentatively the woman bent to her work, and soon the ewe's rich milk was spilling into the bag.

'Ha!' she exclaimed, flashing him a girlish grin.

Her eyes were not completely brown, he noticed then. Flecks of gold dotted the inner rings. Where had they come from? he wondered. Those tiny slivers of sunlight? And what was this woman's station that she had never before milked a beast?

He had spotted the lie when she had told him about her kin, of course. It had been as if she were reading from a scroll of untruths as she'd described her destitute family in Abydos. She had mentioned a city. Had she dwelt in one? It seemed probable, since she had either been born very high or very low indeed. Which was it?

When they arrived at the oasis they passed the bag

between them, drinking long draughts of the sweet, creamy milk.

'It was a good idea to pursue the sheep,' she conceded, as a white moustache appeared just above her upper lip.

Impulsively he smeared his thumb across the stain and then licked his digit clean. She stared at him curiously, her full cheeks glowing red.

What an unusual woman. One moment she was doubting him, with her pompous Khemetian nose in the air. The next she was quiet—appreciative, even. And, he realised suddenly, quite lovely.

'You were very skilled at the milking,' he lied.

'Well, I have been doing it all my life,' she lied, smiling wide.

And in that moment he wished for her to lie again, for he found himself adoring her.

Careful Tahar.

It had been many years since he had spent any time with a woman, but he remembered the day as if it was yesterday. It had been back when the drought was young, and traders like Tahar had still thrived along the routes. Tahar had just completed a large transfer of Garamantian natron to a merchant in Alexandria, and he had been rich with copper.

As a reward for his success Tahar had taken himself to Alexandria's renowned House of Women. He'd settled himself inside its cool tavern and made a gift of goodwill to the owner—five *deben* of grain. In gratitude, the owner had brought Tahar a beautiful woman who wore cymbals upon her fingers and bells upon her toes. Her eyes had been kohled in a luxurious spiral design, and when she'd walked her hips had swayed smartly, whispering their conceits.

'She has seen a full eighteen summers now,' the quick-eyed owner had explained, his lips twisting with mirth. 'She is one of our best.'

In a bedroom, Tahar had showered the woman with copper coins. He'd scrubbed her back with lavender oil and fed her honey cakes and beer. But it had not been enough.

After their joining, the woman had burst into tears. 'You took my purity!' she'd claimed.

'Impossible,' said Tahar. 'You are skilled in the arts of the flesh and you are well of age.'

'Nay, I have seen but fourteen summers.'

Tahar had been shocked, and had soon felt a knot of shame twist inside his stomach. Had he known she was of such a tender age he would never have bedded her. Overcome with guilt, he'd given the girl almost all the copper he'd carried.

'This will keep me fed for many months,' she'd told him in gratitude, tears streaming down her face.

He had taken her virginity, after all. Surely that was worth all Tahar had to give? He had fumbled for his belt. The only other thing of value that he'd owned had been his father's precious old battle axe.

'Trade this,' Tahar had explained, handing her the copper-plated weapon, 'and you will not have to lie with another man for several years.'

'Thank you, kind trader,' the girl had said, accepting the only possession that had remained of Tahar's father besides his horse.

Tahar had gathered his things and hurried to the nearby stables, paying the stable boy and guiding his beloved old beast hurriedly out of town. On his way, he'd passed by the House of Women once again. Impulsively he'd tied his horse outside the mud-brick building and brushed through its beaded entryway, intent on retrieving the grain he had gifted to the deceitful owner.

As his eyes had adjusted to the tavern's low light once again he'd beheld the woman. She'd been sitting on the lap of the owner, handing him the copper coins Tahar had gifted her just hours before. And the battle axe that had belonged to Tahar's father and his grandfather before him had lain askew in a wooden box in a dusty back corner of the tavern, as if it had been thrown there as an afterthought.

Tahar had made a motion towards the box and the woman had quickly stood. She'd held out a long knife. 'You would steal back a freely given gift?' she asked.

Suddenly all her feigned innocence disappeared and the Blue Serpent—the shrewdest, most successful trader in all of the Red Land *and* the Black—knew that he had been taken for a fool.

Tahar had turned on his heel, begging his father for forgiveness and vowing never to let a woman get the better of him again.

But the drought had not relented, and soon there had been no more women, nor copper coins, nor even grain. The woman from Alexandria was the last woman he had known.

Until now.

Tahar watched his Khemetian captive take another draught of milk. He could not afford to be foolish again, he reminded himself. No matter how kind she appeared, she was like any other woman—a serpent in the soft grass. Tahar licked his thumb clean of the milk he had rubbed from her lip, but refused to take another sip.

'The rest of the milk is for you,' he stated. 'You need it more than I.'

'Thank you, kind trader,' she said, and Tahar recalled that the treacherous woman had said the same.

'I suppose this is the last time in your life you will ever have to milk a beast,' Tahar added, assuring himself that he was still in control.

'Why do you say that?'

'As the wife of a Nubian Chief, you will have servants to do the milking for you.' He turned away from her then, for despite the bitterness and suspicion that had long occupied his soul he could not bear to watch the woman's shy smile turn to dust.

Chapter Thirteen

When they set out upon the plateau at dusk, the woman was silent. She had been that way since their rest at the second oasis—over eight hours ago now—and Tahar had the vague notion that he was being punished. He should have known better than to provoke her as he had. She was a woman, after all, with a woman's sensitivities, and he was quite clearly in control. There had been no need to remind her that soon she would be warming some rich man's bed.

It occurred to Tahar that the rich man would be a lucky man indeed. Tahar did not know him, and already he envied him.

Tahar led the donkey onward into the twilight.

The sun dipped below the horizon and cast its pink and yellow spell upon the sky. She observed the spectacle of colour with mutiny in her eyes. 'How long until we reach Abu?' she asked at last.

'We've yet many days,' said Tahar.

Soon the stars began to sparkle above them and the heat of the day lifted mercifully. Still the woman seemed restless. She adjusted herself upon the saddle, apparently unable to find a comfortable position.

'May I lead the horse for a time?' she asked. 'I wish to stretch my legs.'

He did not answer her request immediately. 'Hem,' he said. 'Let me think on it.'

Of course he would let her lead the horse. What a welcome request.

Yes, my lovely. Take the horse. Stretch your shapely legs and feel the crunch of dirt beneath your feet. Let me rest and contemplate your gait, the swish of your hips, the long muscles of your legs.

After a long pause, Tahar gave his assent. 'On one condition,' he said. 'You must admit that you do not come from a family of farmers in Abydos.'

'Fine, I admit it.'

She admitted it? No headstrong resistance? No fiery debate? Tahar felt strangely disheartened. *So where do you come from?* he wished to ask now. But that had not been part of the bargain.

Obligingly, he helped her off the horse, and soon she was guiding it across the empty plain with him upon its back.

'Your hair grows,' he ventured. 'It is as new shoots in an empty field.'

She said nothing.

'Your arm heals.'

Nothing.

'Your gait is strong. There is no memory of the snakebite in it.'

Finally, she spoke. 'You observe me as if I were a newborn calf or a recently grafted vine.'

'What more can I do but observe if you will not converse?'

'I do not converse because I do not have anything to say to one who keeps me as a slave.'

'If you have not noticed, I feed you and protect you.'

'Like a fine cow.'

'I tend to your wounds. I prepare you not for slavery but for marriage.'

'Marriage, slavery—they are the same.'

'Isn't marriage what *every* woman desires?' Tahar asked, disbelieving. 'To bear children? To enjoy the love and protection of a husband? To be provided for?'

The woman turned and continued walking. 'Not every woman.'

'Indeed? Then what is it exactly that *you* desire?'

The woman did not speak. Instead she shook her head and began walking more rapidly.

'You cannot answer my question?' Tahar pressed. 'If you cannot express your desire, then you do not deserve to have it fulfilled.'

The woman stopped in her tracks. She turned to look at Tahar, and even in the low light he could see the magical flicker of her dark eyes.

'Desire? What do I *desire*? I don't have the luxury of desire,' she said, 'unless you consider the desire for a belly full of food—enough to get me through the day. You pretend that you are offering me a better life, but you are not. You are using me to obtain a better life for yourself. What do I desire? I desire to be free of you, or anyone who would use me as a possession. I desire freedom. So, handsome trader from beyond the Big Green, will you fulfil my desire? Do I *deserve* it?'

Before Tahar could respond the woman had turned

her back to him and resumed her march across the empty plain. He was left sitting lamely upon the saddle, his head spinning. He had hoped for a trickle of conversation; instead he'd got a flood of words.

If he had been attending to them closely he might have heard how thoroughly she mistrusted men. He might have discerned her desire for food—the kind of desire only felt by one who regularly went without it. If he had been truly observant, as he normally was, he might even have become discouraged, for her longing for freedom was as clear and certain as his own.

But he did not ponder any of that, for all he could think about in that moment was a single word.

Handsome. She thinks that I am handsome.

Chapter Fourteen

Never again. She would not speak to him ever again. She had finally expressed her true desire to him, had laid her heart bare, and he had said nothing in response. He was never going to set her free.

Her greatest wish was beyond what he was willing to grant. He would praise her skills and feast upon her flesh with his eyes, but when presented with the right thing to do he recoiled like a stunned snake.

They remained on their course to Nubia. To the land of deep mines and rich husbands, or so he had told her. She had been wrong about him, after all. He was not kind, not noble. He wished only for his own gain.

How easy it had been to forget her mother's wisdom, to let her guard down. In her delusion she had imagined that Tahar might actually sympathise with her plight. She had thought him kind. She had thought him her friend. She had even thought—

It didn't matter what she thought now. She could not influence him—not with tears, not with lies, not even with the truth. He was committed to his plan: to sell her to the richest suitor he could find. And now she was rededicated to hers: to take back what was left of her stolen grain and escape his wicked grasp.

The nights passed like colourless dreams. She had to be patient. She could do nothing until they were closer to the Great River. Even if she did recapture her grain, there was no sanctuary to which she could escape. The desert stretched vast and barren all around them. The secret wells that Tahar found with such proficiency were invisible to Kiya. Nor would she be able to find her own food. There were no street vendors or fishermen here— only quiet, lurking animals that did not wish to be seen.

Though Tahar saw them.

How he had sniffed out that swallow's nest at the last oasis was a mystery to Kiya, but, oh—how tender had been the boiled eggs upon her tongue! He'd wielded his newly acquired bow with dexterity, piercing a very fast-moving hare and skewering it for their breakfast. He'd threaded its hide across the top of the addax-skin dress he had gifted her, explaining that the soft fur would help catch the dust. He had even discovered a band of grasshoppers clustering on the sunny side of a small dune. A Khemetian delicacy, the large green insects roasted were crispy and delicious. Seth's bones, the man was almost as skilled as she at making something out of nothing.

Now they rested in the shade of a lone sycamore tree that Tahar had discovered at a bend in the small wash in which they travelled. It was funny, she thought, here she was, in the desolate wastes of the Red Land, and yet she had never eaten so heartily, dressed so elegantly, nor rested so well.

Kiya pretended not to watch Tahar, dozing contentedly, his heavy brows falling back from his closed eyes.

Strange, aqua-blue eyes. She had never in her life seen such eyes. She had never even known such eyes could exist.

Perhaps his mother or father had come from far away. The people of the desert sometimes intermarried with foreigners. As nomads, the Libu ranged widely, always searching for better grazing lands for their flocks of goats and sheep, always hunting for their paradise—a Khemet all their own—but never finding it.

She was not unsympathetic to their plight. In many ways it was like her own—always searching, never finding. Always struggling to survive.

Still, she needed to be careful not to mistake her captor's generosity for caring. He intended to sell her for his own gain. She could not forget that simple fact. If she did, she risked the worst possible fate—the fate of her mother.

Kiya recalled the vials that had littered the space beneath her mother's bed. They'd been made of a beautiful blue glass and had smelled faintly of flowers. Every day her mother had tilted one of those vials to her lips and drunk the mysterious liquid inside.

Afterwards, her mother's eyes would grow cloudy and she would drift off to sleep—often in the middle of the day. When she awoke, many hours later, she would tell Kiya to fetch one of the harem's servants and order food, and while they waited for their meal, she would tell Kiya a story. That had been Kiya's favourite time with her mother.

As she'd told her tales, her mother's eyes would grow bright, lighting up the dark chamber. She would tell children's tales—stories meant to teach Kiya about Khemetian history, its gods, and how things came to be. The tale she'd told most often was called *How the Date Palm Got*

Its Dates. She'd come alive, pretending to be the monkey in the tale, and Kiya would laugh and clap as her mother jumped around their chamber, scratching her ribs and cackling wildly.

But soon she would empty another vial and her gaze would grow cloudy once again.

The day of the raid Kiya had had to clear those empty vials out of the way just to reach her hiding place under her mother's bed. The vial that her mother had drunk from to take her own life had not been very different from the others, just bigger. It had been as if her mother had been saving the bottle for exactly such a moment— as if she had known the raiders were coming.

As if, perhaps, she had *wanted* them to come.

After the raid Kiya had pulled a blanket over her mother's ashen face and vowed never to endure such an ugly fate. She might be the young child of a forgotten concubine of a dead king, but she was not dead yet.

Hungry and scared, she had followed the river trail until she'd reached the great capital city of Memphis. There Kiya had found other children like herself— parentless, unwanted creatures who survived on scraps, their own wits, and an aptitude for survival. Kiya had quickly become one of them.

Now Kiya studied Tahar's placid face and struck upon an idea.

For she was one of them still.

Chapter Fifteen

That evening, for the first time in a week, she spoke. 'May I lead the horse?' she asked Tahar. 'I wish to stretch my legs.'

It was good to hear the sound of her voice. Its soft, gentle lilt was like the tinkle of water amidst the sweltering silence. Further, it gave him an excuse to turn and behold her atop the beast—a vision he found himself craving more and more.

'As you wish,' Tahar said.

The sun had already set and the full moon risen, and there was plenty of light for her to seek her path upon the ground.

She dismounted the beast, and stroked its long neck. 'Good horse,' she said, patting it on the snout. 'What is his name?'

She was standing closer to Tahar than she had in days, and he felt his awareness grow more acute.

'He does not have a name. He is a beast.'

'In Khemet we give our beasts names. May I name him?'

'You may,' he said. Her nearness was a tonic.

'Hello… Meemoo,' she said, a playful smile extended across her face.

Desert wind, what was he doing to her? He did not understand her changing moods. She had called him handsome, and then for a week had ceased to speak to him at all. She had praised his pursuit of the sheep's milk, but when he had landed them a hare she had said not a single word. She wouldn't even lie atop the carpet he unrolled for her day after day. Instead she stretched across the naked ground, as he did, as far away from him as possible.

She touched Tahar's hands and smiled as he gave her the reins, and the sensation was enough to make his heart skip. Her beauty was growing impossible to ignore. He had not anticipated the impact that a regular diet of meat and grain would make upon the woman. Only three weeks had passed since the raid and already her gaunt, pale face had gained colour and fullness. Her shiny black hair grew, though it remained hidden beneath her makeshift headdress. And those lips. Gods. Her lips alone could stop a caravan.

He had hoped that she would soften towards him, and that they might again begin to converse. It wasn't just that he wished to convert her to the idea of marriage. He wished to understand why she rejected it so completely. She was like no other woman he had ever known. Clever and capable. Feisty and headstrong. Mysterious and—curse her—incomprehensibly appealing. Yet instead of desiring the safety and security of a husband she wished for freedom. She was a puzzle he wanted to solve, but it had been so long since she'd spoken to him that he'd grown afraid of asking. Who, he wondered, was training whom?

'There is an oasis ahead, yes?' she asked.

'Aye, about half a day's—or I should say half a *night's*—journey.'

'That is well.' She waited for Tahar to mount the horse and then began to lead it across the flat, moonlit plain.

Tahar was glad for the rest, and he admitted that he did not mind the chance to appraise her from behind. Her gait was strong, confident. Her headdress hung about her shoulders, and in the moonlight it looked like a mane of long, luxurious hair. The leather sandals he had made for her twisted appealingly up her muscular calves, and her addax-skin dress clung snugly to her breasts and growing hips, which moved in a rhythm all their own.

Her body was changing: she had begun to show a woman's curves. And it was as if those very curves were on some clandestine mission to test Tahar's resolve.

'It is beautiful tonight,' she offered as she walked.

'Aye,' he said.

He had not noticed. He wrenched his eyes from her succulent backside and looked around him. The full moon cast its cool glow upon the land. In the distance Tahar could see the bristly palm leaf profile of the Dakhla Oasis. Beyond it the Big Sandy undulated softly, almost invitingly. The woman was right: it was a lovely night.

'It is as if the moonlight were water,' she observed, 'and Thoth were pouring it upon the land.'

Moonlight as water? He had never thought of it that way. He closed his eyes and imagined the moonlight falling from the night sky like rain. A wave of contentment washed over him. It had been a long time since he'd allowed himself to feel the gentleness of the desert, the wonder of it.

The Libu tribe that had adopted him did not see the

wonder of the Red Land, for they had never known anything else. Of course they knew of Khemet, where water flowed through fertile fields and nobody lived in want. But Khemet might as well have been a realm of the Gods, because it was forbidden to them.

The Libu of the Meshwesh region had found Tahar and his horse lost amongst the dunes. They had adopted the blue-eyed boy and his strange beast as their own. They had only asked that Tahar learn the ways of the desert and, as soon as possible, help support the tribe. They'd given him a copper blade and shown him how to hunt addax, oryx and gazelle. They'd taught him to use his ears, to hear the scratch of a hedgehog's feet upon the ground and the whisper of birdsong on the breeze, beckoning him to hidden wells.

Tahar's soul filled with gratitude. Without the kindness of the Libu Meshwesh he would have certainly perished. He had committed himself to learning all they had to teach. He'd ranged across the treeless landscape, unearthing its secrets. His mind had always been working, always trying to piece together the puzzle of creation. He had searched in deep, dry canyons and found them teeming with hidden life. He had reached the summit of the tallest peaks and observed stories told in stone. He'd discovered hidden wells and ancient bones and histories etched on walls a thousand years old.

His soul had filled with wonder. Who needed gods when there were marvels such as these? They were all there, for anyone to see if only they wished to look.

'May I ask you a question?' asked Tahar.

'You may ask any question you like. Whether I shall supply an answer is another thing entirely,' the woman answered haughtily.

'Have you ever had the privilege of entering the Great Pyramid of Stone?'

The woman paused, as if considering which lie she would tell. At length, she seemed to decide upon the truth. 'I have.'

'What is it like inside?'

'What is it *like*? Hem. Well, it is cool and dark. Torches illuminate the sacred passages, of which there are three. Each passage leads to a holy chamber, each chamber more grand and elaborate than the last. They say that the first chamber—the one beneath the earth—is false, constructed merely to confuse malicious spirits. The second chamber is for the King's *ushebti* statue, of course. The third is his true chamber—the place where his mummy will rest. But I think—'

The woman stopped walking and turned to face Tahar.

'Please go on,' said Tahar. 'What do you think?'

'I think that there are two other secret chambers.'

'Two secret chambers?'

The woman's eyes glimmered with excitement. She lowered her voice. 'I have heard that there are no reliefs in the third chamber—nor any hieroglyphs upon the walls. In addition, the third chamber is small. There is only a single slab of red granite to receive the King.'

'Is that unusual?'

'Yes, very unusual. The King needs the text of the spells to protect him on his journey through the Underworld. They must be written upon the walls of his tomb. He also needs a script to recite before Osiris, in the Hall of Judgement. That script should have been carved into the walls of the third chamber, but it has not been. And when he is admitted into the Land of Eternity the King will require all his possessions. It is well known that Khufu's father, the mighty King Sneferu, had two rooms for his possessions—one room for his personal items and the other for his furniture, saddles, yokes and ploughs. The third chamber must have a hidden entrance that leads to these two other secret chambers.'

'Have you heard anyone speak of these secret chambers?'

'Nay—but I feel certain they are there,' said Kiya. 'Just as there are sacred words meant only for holy ears, so there are sacred spaces meant only for gods and kings.'

Tahar smiled to himself. The woman was clever—probably too clever for her own good. 'You observe much; your conclusion rings true.'

The woman gave Tahar a deep bow and smiled. 'Of course if I am ever confronted I will deny that I ever shared any such conjecture with you.'

'Of course,' said Tahar, nodding at the woman.

She returned to her walk.

'There is also a tunnel,' she added offhandedly. 'It winds its way up the great structure, along its inner perimeter, all the way to the top. Anybody may use it who is working on the pyramid, though only a few may step out upon the threshold at the top. The tunnel itself is used primarily for the hauling of stones. It is how the Great Pyramid was built.'

'A tunnel? Inside the structure itself?' Tahar could not conceal his wonder. So *that* was how the clever Khemetians had done it.

'Aye.'

'All the way to the top?'

'Aye, though it will be filled in soon, with stones.'

'How I should love to enter the Great Pyramid before

I die,' Tahar admitted. 'How I should love to climb that tunnel. Have you done so?'

The woman did not respond, and in her silence he read her answer: yes.

'How many more nights until we reach Abu?' she asked, abruptly changing the subject.

It was clear that she *had* ascended the tunnel—many times. *Gods, she had probably been a hauler.* That was the reason for her tightly wrapped breast cloth, the unusually muscular calves—the reason she wore no wig. She had laboured upon the Great Pyramid of Stone *as a hauler.* That was why he had found her at the raid.

'If you do not know how many nights to Abu, can you at least make a guess?' she added brusquely.

'Oh, aye. Seven or eight nights at least,' Tahar replied.

His mind roiled with the implications of her inadvertent admission. She was a woman who had laboured upon a king's tomb. She had defied the gods she professed to believe in so ardently. She had violated the law. She was even bolder than he could have imagined. He wished to probe her mind further, but he knew her too well to attempt to return to the subject of the pyramid.

'So many days?' she asked wistfully. 'I had thought the Isle closer.'

You had hoped it closer. Tahar stared at the woman's soft curves with new wonder. 'Before we can even speak of Abu or Nubia we must first survive the crossing of the Big Sandy.'

'I have heard of it. They say it is vast—larger even than the Big Green.'

'It is larger, and much more dangerous,' he explained. 'Unlike a sea of water, a sea of sand will never carry you to shore. You must carry yourself or die. To cross it at its narrowest point is a three-day march without stopping. If we bring too much water we slow our trek and risk exposing ourselves too long to the sun. If we bring too little water… Well, I don't need to tell you what will happen in that case.'

Tahar swallowed hard. The Big Sandy was a challenge they had to face. To go around it would cost them a many months of travel, through hostile territory, and Tahar could not risk losing the woman again. Still, his stomach turned at the prospect of attempting to traverse the endless swathes of dunes at this, the hottest time of the year.

If only the Big Sandy were a real sea and the woman were his boat. The thought should have made him smile— she *was* his boat, after all—but instead Tahar's insides clenched.

'When we arrive in Nubia I assume you will try to generate multiple buyers, to get the best price for me?'

'That is so,' Tahar responded carefully. 'Why do you ask?'

'No reason.'

But Tahar knew her better. 'I will find you the richest possible husband,' he assured her, shifting into the familiar role of trader. 'I'm sure I do not have to explain that such an outcome will be favourable for you.'

He let his statement linger in the air. He would indeed find her a rich husband, for he was very good at trading. Though the Khemetians viewed trade as a lowly profession, Tahar was not ashamed to call himself a trader. He was like a fennec fox—quiet and observant, with ears large enough to hear everything happening along the trade routes. There was a load of natron salt coming from Fezzan? Well, there was a ship of Etruscans in Alexandria who would pay dearly for it. Five *kites* of silver from Garamantia? He knew some jewellers from Uruk who would be quite interested.

All he asked was a broker's pittance—a cut of grain or a dusting of gold. And he always gave what he earned to his tribe, always in gratitude.

Finding a wife had proved more challenging. Despite the fact that he bore the Libu scar, and had been Libu for more than half of his thirty-two years, the women of the tribe still viewed him as an outsider. He did not look like a Libu man. He was larger and paler and did not wear a beard.

One day he had overheard a group of women discussing the unmarried men of the tribe. 'What about Tahar?' a woman had asked in a soft voice. 'He has brought us much wealth.'

'But he is so…large,' another had said. 'And his blue eyes are strange. They frighten me.'

Undeterred, Tahar had sought out the woman with the soft voice, but when he had finally met her inside her family's tent, she would not look at him. She'd kept her head down, for Libu women were expected to listen, not speak, in the presence of men. Tahar had understood this, but had thought if he could charm a grain trader into an extra half-*khar* of grain, why not a Libu woman into speaking her mind?

'I am here to get to know you,' he'd explained to the woman.

There had been a long, uncomfortable silence.

'We can go for a walk. Is that something you would like to do?'

She had not responded.

'I have come to see if we are a match for marriage. What do you think?'

The woman's chest had moved up and down rapidly with her breaths, yet still she had not spoken.

'What do you want?' Tahar had asked finally.

'I don't *know* what I want,' she had burst out, tears gathering in her eyes.

Tahar had realised that she had probably never once been asked that simple question.

At last she'd looked at Tahar. 'What do *you* want?'

An unexpected answer had come to Tahar's lips: 'I wish to return to my homeland.'

And it had been true. He had not known it until that very moment, but he did not want to spend his life shuffling goods in the desert. He wanted to fulfil the promise his father had made to his mother so long ago. He wanted to return to her. He wanted to go home.

He imagined his mother often. If she still lived, she would now be quite old. She would be in need of him. He imagined the vast grazing grounds where his tribe wandered, always moving with their animals. With patience and a strong boat he was certain he could find that grassy paradise again.

Still, he'd known he owed his Libu tribe everything. How could he possibly leave them and strike out on his own? He would need to amass a large fortune, both to ensure his tribesmen's security and to support his journey. He had thanked the soft-voiced woman, exited the tent, and quietly begun planning his new life.

His first goal had been to amass the fortune. He would work hard, and in five or ten years he would have enough money to buy a boat. With a boat he could move cross the Big Green and the Dark Seas. He could seek his tribe and his mother.

He might even find a bride—a woman who would not

be repelled by his blue eyes and Libu scar. A woman who would speak her mind. A woman who was interested in learning more of the world, which he knew was wider than even he imagined. Indeed, his father had proved it.

But then the drought had crept in on quiet feet. One year. Two years. The rich Khemetian merchants with whom he usually did business had had nothing left to trade. His Libu tribesmen had been no less destitute. With their meagre grazing lands desiccated by the drought, their goats were dying in large numbers. Tahar had not been able to shirk his obligation to the people to whom he owed his very life.

In only two cycles of the sun, Tahar had given his tribe half of what he had saved in ten. Gradually he had given up on his dream. Until the day he'd seen her lithesome figure running across the plain.

'If you cannot find a husband for me, do you intend to offer me as a slave?' she asked now, her voice coppery and high.

'I *will* find a husband for you,' Tahar said, glancing at her developing figure. 'Of that you needn't have a doubt. Nubian men who do business with Khemetians seek Khemetian brides.'

'But you will need to provide some kind of assurance, will you not? Proof that I am indeed Khemetian and that I am a…a virgin?'

'They will be able to discern that you are Khemetian well enough when you speak.'

'And my purity?'

'They will be able to discern that, too.' *What was the little cobra up to now?*

'How, exactly, will they be able to tell?'

'There are ways.'

'What ways?'

'They need not concern you.'

She was not without curiosity, and he admired her for it. Her busy mind would serve her well in her future life, for she would likely become part of a rich man's harem.

Part of a rich man's harem.

He felt his chest tighten. He could not imagine her in a harem. She was too independent, too curious and headstrong. She would quickly grow bored with a life within the bounds of some stifling walled compound. She would pick fights with the other wives just for sport! Worse, she might seek her comfort in vials of milk of poppy, as many concubines did. Not that it was any of his concern.

His concern was to get them across the Big Sandy to the Isle of Abu, then up the river to Nubia. To do that he needed her full cooperation. He needed to show her that *he* held the reins. And yet there she was, walking ahead of him, actually holding the reins.

After several hours they arrived at the edge of the large Dakhla Oasis. The sprawling lowland was abundant with date palms and fig trees, and there was enough water to support small crops of millet and wheat. A small town had taken root amongst its abundant shade—a place where traders could rest their mules and quench their thirsts and find a woman to massage their weary shoulders.

But Tahar divulged none of this to the woman. Instead they stopped on the outskirts of the oasis, where a small, inviting pool beckoned.

'Ah!' the woman exclaimed, staring at the moonlit waters. 'This is lovely.'

With Khemetian soldiers and Libu raiders about, it was too risky for Tahar to show his scarred face in town.

Besides, there was no need for them to seek the comforts of civilisation. They carried plenty of meat and grain, and the pool offered a perfect place for them to bathe and take their rest. What more did they need? They would stay here and gather their strength until the following evening, when they would skirt the perimeter of Dakhla and begin the difficult trek across the Big Sandy.

The air was still and swelteringly hot. The crickets sang their ancient song, though it seemed louder, more urgent this night. A slight breeze tickled the palms, but it took none of the edge off the stifling heat. A full moon rode high in the sky, shining like a sparkling path of light upon the small central pool.

Tahar began to unpack the horse and make camp.

'I shall drink,' the woman stated, sweat beading on her forehead. She was standing beside the pool. 'And then swim.'

'You should not drink from the pool, for there is a well here,' said Tahar. 'The well water will be sweeter—and safer.'

'And where is the well?'

Tahar held his tongue. 'First tell me your name.'

'My name?'

'Aye.'

'My name is… Hathor.'

Tahar chuckled in disbelief. 'You are named for the Khemetian Goddess of Love and Abundance?'

'You think it strange?' the woman said, affecting offence. 'It is an honour to bear such a name.'

'I do not believe you, but I will call you Hathor if you wish.'

'You do not believe me? Why?'

'Because only highborn Khemetians may bear the names of Gods, and you are not highborn.'

Tahar watched the blood of anger flood into the woman's cheeks. 'You know nothing about me.'

'I know much about you.'

'Ha! You know only what I wish you to know,' she said, and she set her jaw in the air.

'You might be surprised by what I know, Hathor, for I am very observant.' He approached her.

'I doubt that very much,' she said, stepping backwards so that her feet skirted the water.

'I know that you can move silently, like a spirit, but you cannot milk a beast. I know that you can fight like a man, but are unaccustomed to a man's eyes upon your skin.' He stepped closer. 'I know that you are faster and stronger and cleverer than any woman I have ever known, and yet until I captured you, you had never ridden atop an animal.'

He was standing directly in front of her now.

'I know you can steal a blade from beneath a man's wrap—' He wrapped his hand around her head and pulled his own blade out from beneath the folds of her tattered headdress. 'But you are unaccustomed to a sky so full of stars.'

He wedged the blade beneath the belt of his tunic and motioned to the stars above them.

He leaned down so his face was just inches from hers. 'You tilt your head in the self-satisfied way of a highborn,' he said, tracing the length of her chin with his finger, 'but you bear a labourer's calluses upon your hands.'

On an impulse he reached out and found her hands. He ran his thumbs across the small hardened mounds at the bases of her fingers. His heartbeat quickened. As he moved his thumb up and over each rough mound it was as if he were exploring some forbidden part of her.

The woman's chest began to heave with her breaths, but he could not tell if they were breaths of yearning or of fury. He pressed his thumbs more forcefully against her palms and his desire begin to spike.

Tahar released her hands and stepped backwards, dazed. Streams of sweat dribbled down the sides of his face and he wiped them away with the fabric of his headdress. The woman, too, seemed to snap awake. He watched her expression change from trance-like stupor to bitter resentment as she recalled that her pride had just been bruised.

She gathered herself, folded her arms, and gave a small *harrumph*. 'Well, I assure you that you are wrong, *trader*,' she said. 'For I am almost as highborn as they come.'

Gods, she was sweet. He had never thought he could enjoy the sound of a woman's lies so much. He enjoyed them almost as much as the way she smelled, which was incredible. Even after days of travel she exuded a delicious earthy scent that was vaguely floral and unmistakably woman. He wished he could get closer to her neck to catch some more of it.

'Where is the well?' she asked again.

Tahar was relieved when he discovered the small, rock-lined hole in the ground a dozen paces from the edge of the pool. He removed the woven palm leaf cover and peered down into its depths.

'The water level is high,' he announced. 'Please, drink… Hathor.'

She bent over the well, and as she did a gap appeared in the addax-skin dress he had made for her—a cleft between her small, plump breasts. A pang of lust vaulted through Tahar's body and he fought to look away, but he could not. There they were, and they were perfect. They hung like ripe fruits that he wished to pluck with is mouth.

She plunged her hands into the water and splashed her face. The droplets dribbled down onto her skin and soaked her chest. Tahar felt himself stiffen. She scooped up another handful of water and brought it to her wine-dark lips.

Those lips.

He needed to regain possession of himself. Or, better, he needed to say something that would cause her to push him away, for clearly he could not move away himself. What could he say to make her spit her venom? Facts! Khemetians hated facts. They believed only what they wanted to believe. He would ply her with a fact that no Khemetian—nor most Libu, for that matter—had ever believed, and she would walk away in fury.

'In fact,' he began, 'the well from which you drink is larger than you can imagine, and much older.' He spoke loudly and confidently, for he knew his certainty annoyed her. 'The ancient well lives below the sands. It is thousands upon thousands of years old.'

Tahar braced himself for her Khemetian indignation—a full frontal assault.

'The well water was above the ground once. It was an ancient sea. It covered the Red Land and the Black Land, too.' *And I remain in control of you and of this situation.*

'Really? That is wondrous.' She stared up at him with her big dark eyes.

'You do not doubt the veracity of what I say?' he asked.

Never in his life had anyone believed his theory of the

ancient sea, yet he knew it to be true. He had seen the evidence in his travels—the bones of ancient sea creatures buried in layers of sand and rock. Tahar was certain that the creatures had swum across the desert once, before their watery home had disappeared beneath the ravenous sun.

'I believe you,' she said. 'Your ocean is like the water from the Cave of Wanderers. It is…water from another time.' With two hands she scooped another handful of water and held it up to him, like an offering. She spoke softly and sweetly. 'Now you drink… Tahar.'

Tahar froze. What strange spell had the moon cast this night that the woman now wished for him to drink out of her very hands?

Reverently, he lowered his mouth and drank.

'And now I shall drink from *your* hands,' she pronounced. 'That is the Libu custom, yes?'

Indeed it was. He bent to the well and dipped his hands into the cool waters, then lifted them to her waiting lips. When she had finished she did not immediately lift her head. Instead she kissed each of his ten fingers, one by one.

She looked up at him. Her eyes danced in the moonlight and her copper skin shone with an otherworldly glow. 'I am going to swim now,' she said.

She cocked her head shyly, then turned and walked towards the oasis pool, loosening the leather straps that held her addax wrap in place. In the distance, a jackal let out a lonesome cry.

Tahar wiped his brow. He had begun to sweat profusely, as if it were the middle of the day and not the deepest part of the night. Why had she kissed him in that way? Each one of his fingers—with such tenderness?

Soon he heard the delicate complaint of disturbed water. He approached the oasis pool and beheld her entering its depths. She had completely disrobed. Her short black crop of hair was almost boyish, but her long, delicate neck and soft curves were all woman. He traced the length of her back with his eyes, studied its lovely dips and bends and fixated upon her firm, round buttocks. An eruption of lust plugged his throat.

He must have sighed, for she turned towards him, revealing her erect nipples. He shivered with desire. She scooped water and splashed it upon her chest several times, until her breasts glistened in the pearly light.

He was struck dumb. If he'd been able to think he might have wondered why her feelings had so suddenly changed. He might have asked her—*Why me? Why now?* But he could not think. He could not even speak.

I have lost control of the situation.

She beckoned to him. *Come.* And in that moment her true name did not matter, for she *was* Hathor, Goddess of Love and Abundance, and she had bewitched him.

Chapter Sixteen

When she saw him unwrapping his headdress and stepping out of his long tunic she knew she had overestimated the power of her own will. He stood to his full height and gazed at her from the bank, and already she yearned for him. His luxuriant mane hung about his face in thick, wavy ropes, and it was the only thing he wore.

He was a man. That was clear.

Stunningly clear.

But as she appraised the whole of his body she realised that he was also a god. Every chiselled bit of him radiated strength and masculinity. There was not even a hint of the softness of age or leisure, not a single inch of fallow flesh. He was as taut and ready as a drum.

And he was coming for her.

The strong sinews of his lower legs tensed as he stepped barefoot into the water. He began to walk towards her and his upper leg muscles bulged and contracted, creating rings of small waves that radiated out from his body. Those waves travelled slowly across the pool, and when they crashed into her body they made her shiver.

He walked towards her slowly and deliberately. If she

had seen him among the tomb workers she would have thought him a loader. She pictured him bare-chested and sweating in the sun, lifting some large boulder onto a cart, his dense muscles flexing. He would have been the most irresistibly handsome loader that ever was.

And he wanted her—nothing could be clearer.

She had thought that she repulsed him. Both times he had responded to her—in the pool and then in the cave—he had made his regret known. Now it seemed he was making the opposite known. She noticed his thick member, which stretched to an alarming length before it disappeared under the water.

Just the sight of it made her heart thump wildly.

He continued towards her, his narrow hips sinking beneath the velvety water, his muscular arms stretching out to caress its still surface. With the moon above him, the contours of his massive chest cast shadows upon his pale skin. It was as if he had been carved in alabaster: a temple relief showing the picture of an ideal man. Only this man was real—very, very real—and he was advancing towards her.

Everything is going according to plan, she told herself, though her whole body trembled. Her goal was to seduce him. To drive him so mad with desire that he would unwittingly take what he valued most about her— her virginity. Yet it seemed that *she* was the one going mad, for suddenly her body ached with a need that she had never felt before—a need so powerful it made her confused and afraid.

It was his eyes that scared her the most. They held her gaze in their deep blue snare—probing, searching, penetrating. They seemed to smoulder with something like anger. Or was it hunger?

Gods, what had she unleashed?

She felt her nipples tighten as he approached. Her whole body was flushed with heat. *I remain totally in control*, she told herself, though she could not slow her breaths. He was only a few arm's-lengths away from her now. His chest heaved and his jaws clenched, as if he were experiencing some terrible intensity—the very same intensity she felt pulsing through her own body.

No.

Yes.

He was so close now. Kiya knew that somewhere under the water his desire had stretched to its engorged length. Her body quaked with a riotous mix of fear and desire. Her womanhood ached.

He is doing just what I hoped he would do, she repeated to herself, trying to stay calm. *I've got him right where I want him.*

Still, she stepped backwards, terrified of him, of her own desire, of what she had started and was now unsure how to finish.

'Tahar—' she began, but could not remember what she'd been going to say.

She felt herself falling backwards. She was almost completely immersed underwater when he caught her in his arms and pulled her to the surface. She felt herself trembling. She feared his touch even as her whole body cried out for it.

'It's all right,' he said. He pulled her against him and held her tightly. 'I mean you no harm. You are safe.'

His words were solace to her soul. His body felt so good against hers. Her breasts pushed against his stomach, just beneath his chest, and her arms wrapped comfortably around the flanks of his lower back. Her head rested upon the bulging muscles of his chest as if upon pillows. His desire throbbed softly—safely—against her stomach.

She sighed. It was as if their bodies were meant to fit together in their embrace. Or perhaps she had finally found a lost part of her own body. Whatever danger she'd read in his eyes had dissolved with his touch. She buried her head in his chest and felt as if she could stay like this for ever. She felt safe. She felt desired. She felt…grateful.

'You have shown me amazing…things,' she said. 'I am—'

Chapter Seventeen

'Shh. Don't speak,' he said. He had spent a week trying to convince her to talk, and now he wished only to communicate with touch.

He pressed his finger against her soft lips, then traced their contours. His need throbbed painfully against her stomach. To touch her like this, to feel her skin against his, was driving him mad with lust.

He smiled and raked his fingers through her short, dark hair, reminding himself of her inexperience. She was as lovely in the moonlight as she was in the light of day. Water glistened against her honey skin, gathering in tiny rivulets that he wanted to taste.

He pulled her back into his arms. He could not restrain himself any more. He wanted all of her. He had felt it at the first oasis, when she had seated herself upon him in the pool, daring him to move. And in the cave, when he'd sucked the soft flesh of her thigh and been so close to her paradise that he had almost been able to taste its sweet nectar.

But even before those moments, even when he had first seen her lithesome figure running across the plain, he had felt it. She was like no woman he had ever known. Fiery and changeable. Wilful and strong. Restless and impossible to tame. He had captured her, and yet deep down he knew that she would never be truly caught. And that, more than anything, was what made him want her so badly.

He cradled her head in his hand. Gently, he tilted it back. He hovered over her mouth, letting her feel his hot breath upon her lips. Then, tenderly, he pressed his lips to hers and parted them. He felt her body stiffen. She pursed her lips, then let them loose, her awkward motions revealing her inexperience in even this, the simplest act of love.

Could it be that a woman as lovely as she had never shared the tenderness of a kiss? It seemed impossible, but there was much he didn't know about her. Perhaps she had disguised herself among men for so long that she had forgotten her power over them. More likely she had never even known she wielded such power.

He would show her now—but gently. Softly. He coaxed her mouth open, kissing her top lip and then her bottom lip. He felt her body relax into his once again. She closed her eyes, and he could see her slipping completely into the invisible space they shared. He probed her mouth with his tongue until he felt her timid tongue begin to respond in turn. How deliciously tentative she was!

His hands were like thieves. They crept down her back and looted the contours of her beautiful round buttocks. They slunk across her waist, raiding her lovely curves, taking everything they wanted. He could feel her heart beating rapidly against his own chest. His kisses grew deeper, more intense. She brushed her fingers down his back and the gentle uncertainty of her touch made him want to howl.

Her mouth began to move in rhythm with his. Her lips were so large and soft he wanted to devour them. He felt the mound of her womanhood push against his firmness, felt her desire transforming his own into a kind of desperation. He only knew what he wanted: to fill her with himself, to feel her as near to him as possible.

The force of his attraction to her verged on the overwhelming. She was a woman in full, unfolding before him like a lotus flower. He stared down at her face in awe. 'You are the most beautiful imposter that this world has ever seen,' he said, and then he moved his lips close to her ear. 'I want you so badly...'

Days later, Tahar would go over and over that moment in his mind, wishing he had never said those words. It had been hearing him voice his desire, he realised, that had reminded her of her own desire. It had wrenched her from the dream. The impossible, impractical, unreasonable dream of their love.

He felt her body stiffen. 'Then take me,' she said, but her voice was flat and without feeling. 'Yes, take it.'

She opened her eyes and he saw that they had changed. They were not rolling with ecstasy, but aware and steady. Her lips were no longer chafed and reddened with the evidence of his kisses. She held them in a thin, colourless line.

Take it, she had said, and it was as if all the desire had been squeezed out of her words so that only a hollow kind of fear remained.

She opened her legs wider and turned away. 'Go ahead,' she said. She drew in a breath and closed her eyes. 'Take it.'

He felt as if he had been snapped in two. *Take it*. She was referring to her maidenhood. She did not want him—not at all. This was a trap. Now her strange, probing questions of hours before made sense. She did not want him. She did not wish for his touch. She wished for him to take her virginity. She wanted to be rid of the thing that gave her so much value to him.

Tahar stepped backwards, stunned. 'You do not want me,' he choked. 'You seek to trick me.'

'I seek vengeance against he who would sell me for profit,' she said, her lips quivering. 'I seek justice.'

He dragged himself from the pool, the pain of his un-fulfilled desire making his whole body ache. She stayed in the water, and he could see that she was sobbing.

How could he have been so foolish? How could he not have seen the obvious signs? Her sudden interest in him, her impulsive flirtation, the brazen boldness of her touch…

'Ha!' he shouted in bitterness. He was like the Khe-metians, believing only what he wanted to believe—that she could want him, could love him, even—and not the truth that was right in front of his nose: that she hated him more and more each day.

Chapter Eighteen

The royal dancer was buxom and well-muscled: a vision of Hathor, Goddess of Love and Abundance. Hemp oil glistened upon her sumptuous golden buttocks, and her firm, naked breasts were hennaed to accentuate their perfect roundness. Upon her head was fixed a golden crown of horns; between the two horns hung Ra's fiery ball.

The music commenced. Her movements were effortless, liquid. She began her journey across the expanse of the royal audience hall, keeping her footfalls light upon the tiles. As she ran she released a gauzy blue veil. It undulated gently behind her like a wave. The chorus of harps grew louder and she unfurled another blue veil to join the first. She did this several more times—stealing gracefully towards the pillars until the music crescendoed and a spectacular moving wave of cloth filled the space.

'Halt!' King Khufu commanded.

The musicians paused. The dancer ceased her motions. Ra's first light shot through the high windows, just missing the blue veil as it collapsed upon the floor. The dancer stared at the lifeless sea of cloth, her face a sheet of white.

King Khufu swallowed his wine, saying nothing. Hundreds of highborn guests stared at the King in widemouthed disbelief.

After several moments Imhoter stood up from the priests' table. He had long ago been elevated to King's Advisor and Holy Seer, but today he wore the ceremonial leopardskin cloak of his former position as High Priest. He walked towards the base of the high throne, adjusting the leopard's head so that it would not face the King directly.

'Permission to speak?' he asked humbly, keeping his eyes down and his palms up in obeisance.

'Speak, Imhoter.'

'Does the dance not please the King?'

'The dance, the dancer—none of it pleases me,' the King growled. 'It is all rubbish.'

Imhoter felt his heart twist. For many weeks he had been preparing for the Feast of Hathor—the most important feast of the year. He'd wanted to create a spectacle worthy of the Goddess of Love and Abundance, and had settled upon the illusion of water flowing across the royal terrace in the form of a floating blue veil.

To Imhoter's eyes the dance had been beautiful—a marvel of movement and colour. The guests, too, had appeared delighted by the mirage. Imhoter had even heard a few awestruck gasps. It was only a feast, but the drought had fomented doubt among the highborns about Khufu's authority as King. Imhoter had been trying to inspire their awe and also their fealty.

'And the dancer is unappealing,' the King added, stroking the long black column of his ceremonial beard. 'She is not Hathor.'

From the corners of his eyes Imhoter noticed several

guests exchange worried glances. As part of the Feast of Hathor, the King—Horus Incarnate—was supposed to join with the dancer who had been selected as Hathor Incarnate. By spilling his royal seed inside Hathor, the King would help ensure the arrival of the flood. It was a tradition that had never been broken.

But in the days since the Libu raid on the grain tent the King had been angry and impulsive. Instead of rising to face the challenge of feeding his people he had sent the rest of the King's Guard into the Red Land in search of the Libu raiders. It was a futile mission, for it was well known that the many different Libu tribes came together only for raids.

Imhoter had tried to persuade the King to call the soldiers back, but the King would not hear of it. Now it appeared the King was making another grave error, for he would not rise to the occasion of the Feast of Hathor: he was refusing to join with the woman.

As Imhoter fumbled for words another priest stood. He was tall and very thin: his eyes were set inside deep pockets and his skin was so taut over his bones that he appeared almost mummified. Menis was his name, and he was as old and rich as a tomb.

'My King, I must say that I, also, am displeased.'

Imhoter knew that Menis was not speaking of the dance, for the wretched old priest had lost his appetite for beauty long ago. What Menis craved was power.

'I am touched by Osiris,' he often whispered in the corridors of the palace. 'I am meant to rule.'

Menis had always been loath to describe his origins, but by plying him with wine and flattery Imhoter had discovered Menis's disdain for common folk, including his own father—a 'lowly' farmer. As a boy, Menis had refused to join his father in the fields. Instead he had loitered on the steps of his village temple, filthy and starved, begging for the honour of shaving the priests' toes.

When the holy men had finally opened their gates to Menis he had been almost grown, and his heart had become twisted with bitterness and ambition. By the time he'd been draped in the fine cloths of a *wab* priest the garments had no longer been good enough for him.

Unlike the other *wab* priests, Menis often trod the river paths between the villages of Lower Khemet. He offered blessings to the sick and the mourning, explaining that he could grant the favour of the God of Death and Rebirth. All he asked was a small offering to help him on his travels.

By his thirtieth summer Menis had accumulated enough wealth to buy his first plot of land. He'd charged his farmers rent, in the form of a third of their harvest, and had soon begun to hold feasts—each more elaborate than the last, and each thrown in honour of the High Priests of Memphis. In his fortieth summer he was made one of them.

'I have read the ancient scrolls,' Menis had once told Imhoter, 'and I have learned that only the strong survive.'

Now in his sixtieth year, Menis had accumulated so many *arouras* of land that he was by far the wealthiest priest in the kingdom. The old priest enjoyed the support of dozens of *nomarch* mayors, and a host of tenant farmers willing to fight for him in exchange for rent. If the floodwaters of Hapi did not arrive soon, Imhoter knew that Menis would attempt to capture the throne. Beneath Menis's fragile, skeletal exterior was a hyena ready to pounce.

'Speak your mind, Menis,' said King Khufu now, his eyes dancing with derision.

'Your will, Great One,' said Menis, bowing low and stealing a glance at the other priests. 'As Your Majesty well knows, we, the priests of Memphis, continue to work tirelessly to encourage the arrival of Hapi, the life-giving flood.'

Khufu nodded. The hyena was circling.

'Today is the Feast of Hathor—the holiest of days— when we honour the Goddess of Love and Abundance, who is also mother of the flood, and ask for her blessing.'

Khufu nodded again. The beast had smelled blood.

'The remaining Apis bull has been prepared for sacrifice.'

A preliminary bite…

'The dancer, Hathor Incarnate, has fasted, has been bathed, shaved and anointed, and is ready to receive you. Now more than ever the land of Khemet requires your seed. The Libu raid upon the grain tent has left the land of Khemet without grain—'

Pounce.

'Enough, Menis!' exclaimed the King, who clearly did not need to be reminded of his failure to protect the last of the royal grain stores. 'Your audacity is breathtaking. I am the King of Khemet. I am a god who consorts with gods. I am the embodiment of their will and you are nothing!'

The King smoothed his wrap and took a breath as Menis fought to conceal his triumph. He had pushed the King too far, and the beleaguered monarch had revealed weakness before his guests.

'Go now!' the King barked at the dancer. 'I command you!'

The distraught woman gathered up the swaths of cloth that surrounded her and darted across the terrace.

'Wait!' Menis called to the woman. 'You must not leave. You have not yet performed your sacred duty.'

The young woman paused. Tears traced their paths down her well-anointed cheeks.

The King pounded his sceptre upon the ground. 'Leave now, woman. That is an order from your King. Imhoter, see her out.'

Imhoter rushed to the young woman's side.

Menis turned to the King. 'Your Highness does not wish to join with the Mother of the Flood, the Goddess of Plenty Incarnate?' His tone was rich with exasperation. He looked out over the guests as if they were his own subjects.

Having regained his composure, the King laughed. 'I have joined with many Goddesses of Love and Abundance, and they have given me an *abundance* of children.' Several of the nobles chuckled. 'What they have *not* given me is Hapi,' the King concluded, and Menis's wrinkled lips twisted into a scowl.

Khufu and Menis continued to spar. Imhoter could hear their haughty voices growing ever louder as he found the servants' exit and the stairway that led down to the street. The young woman beside him had lost the buoyancy in her step. The glow in her cheeks had faded and she sobbed quietly, unaware of the beauty she had embodied, the wonder she had evoked with her dance. She had told a tale—the tale of the flood—and she had told it well.

She reminded Imhoter of a woman he had known long ago.

'Young Hathor,' Imhoter said to her as she began to

descend the stairs, 'you are as beautiful as the sky that gives birth to the sun.'

The girl ceased her flight. She tilted her head towards Imhoter, listening closely.

'Do not despair, for you *have* fulfilled your duty. You have honoured the Gods, and the Goddess will bless you for it.' Imhoter removed the most delicate of the rings on his fingers and placed it into her hand. 'Take this and go. You have earned it.'

The young woman wiped her tears and a sad smile spread across her face. 'I cannot accept your ring, Venerable One. It is much too fine.'

She held out the ring, but Imhoter refused to take it back.

'Your dance was more beautiful than a thousand gold rings, dear woman. Now, go and be well.'

Tiny tears seeped from the corners of her eyes and her hand closed around the ring. 'I am honoured and humbled by your kindness.' She bowed deeply and departed upon lighter feet.

Imhoter returned to the royal terrace to find Khufu draining another goblet of wine. His guests picked at their food, peering at him with accusing eyes. Even the leopard's head on Imhoter's shoulder seemed to stare at the King in reproach.

The deed had not been done. The King had not joined with Hathor, Goddess of Love and Abundance, Mother of the Flood. He had not spilled his seed and fulfilled his duty as King. In the guests' minds, the flood was now even less likely to come.

Suddenly, King Khufu stood. He raised his sceptre and spoke: 'The source of the Great River is the Island of Abu, a month's journey upriver,' he pronounced.

Imhoter's mind raced. *No, don't do this. Do not leave the great city without its King.*

The King's voice echoed across the great hall. 'We do not need any more feasts or dances or joinings with virgins. They do not help bring Hapi. Only I, Horus Incarnate, can convince Hapi to come. To do this I shall appeal to Khnum, God of the Great River, directly. On my soul, we shall have our flood. Tomorrow I journey to the Isle of Abu.'

The people appeared pleased. One by one they stood and began to applaud. They had come to be entertained, after all, and with this startling pronouncement the King had not disappointed them.

Imhoter glanced at Menis. The old priest's eyes sparkled like tiny black jewels.

Chapter Nineteen

She never should have done it. She never should have tried to seduce Tahar. She should have simply waited until they'd arrived upon Abu and then made her escape.

But, nay, she'd had to act. After almost two cycles of the moon he had not wavered—he was going to sell her into marriage against her will. What choice had she had? Each day they had got closer to Nubia and closer to the inevitable exchange. She could not simply escape into the desert. She had tried that already. The only manner of stopping his malicious scheme, it had seemed to her, was to sabotage it from within.

Foolishly, she had thought it would be easy—like stealing a fig from a street vendor's carefully constructed tower. But this time the moment she had pulled at a single fruit the entire tower had come tumbling into her lap.

It had been that kiss. She had not been prepared for that at all. The feel of his lips upon hers had awakened a thirst that the water of a thousand wells could not quench. He had been tender and insistent. Guiding. Probing. *Loving.* She'd had no idea that a simple kiss could make her forget the terrible life he intended for her, and as she'd kissed him back she had realised for the first time the depth of her own feelings. She trusted him. She cared for him. She admired him. She…

She was overmatched. Seduction was a game whose rules she did not understand—a game of which she had neither experience nor understanding. A game she should not have rushed to play. Not with him.

Now she watched his hands wrap the twine about her wrists over and over, wishing she could go back in time. She wanted to feel his arms engulfing her again. She wished to drink again from those strong, capable hands and to kiss each of his fingers a dozen times.

Seth's blood, she was a fool. She could not accept her desire for him. Her body had acted against direct orders from her mind. But it had been more than that. It had been as if the moment he had embraced her all the dis-ordered parts of herself had fallen neatly into line, and she'd wanted to stay with him like that for ever.

Or maybe the Red Land had finally driven her mad.

It mattered not. Whatever chance they'd had, she had ruined it. Whatever bird had taken flight that night, she had clipped its wings.

Now he gathered her up and seated her before a date palm trunk. The tenderness had disappeared from his touch. He grabbed her sharply by the ankles and wrapped her legs around either side of the trunk. He went to work with the twine once more, encircling her ankles again and again, just as he had done the day he'd captured her.

I want you so badly, he had said, and it had been those words that had broken the spell he had cast upon her. When she'd heard them she had thought of what *she* wanted—which, in that moment, had been him. Him, him, him. Him all around her, against her, intertwined with her. But then what? That was the question her soul had asked. No moment of ecstasy could ever measure up to a lifetime of servitude. *Stay away from men*, her mother had warned, and this man was no different from any other. If he wanted her—really wanted her—he would have to set her free.

'I am leaving,' he told her now. 'I won't be back until sunset.'

He had placed her in a position as humiliating as it was clever. Her arms and legs straddled the trunk of the date palm and were tied together at the wrists and ankles, so she appeared to be hugging the tree. It was a wretched embrace. Even if she could free her hands she would never be able to reach the twine around her feet.

Again, she was outplayed.

He placed a water bag between her arms, grabbed the horse's reins, and began leading the beast away from camp.

'Where are you going?' asked Kiya, then added, 'With my grain.'

'It is not your concern.'

'It is *my* grain. Of course it is my concern.'

Tahar stopped. 'Nay, it is my grain now, and you are still my captive.'

Nothing had changed between them, and yet the word split whatever had remained of her heart in two. *Captive.*

'I shall draw attention to our camp,' she continued, humiliation searing her thoughts. She lifted her head and called loudly, 'Where do you wander, oh, Tahar the Trader, with such a heavy load?' Her insides squeezed with bitterness.

Tahar retrieved a strip of fabric from his saddlebag and tied it around her mouth. Still Kiya continued to yell, but

DO YOU WANT TO GET REWARDED WITH FREE BOOKS?

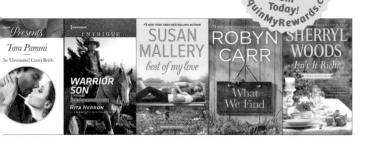

her muffled rantings barely broke the silence of the waning night. She kicked her bound legs, but all she managed to do was rake her inner thighs against the palm's rough trunk. Tahar was already almost out of view.

'Drink the water that is in that bag and rest,' he called as he led the horse away. 'Tomorrow night we begin the most dangerous part of our trek. We shall cross the Big Sandy.'

Kiya shouted a dozen questions at his retreating figure, followed by as many curses, but the thick cloth over her mouth stifled all the sound.

'Where do you go now?' she cried. 'Why do you leave me here alone?'

'Cease!' he shouted finally. He looked back at her in defeat. 'I am to a House of Women. To seek my relief.'

Chapter Twenty

But there was no relief. Not from the heat, not from the sun. Not from her. Especially not from her. He could not expel her from his mind. She had invaded it utterly. She had sent in her legions and pillaged and plundered and now she hovered there, heedless of the wreckage.

The Dakhla Oasis was far behind them now, and they were well on their way across the Big Sandy. He had tried to explain to her that *he* should lead the horse, that her body was not accustomed to treading across dunes. But there was no reasoning with her. He sat powerless atop the horse, watching her wither as she marched furiously beneath the hot sun—bent, it seemed, on her own destruction.

It was his fault. When he had returned from the House of Women that afternoon she had changed. The curious woman who had stolen glances at his body, who'd eaten and drunk heartily, who had watched the desert with wonder in her eyes, was gone. In her place was a lifeless husk. The water bag had lain at her side, untouched. Her body had been limp. Her gold-flecked eyes had lost their sparkle, and he'd been able to see the stains of the tears that had flowed upon her cheeks. He'd felt his heart pinch as he had observed the strip of cloth that he had tied about her mouth.

By all creation, what had he been thinking?

He hadn't been thinking, in fact.

After she had repeated her command, *Take it*, all his abilities for reason and observation had dissolved. There had been no thinking, only reacting, as his whole body had contracted with the pain of rejection. In one moment he had been kissing her with a thirst that he had never known; in the next she had snatched away her love and left him drowning.

And he deserved it. He had given her no alternative. He planned to sell her—plain and simple. He had become the kind of man he loathed. A man so consumed with the accumulation of wealth that he would sacrifice the life of another for his own gain. In a sense, he was no different from Chief Bandir. And the woman, wily though she was, could not escape him. She'd had nowhere to go, nowhere to run, no choice but to fight back.

It was the form of her attack that had been so unexpected. Seduction. Soft and sweet. He had never been so completely taken in by a woman. Even now, two days later, he could not concentrate on the journey ahead. Curse his boat and his foolish plans. They had all seemed so meaningless when she had pressed her naked body against his.

But she had seduced him out of spite, not desire. Though her warm body had opened to his, though he had felt her breath quicken at his touch, she had apparently not wanted him after all. And why should she? He meant to trade her. She was justified in her anger. How had he not seen it before? Every new day that he kept her in captivity he wronged her. She'd had no choice but to strike back. He just had not foreseen that it would sting this badly.

As if a House of Women could even *begin* to ease the pain she had inflicted. The working woman who had attended him had donned an elegant Khemetian wig. She had even danced about the tiny room for him, her large breasts bouncing. Tahar had waited for his lust to rise. He had waited for that inevitable moment when he would grab the woman, pull her atop him and take what he had paid her to give. The moment had not come.

Finally the working woman had taken him in her mouth. He'd felt himself grow large with the sensation. He'd closed his eyes, trying to concentrate. But Hathor had invaded his fantasies, too. Hathor the Beautiful. Hathor the Strong. Hathor the Imposter.

What was her true name? He yearned to know for certain. But more than that he yearned for her to tell it to him. And he wanted to run his fingers through her short, dark hair. He wanted to touch her petulant lips and look into her enigmatic eyes and tell her how much he wanted her.

But even in his fantasies she had confronted him. She had glared at him with anger and accusation. How could he do it? How could he sell her into marriage? The Goddess of Love and Abundance was not meant to be sold. She was meant to be revered. Honoured. *Loved*.

He had pulled himself from the working woman's grasp. 'I am sorry,' he said. 'It is not your fault.'

The woman had stared up at him, confused.

'You see…' Tahar had fumbled. 'I have been enchanted by a goddess.'

The woman had looked at him curiously, but had

seemed to understand. 'Go to her, then,' she'd said, accepting his bag of grain. 'Go to her and never look back.'

But when he returned to the oasis, Hathor had refused to look at him. And when he untied her, she had said nothing. She had simply stood and began to walk toward the Big Sandy. She remained ahead of him now as they trudged across the grim procession of dunes. There was no sanctuary, no safe harbour from the waves of emptiness that filled his vision and buffeted his heart. The afternoon wind pelted his face with sand and the sun bored into his soul.

'Hathor...' he said, but the utterance was more like a prayer, for he knew that she would not answer to it. She had shut him out of her world.

Forgive me.

She led them relentlessly across the dunes, refusing to stop or to drink. Even in the relative cool of the night before she had not taken a moment of rest. She was steady in her purpose, as if some inner fire were fuelling her beyond what any woman could possibly endure.

Take control, you fool. Take the reins.

But how could he? He knew her well enough to know she would certainly put up a fight. Even if he managed to get her seated upon the horse she would somehow make him pay. He had wronged her—he understood that now—but she gave him no way to repent.

Now began the test. To traverse the Big Sandy in the middle of *akhet* would be no small feat, even for the most experienced desert traveller. There was nowhere to take shelter—no measure of shade upon the endless, undulating dunes. Even with an infinite supply of water, any traveller would eventually become exhausted by the heat. The sun always won. It would always win. The only way to survive the journey across the Big Sandy was to do it quickly.

They carried only enough water for a three-night journey. Any more water would weigh them down and hinder their progress. Any less and they would grow mad with thirst. By allowing her to lead the horse, he had already made their three-night journey become three nights and half. They would surely run short of water before the next oasis. Then the heat would overtake their minds. They would begin to hallucinate.

When that happened, they were as good as dead.

'Hathor!' he yelled.

She stumbled forward, coughing, and he watched in horror as her strong, beautiful figure collapsed upon the sand.

Chapter Twenty-One

He had to keep her alive. If he could not, then he might as well die himself.

Her strength was gone. The dunes had claimed it. They had claimed her mind, too. She was so dizzy with thirst that she no longer remembered that she needed to drink. She could neither walk nor speak. She lay atop the horse with her head against his grey mane.

'Meemoo,' she muttered.

Darkness enveloped them. Soon Tahar was jogging across the moonlit dunes, trying to make up for lost time. Meemoo grew tired, unable to keep pace with Tahar. Tahar begged and cajoled, dragging the beast behind him, stretching his long legs into giant strides. Soon, however, Meemoo stood still. The poor creature was spent.

Meanwhile the eastern horizon grew ever lighter in anticipation of the new day.

The deadly new day.

Tahar poured a ration of water into Meemoo's bowl and watched the tired animal drink his fill. Then he dribbled a few drops of water upon Hathor's parched lips.

'Meemoo drinks, dear Hathor, so you must drink, too,' he told her.

She muttered some incomprehensible thing, then licked the drops. Tahar's heart raced with joy. He allowed the dribble to become a trickle, watching closely as she accepted the precious liquid. She drank for several moments and began to cough. Then she ceased drinking and returned to muttering.

He needed to lighten the horse's load. It was his only hope to keep the horse alive. He lifted Hathor from the saddle and slung her over his shoulder. Relieved of its burden, the beast obediently followed Tahar onward.

They walked that way for many hours: Tahar in the lead with Hathor over his shoulder and Meemoo following close behind. Tahar's powerful legs were an asset now. He trudged up and down the dunes, trying to maintain his pace as the sun grew hotter. When his right shoulder became tired, he placed Hathor over his left shoulder.

Soon he held her limp body in his arms. The sun was now exactly overhead, he was covered in sweat, and the Big Sandy stretched out before them in every direction. They had two days of travel still ahead, and only enough water for one.

What had he done? Leaving her like that at camp, alone and exposed. She had been overcome with emotion: that much he had been able to tell as he'd bound her limbs. So why had he left her?

Because he was a fool. Because he had done the first thing that had come to his mind,—as fools did. He had escaped to a House of Women, where he'd thought he might find comfort, though deep in his heart he had known he would never be able to touch another woman.

His desire could not be sated with the simplicity of paid-for pleasure. Not any more.

Nor could it be cured with dreams of a boat. Indeed, whenever he imagined a boat's full sail and long white curves, the woman's full hips and long bronze neck took its place. So why, really, had he left her there alone, tied to a tree like a beast?

Because he himself was a beast. She had begged him to set her free, but he had refused to listen to her. Instead, he had denied her the very thing he valued most about his own life: freedom. If her plan to seduce him had been cruel, his plan to trade her had been barbaric. To sell her into marriage was no different from selling her into slavery. He understood that now. The bonds were the same—only the duties were different.

It was true that the drought had dashed his dreams and destroyed his spirit, but what kind of monster had grown in its place?

And why, *why* had he left her alone?

Because, ultimately, he was a coward. He refused to face his own feelings towards her, which grew stronger every day. When he had finally embraced her those feelings had overwhelmed him. He had wanted her more than he had ever wanted anyone in his life, and when she hadn't wanted him back he had not been able to bear it.

Take it, she had said, and the coldness of her words had slayed his heart.

Still, nothing she could say would match the warmth of that kiss. She had spoken to him with that kiss. She had told him all the things she had been afraid to say, or had not been able to say. Even if her plan had been cold-hearted seduction, her lips had told him otherwise.

And her eyes. Those, too, had betrayed her. He had

read them like scrolls. They had lost their purpose: they'd been full of confusion and regret. The situation had gone beyond her power to control. She had been swept up, as he had, into something bigger than either of them.

He should have stayed with her and talked to her—not tied her hands with twine. He should have held her close despite her protestations. She had wanted him, but she had not been able to tell him that, for he had condemned her to a life she could not bear.

He should have told her that as soon as he'd felt her body against his he had never wanted to let her go.

He should have told her how much he loved her.

Because he did. He loved her. It felt so good to admit it to himself, finally. He had known it the instant he had embraced her for, despite his unreasonable, almost un-controllable lust for her, in the end he only wanted to make her happy. Her happiness, he realised, was his. She was his boat, his homeland, his dream come true. Whatever she wanted from him, he would give it. Whatever command she gave, he would obey it. Wherever she went, he would follow. She had his heart, totally and completely, and she would have it for ever.

'Hathor,' he said. He lifted her limp body and whispered in her ear. 'Forgive me.'

Chapter Twenty-Two

At first he believed he was dreaming them. Palm leaves in the distance—ancient and wild. They swayed together in the heat haze like a tribe of wine-drunk men.

Dizzy. He was so very dizzy. He could not determine if he walked or simply floated down the dune.

Where is your grandfather's battle axe? whispered a voice in his ear.

Turning, Tahar beheld a towering man at his side, not an arm's length away, yet somehow out of reach.

I do not know, Father. It is gone. I am sorry.

Why do you linger in the Red Land, Tahar? Your mother grows old. She needs you.

I do not know why I stay, Father.

But you do know, said the ghost, disappearing into the dry air. *You do know.*

Tahar stared down at the woman asleep in his arms. Yes, he did know. It was her. It had always been her. She was the reason he remained in this godforsaken place.

She was feather-light, barely breathing. Her eyes no longer moved beneath their lids. Her lips were cracked; her body was limp and still. Yet she glowed with inner light. He had been seeking this woman all his life, he realised, and if they did not find water soon he would lose her for ever.

Meemoo followed wearily behind, stumbling. Tahar did not have the heart to turn and observe his condition. The noble old horse had been his father's final gift to Tahar. He had left the beast as a means for Tahar to return to his homeland, to his mother, who had surely grown more hopeless with each passing year.

Tahar pictured her staring out at the endless grassy plain, watching for her husband and son, praying they would suddenly appear on the horizon. *I will not disappoint you, Father, not again.*

Tahar willed his head up, calling upon all that was left of his strength. There they remained, at the edge of his sight—the palm leaves. They had not disappeared. Nay—they seemed to be growing larger as he treaded down the dune. Was this another mirage?

They clustered at the far side of a long, overhanging rock that cast a finger of shade upon the rust-coloured ground. The shade, too, seemed to be growing. Or was that just the darkness invading his mind?

Then he spotted it—a small, stone-encircled well. It was located at the base of the largest of the palms. Someone had piled new palm leaves over the hole, as if it had been recently used. *As if it contained water.* Tahar slapped his cheeks and closed his eyes. He opened them, and the rocks were still there. So were the leaves.

When Tahar's feeble legs reached the flat hardpan his wilted mind would not let him believe it—the possibility of a well at the edge of oblivion.

As he neared the small opening he began to sob,

though he had lost the ability to produce tears. It was real. The well, the shade, the palms. All of it—real.

He laid the woman down in the shade and scooped a draught of water into her mouth, praying she would remember her thirst for life.

Suddenly she coughed. She opened her mouth wider and began to drink. Tahar lifted another handful to her lips. Her eyes remained closed, as if she, too, believed herself to be dreaming.

Meemoo dipped his long snout into the cool depths and Tahar saw a lively shiver ripple down his flanks. Tahar splashed the water onto his own face and drank his fill, feeling his thoughts begin to unscramble. He lifted another handful to Hathor's lips. Finally, she opened her eyes.

'Thank the Gods!' he cried. He lifted her into his embrace, rocking her and petting her hair.

'I thought you did not believe in gods,' she whispered into his ear.

He pulled her closer, squeezing her as tightly as he dared. 'I do when they bring you back to me.'

Tahar breathed in the dusty scent of her hair, then opened his eyes. There in the distance was his father's hulking shape—a leather-clad ghost swaying at the foot of the dune. Tahar thought he could see a smile spreading across the beloved man's face. Tahar closed his eyes and lay back with Hathor in the shade.

They passed the remainder of the day in such a fashion, guzzling like drunken sailors and marvelling at their good luck. Meemoo let out a cheerful whinny at sunset, and ate three pots of grain in as many minutes. Tahar cooked their own dinner of porridge over a small fire, and as the stars revealed themselves one by one a profound exhaustion overtook them.

For the first time they fell asleep side by side.

'The Blue Serpent sleeps,' said a familiar voice.

It reached into Tahar's mind, wrenching him from slumber.

'These are strange times indeed.'

Tahar opened one eye and studied the thin, leather-skinned man hovering above him. The man was watching Tahar with a single eye of his own, the other eye concealed by a familiar patch.

'If you think I was asleep then you have lost your formidable judgement, Chief Bandir,' Tahar replied.

'You claim to have been awake?' the Chief said with mock astonishment. 'Ha! If you had been awake you would have seen my army by now. We have been approaching all morning.'

Tahar sat up to behold a massive caravan arriving at the oasis—a hundred men at least.

'It appears that we have caught up with you, Tahar. I never thought we would.'

Tahar jumped to his feet, his eyes darting about the camp. Thankfully she was nowhere in sight. Tahar allowed himself a breath.

'Well met, Chief Bandir, Guardian of Siwa Oasis and Leader of the Libu.' Tahar struck the traditional Libu welcome pose, opening both his arms and bowing low.

It had been almost two cycles of the moon since Tahar had stolen Hathor and escaped the Libu Chief and his minions. There was nothing he could do now but hope for mercy.

'Well met, Tahar the *Traitor*,' the Chief said, satisfied with his cleverness.

He motioned to his men, who guided their donkeys into the shade beneath the long rock outcropping where Tahar and Hathor had been sleeping.

'You look tired.'

'Not tired—only resting,' said Tahar.

He scanned the men's faces and sighed with relief when he spotted Dakka, who still travelled with the entourage. By the Libu code, Dakka's loyalty to his fellow tribesmen came before his loyalty to the Chief. Dakka and Tahar exchanged nods.

'Nay, you are spent,' the Chief continued. 'The Big Sandy almost took you.'

The Chief spoke casually, but his one eye never rested. It darted about the camp, probing for answers to unspoken questions. Like Tahar, the Chief was a master observer. His camp in the Siwa Oasis was the largest and richest in all the Red Land. He claimed that it was fate that had catapulted him to his success, but Tahar knew better. Bandir's riches had been gleaned by careful, keen observation of men and their behaviour. He manipulated men's minds as thoroughly and evilly as the desert sun.

'With respect, Chief, I never tire. In fact my trek across the Big Sandy seemed unusually short,' Tahar lied. 'Far too short. If only there were just a few more grains of sand to traverse.'

'Hem…' the Chief muttered.

Tahar watched the old man's eye find Tahar's horse, tied beneath the palms. He was searching for signs of the woman.

'If you give her to me now I will not punish you,' he

stated. 'In fact I will reward you. We have need of strong men like you on our mission.'

Bandir unfurled his purple headdress and Tahar caught the glint of gold around his neck.

'But first I must drink.'

The Chief walked ceremoniously across camp to the small rock-framed well. It was tradition for the leader of a caravan to have the first drink from any well, and the men watched him patiently as he drank his fill.

It was an army of men. Many more had joined since Tahar had encountered Bandir and his dozen followers at the first oasis. Tahar counted five score donkeys at least, with two men for every one beast. And it was not just grain the donkeys carried. Upon the back of each animal was a large load covered by cloth. Tahar could not see what lay beneath, but he noticed the glint of gold protruding from several of the bundles.

Chief Bandir dipped his head into the well. He lifted it out in a spray of water and the men cheered. He returned to Tahar's side as the parched raiders gathered at the well to drink.

'We have survived the Big Sandy!' the Chief exclaimed. 'And I have only lost a half-dozen men.'

Such a high cost, thought Tahar. 'But where do you journey with such an army?' he asked.

'We are to Nubia. To the land of riches.'

'You have already become wealthier than any Nubian, I suspect,' ventured Tahar. 'I assume that is not natron upon the backs of your asses?'

'It is not,' said Bandir cautiously.

'But there was no gold to be had at the raid—or did I leave too soon?'

'Nay—not a bit of gold at the raid, nor any slaves to

be claimed. Not even inside the tomb,' Bandir said, spitting on the ground.

Tahar recalled the Khemetian workers who had sought refuge inside the Great Pyramid. They must have hidden themselves well—probably inside the secret tunnel that Hathor had described to him.

'We followed the corridor downwards for hours, only to find a half-finished cellar under the ground. The Great Pyramid of Stone yielded nothing for the Libu. But why do you smile, Tahar?'

'Ah,' mused Tahar, thinking quickly, 'I smile because clearly you *did* find treasure. How?' Tahar nodded at the heavily burdened donkeys, trying to appear impressed.

'Ah! Yes, indeed. Well, there are many other tombs in the ancient land of Khemet. You should know that.'

It took Tahar a moment to absorb the Chief's meaning. 'You raided *another* tomb?'

The Chief watched him steadily.

'An *occupied* one?'

'You put it so crudely,' the Chief said.

Tahar did not believe in the divinity of dead Khemetian kings, but there was something unnerving about the prospect of raiding their occupied tombs.

'Not crude, Chief—just bold,' Tahar said, trying to conceal his disgust.

One of Bandir's gold rings flashed in the sunlight. Upon it Tahar noticed the image of an arm holding a blade—the symbolic cartouche of the ancient King Zoser.

'You admire my ring?' said Bandir.

The man missed nothing.

'Yes,' Bandir continued, 'to answer the question I can see behind your eyes, I stole it. Or, better yet, I took what

I was due. It was how I paid my respects to the Murderer of the Libu.'

'There is no need to say more,' said Tahar. 'I understand.'

'I hope you *do* understand,' said Bandir, eyeing Tahar closely. 'It is justice for all the Libu that I seek.'

Justice? Exactly what kind of justice? Zoser had reigned over a hundred years ago, and stories of the ancient King grew more outlandish with each passing season. In one story Zoser overcame the Libu with an army of lions. In another Zoser conceded Khemetian grazing grounds to the Libu and took a Libu wife. Only scribes and priests knew the true history of Zoser's reign.

'Aye, justice,' Tahar said. 'But why do you go to Nubia?'

'Isn't it obvious?' asked Bandir. 'We shall need an army to take Memphis—strong men to scale the walls of Khufu's palace and overcome his soldiers. I believe it will take a thousand men at least.'

'And you think that the Nubian tribes will join you?'

'For enough gold and grain, they will,' said Bandir, motioning to the donkeys. 'They have been wronged by the Khemetians, as we have been. Besides, the Khemetian King is weak. Now is the time to strike.'

'It is a bold plan, my Chief,' said Tahar. *To make yourself into the new Khemetian king.*

'It takes bold men to seek justice. Will you not join us, Tahar of the Meshwesh?'

Tahar should have known such a question was coming. Bandir had withheld mention of Tahar's tribal affiliation for a reason: he wished to wield it like a blade. Tahar owed the Libu of the Meshwesh region his loyalty and his life, and Bandir knew it. Now, like a good merchant, Bandir would exact his toll.

Tahar flashed Bandir a crocodile grin. 'It would be an honour to join you, my Chief. Let us find our justice.'

Never in a thousand cycles of the sun would I join you on your bloody mission.

'Good,' said Bandir, and the two men embraced. 'Now, tell me, soldier, where is the woman?'

Just then there was commotion at the well. Several of Bandir's men were shouting and throwing rocks at the trees. There she was, perched like a bird in the palms, her face contorted in thinly concealed terror.

Bandir's eyes narrowed upon Tahar. 'Just as I thought.'

Before any of the men could scale the trees to reach her she managed to descend. Two men took her by the arms and led her to where Tahar and the Chief stood in the shade. Like a pack of hyenas, the men gathered all around her. Most had not seen a woman in many months, and they studied her exposed limbs with wide-eyed lust.

Tahar struggled to keep his breaths even as Bandir's single eye raked across her body.

'She is much improved since I last saw her,' Bandir said. 'There is meat on her bones. What does she call herself?'

'Hathor,' Tahar muttered.

'Hathor?' cried the Chief. '*Hathor?* Fie! If this woman's name is Hathor then I am the Son of Ra!'

The agitated men erupted in laughter.

'When may we worship at Hathor's altar?' one man shouted, and bawdy chuckles filled the air.

'Does she give her love *abundantly*?' another quipped, to riotous laughter.

'It is the name she gives,' said Tahar. His hands were beginning to tremble.

'I am certain she gives more than just a *name*,' Bandir said, winking at Tahar.

Tahar's throat tightened.

The Chief studied the thick, shiny black hair that carpeted her head like a hat. 'She is indeed more womanly,' Bandir stated, taking stock of her backside.

Tahar thought he noticed Hathor's lower lip quake.

'Where did you think you were going with such a fine captive?' asked Bandir.

'We make for Abu,' Tahar said.

'Ah! The sacred Khemetian Isle. Your purpose?'

'The woman wishes to make an offering to the God of the Flood,' Tahar lied.

'She does indeed,' said Bandir, motioning to Hathor. 'Woman, come closer,' he said in Khemetian.

Tahar wanted to tell her to have no fear. He wanted to say he would protect her. Nay—he would give his very life to keep her safe. He wanted to tell her that he would scoop her from these evil men's clutches and deliver her to the life she wanted—whatever life that was. He loved her. By the Gods, he *loved* her—and with a ferocity he did not recognise or understand.

He wished to slit the Chief's throat and steal all his gold and ride off with her into the desert.

But that was impossible—for the Chief's army of minions hovered, watching his every move and awaiting her every breath.

Chapter Twenty-Three

The woman took several steps towards the Chief and a flirtatious grin spread across his face. 'You see?' he looked around at his men. 'That is the effect I have on women.'

The men howled.

'Gods, you are beautiful,' said Bandir. He put his hand on Hathor's chin and lifted it. 'Now I see why you are called Hathor.'

Tahar could no longer think. He could no longer see. If the Chief kept his hands on her skin one moment longer Tahar feared he would smash that wicked grin from the Chief's face and stick an arrow in his middle. It was only after many moments that Tahar realised Bandir was speaking again, and placing something shiny around Tahar's neck.

'Forged in the mines of Meroe, honed by the craftsmen of Napata, and stored for safekeeping in the tomb of Zoser the Great—ah, I mean the Terrible,' Bandir pronounced.

Tahar touched the heavy chain that had been hung around his neck. It was made of thick gold. He had seen such a chain once before, hanging about the neck of a travelling prince.

'This gift I present as a token of my gratitude,' Bandir said, 'for allowing me to take Hathor as my wife.'

If Tahar had believed in gods he might have thought they were laughing at him now, for they had just given him everything he had always wanted. The only problem was that he didn't want it any more.

'I could just take her, of course,' Bandir added, 'but you are a soldier in my army now, and you have protected her virtue well. I am assuming she is healthy, and sufficiently skilled at performing a woman's duty?'

'Hathor is a virgin.'

Bandir stumbled backwards exaggeratedly, and his men laughed. Righting himself, the Chief lifted another gold necklace from around his neck and placed it around Tahar's.

'There you are, brother—enough gold to buy ten asses, a field of wheat or a very large boat. After you help us defeat the Khemetians you will never need to ply the trade routes again.'

Tahar stole a glance at Hathor. She stared at the ground with stony eyes. Though she could not understand the language the men spoke, she could surely guess what was taking place.

Bandir addressed his men. 'Tonight shall be our wedding night!' The Chief raised his arms and smiled while his men cheered. He stepped before Tahar and opened his arms. 'Congratulate me, soldier!'

The dagger Tahar kept on a belt beneath his robe seemed to burn against his skin, but there were simply too many men for him to attempt to use it. There was nothing Tahar could do but accept the Chief's embrace.

The old man whispered in Tahar's ear: 'She looks good enough to eat. Tonight, I feast.'

Tahar burst into a fit of coughs, struggling to swallow his rage. He managed to bow to the Chief, as was the custom.

The crowd of men exploded in a storm of whistles and shouts as the Chief bowed back. Then the wretched old man wrapped his arm around the woman's waist and pulled her close.

'Look at me, brothers,' he shouted. 'I am wed!'

The men converged upon the Chief and his bride, shouting their congratulations, and Tahar felt his body grow cold. If it was the last thing he did in his cursed life it would be to free the woman he loved.

Chapter Twenty-Four

She did not need to understand the Libu tongue to know what had transpired. Tahar, who claimed to have renounced the Libu, had embraced their Chief like an old friend. Moreover, he seemed to have struck a deal. The two men had bowed to each other in the way of traders, and it was clear that something terrible had been agreed upon—a demon's bargain that had seen two gold necklaces around Tahar's neck and the Chief's wiry arm about her waist.

So he had finally done it. Tahar had traded her. And to a Libu Chief, no less. He had sold the right to wed her and bed her for the price of stolen gold from a murderer. She had been right about Tahar after all—he had no soul, no heavenly *ka*. He was lower than the meanest rat in the deepest pile of fish bones in the dustiest corner of Memphis.

'This should fit you nicely,' said the Chief now, holding up a richly embroidered skirt. He studied her with his single roving eye. The spacious tent had been erected especially for this, his wedding night. 'I would like you to wear it without your wrap, so that I may admire your fine breasts.'

A golden lamp flickered in the corner of the small space, and she saw that two thick carpets lay side by side on the ground.

How could she have been so blind to Tahar's true character? How could she have eschewed the several opportunities she had had to escape? The day they had encountered the archers, for example. She could have simply kept running. Or inside the cave. He'd left her alone there for quite a while, apparently believing her too injured to flee.

But she hadn't been too injured. She could have easily slipped out of the cave in his absence and disappeared among the cliffs. Instead she had stayed with him, telling herself that she was biding her time for a 'better' opportunity. Telling herself she was only using him for his survival skills. Telling herself that she might somehow convince him to do the right thing.

It had all been a fantasy—a wistful tale filled in with details she had conjured in her fanciful mind. He had recognised that fantasy and carved himself into it. He was an imposter—just like her. All along Tahar had just been pretending to be honourable. He was like the Libu Chief…although the Chief did not even pretend.

She had watched his wrinkled face twist with contempt as he had pronounced the name of King Zoser. Clearly his caravan carried more than just Khemetian grain—it carried gold: Zoser's gold. Her stomach turned as she imagined the Chief—her new husband—raiding Zoser's sacred tomb.

'Do you like the skirt?' Bandir asked.

'Aye, My Lord, it is beautiful,' Kiya said, pretending to admire the garment. *From which of Zoser's dead wives did you steal it?*

And why was the Chief not returning to his home-land with Zoser's loot? Libu grazing grounds lay to the west, yet the caravan was headed in the same direction as Tahar—south. Did the Chief intend to conquer the Nubians, then? To slay more souls in his mindless quest for riches?

Kiya had believed that Tahar had detached himself from these murderers. She had even begun to think him noble. When they had been crossing the dunes his voice had broken through the chaos of her addled mind and he had asked her for forgiveness.

He had also saved her life.

But Tahar was not a noble man—nay. He was not special, as she had begun to believe him to be. The Chief had made him an incredibly generous offer—two gold necklaces!—and, like most men in his situation, Tahar had not refused them. He had never intended to let her go. She had always been just his means to an end.

Stay away from men... They only mean to possess you, to enslave you.

She felt tears filling the wells of her eyes as she let her addax-skin dress fall to the ground.

Chapter Twenty-Five

Perhaps it had been the sight of her naked flesh that had persuaded him. Or perhaps something smaller than that. The way she had cocked her head at him or the way she had sighed demurely when his breath had begun to quicken. Bandir was a man, after all, and Kiya had certainly had some practice playing roles. Whatever it had been, the Chief had trusted her feigned desire for him enough to allow her to 'purify herself' at the well.

She wrapped his headdress about her naked body and explained that she wouldn't be long. Then she exited the tent and walked in the direction of the well. Scattered about the camp were a hundred men lying upon mats, most of them already asleep. She hiked up her covering, pretending to be in a hurry to relieve herself, then slipped behind a bush near the well.

Behind that bush was another bush. Beyond that the open desert.

She kept walking.

She was almost out of earshot when she ran into a large boulder. A large, breathing boulder, with ripples of stony flesh.

'They will notice your absence soon,' Tahar whispered. He was placing the horse's reins in her hands. 'I will distract them for as long as I can. The River is only a day's journey to the east of here. Do you see that star?'

It was him. *Him, him, him.* He had come for her. He was not going to sell her—no matter what the price. He was going to save her after all.

'Hathor, do you see the star?' he repeated.

He was pointing to a large bright star above the eastern horizon.

'If you follow it faithfully by morning you will see a single tall peak. From the top of that peak you will see the River...and the Isle of Abu.'

She stared at him, unable to speak.

'You will also see if they have followed you. If they have not, you may stop running.'

'You are not coming with me?'

'I must stay and try to prevent them from following you.'

He is not coming with me. 'But how will you stop them?'

Tahar pointed to the golden necklaces around his neck and smiled. 'Do not worry—I have a plan. One of my tribesmen is here and will help me. Already he is riding south, creating a false trail.' Tahar sobered. 'There is a blade in the saddle, and plenty of grain—*your* grain.'

My grain. She could not believe it. He was returning her grain to her. There was still enough to see her through the season.

'I don't understand—'

'Go now, Hathor. You must fly. Go to the Isle of Abu. You will be safe there.'

With an ease that exposed his strength, Tahar lifted

her and set her atop Meemoo. He let his hands linger on her waist for a moment, then shook his head.

'What about your boat? The deal you made with the Chief—?'

'I made no deal. And I no longer wish for a boat.'

Kiya could not believe it. Her dream was coming true—she was being set free—so why did it feel as if her hopes were dying?

'If you no longer wish for a boat, then what do you wish for, Tahar?' she asked suddenly.

'I wish for you to be free from the clutches of such an evil man. I wish for you to have a better life. You have made my life better than you will ever know.'

The moon had not yet risen, but through the darkness Kiya thought she could see a sheen in Tahar's eyes.

'Now, go—there is no time to lose,' he said, and he smacked Meemoo on the flank.

And just like that she was free.

Chapter Twenty-Six

The air was changing. It felt thicker, weightier. Even as she ascended the steep slopes of the mountain Kiya could sense her proximity to the Great River. She should have been ecstatic. To all Khemetians, the Great River was home. It was where they grew crops and raised families, where they washed and played and hunted and fished. The River was everything, and it flowed through Khemetians' hearts, filling their spirits with joy.

So why did Kiya feel nothing but sorrow?

She had ridden all through the night, just as he'd instructed. She had kept her senses alert, never resting, allowing the memory of Chief Bandir's twisted grin to spur her onward.

When she arrived at the base of the mountain the Sun God's light was already spilling onto the eastern horizon. Kiya tethered Meemoo to a small tree and began her trek up its steep, rocky slope.

She was grateful for her sandals now. *The sandals he made for me.* Khemetians did not wear shoes because they were unnecessary. She had always meant to explain that to him. The bottomland mud upon which Khemetian farmers trod was soft and cool, and even in Khemetian villages and cities the sand was pulverous and yielding.

The earth of the desert was different. It was rocky and much less forgiving. Without Tahar's well-made sandals now, the sharp granite talus that comprised the slopes of the desert mountain would have surely shredded her soles.

Why had she never thanked him for the sandals?

She stopped and took a draught from the water bag she carried. He had packed it for her in the saddlebag, along with a clutch of ripe dates.

She could not believe he had managed to find dates in the palms growing where they had camped. She had hidden among the leaves of those very palms and had not seen them. But, then again, Tahar was always discovering food where there seemed to be none. It was one of his many talents.

Another of his talents was observation. If he were watching her now she wondered if he would observe the stains of tears upon her cheeks. Would he notice how she neared the summit of the peak but still did not look up? She bit into a date, though its sweetness was lost upon her tongue. Would he notice her spitting the lovely fruit onto the ground?

She stopped in her tracks. What was wrong with her? She was supposed to be happy. She had got her wish: he had set her free. And he had faced great challenges to do it.

The first challenge had been temptation. The Chief had made him an offer he hadn't been able to refuse: two gold necklaces—enough to procure a large boat indeed. And yet Tahar had only pretended to agree to it. By then he had already been preparing for his second challenge: engineering Kiya's escape.

How he had managed to ready the horse without being noticed was incredible to her. Nor did she comprehend how he had known where to find her in the dark desert surrounding the camp. But find her he had. It seemed he had placed himself directly in her path. He could have simply run away with her then. But, no—he wanted to increase her chances by drawing any would-be pursuers away from her path.

That was the third challenge he faced right now. And it had begun the moment Chief Bandir noticed that his most recently acquired possession—Kiya herself—was gone. Tahar had declined to tell her his plan for diversion but she had guessed it, and it was as clever as a leopard's tail.

Tahar had already sent his tribesman towards Nubia to create a trail that headed south. Kiya's own trail headed east, towards the Great River, so her pursuers would have to decide between the trails. But there would be a third trail—Tahar's. That trail would head west, deeper into the desert. It would be similar to the other trails in all ways but one: Tahar's trail would be marked by two gold necklaces.

Which trail were the Chief and his minions most likely to follow then?

The answer seemed clear to Kiya, and in a dozen more strides she would find out for sure if she was correct. If the Chief's men were doing as she expected she would not see them at all, for they would be headed westward in pursuit of Tahar.

Luckily Tahar would be half a day's ride into the desert before the Chief and his men set out upon Tahar's trail. He would lure them farther and farther westward, giving Kiya more time to reach the safety of the boundary of Upper Khemet. She imagined him spurring Meemoo onward as he raced ahead of the militant thieves...

It was in that instant that Kiya realised her error. *I have Meemoo.*

Kiya's legs became weak. They refused to take her the last dozen strides she needed to reach the summit.

He is without Meemoo.

While she had galloped away to freedom Tahar had travelled on foot, with an entire mounted army behind him in pursuit. They were probably overtaking him right now.

Kiya pictured Chief Bandir's evil grin. When he finally caught the man who had freed his bride he would surely show no mercy.

Kiya felt ill. In setting her free, Tahar had sealed his own fate.

She bounded up the last stretch of slope and stepped out upon the small flat table of rock that defined the summit. She took a breath and focused her eyes westward, towards the desert. She scanned the vast flat plain and saw not a single soul. She could just make out the outline of the low escarpment where they had made their camp. Nobody was coming for her. They had apparently gone west—in pursuit of Tahar.

If they have not followed you, you may stop running, he had said.

She closed her eyes and let the tears come. By saving herself she had condemned him. The man who had saved her life a dozen times. The man who had shown her wonders beyond her wildest dreams. The man whose very smile had made her whole body quake.

She collapsed upon the ground. The whole of the universe seemed to have turned upside down. Somewhere in the distance Tahar was either running from his death or meeting it.

It was hours before she was able to lift her head. Ra's heavenly body floated high above the horizon and her skin burned beneath his rays. What had happened to Tahar? Perhaps she would never know. But she would not give up hope that somewhere, somehow, he was alive.

Kiya could hear Meemoo's plaintive neighs at the base of the mountain, urging her to return. Before beginning her descent, she gazed eastward, and a majestic view spread out before her. In the distance the Great River wound across the plain in giant serpentine bends. Glittering in the sunlight, its blue-green waters appeared to flow for ever—Kiya could not discern where the River began or ended. It seemed as long as time itself.

When she was young she had swum in the River almost every day. The other street children had feared its waters, for crocodiles hunted in them, toppling fishermen's boats and taking laundrymen's limbs at will. But Kiya had tempted fate, swimming until she almost grew gills and her feet became fins that could outswim any foe.

There had been other children who often swam in the Great River's waters, as Kiya had, but they had done it without risk. They were the King's bastards. They had lived with their mothers—the King's concubines—in the royal harem on the far side of the palace. The harem's removed location was far enough away from palace activities to be forgotten, and its location offered its residents easy access to the artificial lagoon that had been created for the King's fishermen.

The lagoon was called the King's Shallows, and it was protected from crocodiles. A fence of tightly coiled papyrus guarded the narrow underwater entrance, allowing the Great River's perch, tilapia and catfish to swim in but keeping its crocodiles out.

It was a fishermen's paradise and a child's playground, and many of the King's concubines chose to bring their children there, despite their access to the well-tended pools of the inner palace. It was a realm of white sands and shimmering fish and palms that danced wildly in the breeze. It was a place free of rules, where children could be children, regardless of their lineage. And its ample beach was surrounded by a high wall, affording the royal women and children a privacy that was almost complete.

Almost. A hole in the wall had allowed Kiya to spy on them—something she had done for hours on end. The young children had splashed in the shallows, their chubby hands groping for the silvery fish. The older children would range more widely, finding shells and digging up creatures along the banks. They would present their newfound prizes to their mothers, who had lounged like contented hippos upon the shore, with nothing to worry about but what they might eat for lunch.

Kiya's envy had grown. She had yearned to be like those children, to enjoy a life of abundance and levity— a life free of crocodiles. It was the life she had been born to, the life she had always searched for but had never seemed to find.

And now she realised she did not want it—not if it did not include a certain stubborn trader with liquid blue eyes and hair the colour of wheat. She refused to believe him dead. As long as the Great River flowed, as long as Great God Khnum presided beneath the Isle of Abu, she would not give up hope to see her desert trader again.

And there it was before her now—the fabled Isle

of Abu. She had imagined it as a tall, floating cavern through which the river waters spewed, but it was only a long, narrow swath of land that split the River lengthwise, like a frozen teardrop.

Tahar had been right. The Great River did *not* begin at the Isle of Abu. If only she could speak to him now— how satisfied he would be to hear her say those words, and how glad she would be to finally say them: *Tahar, you were right.*

She would never doubt him again. What had he told her to do? *Go to Abu.* She would be safe on Abu. Fine. She would do that. She had plenty of grain, a sharp dagger, and the strongest, most wonderful horse that had ever lived. Tahar had furnished her with everything she needed to survive.

She would go to the Isle of Abu and wait. He had told her that she made his life better. If that was true then he would come for her. Surely he would. If Tahar yet lived he would seek her out upon the Isle of Abu.

She would wait for him and he would come.

Chapter Twenty-Seven

King Khufu had never seen a creature so daring or so beautiful.

She had been swimming between the island and the riverbank for nearly half the day. He'd watched her from behind one of the large boulders that littered the island's shoreline. First she had swum the distance alone, her long limbs stroking comfortably against the current. Then she had begun to carry loads. A bag of grain upon her head. Then another. A saddlebag. A clutch of dates.

She'd worked quickly and efficiently, scanning the surface for crocodiles, though it appeared she had little fear of them. Before long she had all of her treasures safely transferred to the island but one.

The King had never seen such a large donkey. Or perhaps it was something sent from the Gods.

She'd tugged at the beast's reins, but he had refused to venture into the water. Finally the clever woman had crossed back to the island and filled a bowl of grain. She had returned to the shore, given the beast one taste, then held the bowl above her head, just beyond his reach. The beast had not even known he was swimming, and when he'd reached the island he'd got his reward.

She, too, had got hers—rest. She had collapsed upon the shore, exhausted.

Now, no longer in danger of crocodiles, she moved slowly, savouring her accomplishment. She inspected the purple headdress she had twisted about her body, now completely wet. The garment clung to her curves like a second skin.

King Khufu felt a long-forgotten stirring deep in his stomach. He had come to the Isle of Abu in search of a god. Instead, it seemed that he had found a goddess. He stole closer, hiding himself behind a large boulder at the water's edge.

The late-afternoon sunlight sketched her soft curves and he studied them, as if beholding a gloriously carved relief. Slowly she removed her wrap and stood naked upon the shore. Khufu had to catch his breath. She entered the water to her knees, then dunked the garment and wrung it out. She spread the large cloth upon the rocks to dry. Completely disrobed, she returned to the water and began to give herself a bath.

Her face was dirty—stained with perspiration and dust, as if she had endured a long journey. Now, every splash of water seemed to reveal a new layer of loveliness. Her breasts were round and ripe—her nipples becoming perfect peaks at the touch of the droplets. She bent over and dipped her short black hair, then lifted it in a spray of sparkling water. Her movements were so fluid and graceful it looked as if she were performing a holy dance.

Khufu could not believe what he was seeing. Two days before, when his entourage had first arrived at Abu, he had spat upon the ground in vexation. A month's journey for this small piece of rock? There was no cavern, no temple, nowhere to seek communion with Khnum, the God who was supposed to be at his command.

He had begun to feel foolish. He had left the capital city without its King during a time of drought. *Horus spoke to me*, he had told Imhoter. And so the God had. He had told Khufu to come to Abu, but why?

Now he understood why. It was *her*. She was the answer. Horus had sent him the epitome of beauty and grace to rescue him and all of Khemet from despair. She seemed to have been born of the Great River itself. She was harmony, she was loveliness, she was beauty incarnate, she was…

'Hathor…' he uttered.

The woman turned. 'Yes?'

Chapter Twenty-Eight

She fought the two guards mightily, but was powerless against them. They dragged her to the other side of the island, where five large sailing boats floated offshore.

'Meemoo!' she yelled, but a callused hand pressed against her mouth.

She was placed upon a papyrus raft and was piloted to the prow of the largest boat in the fleet. The men lifted her aboard and ushered her past seven massive oars and through an entrance to a long cabin that sat atop the wooden deck.

There was no seeing in the cabin at first. The rich smell of incense assaulted her senses, and she could hear the soft musical clinking of chimes. As her eyes adjusted to the low light she beheld a space like none she had ever seen. Thick, luxurious carpets and massive cushions covered the floors, and the walls were decorated with richly coloured tapestries. There were small low tables stationed throughout the room. Upon them sat glazed earthen pitchers, and platters overflowing with fruits, nuts and breads. Above it all several high, thin windows let in rays of sunlight that bounced off the gilded furnishings.

For a moment Kiya thought she had died and been transported to the heavenly quarters of some benevolent god. Then she felt the squeeze of the guards' grips upon her arms. She strained against them, fighting to free her arms as they escorted her across the room. The guards motioned to a stack of cushions and bade Kiya sit, but she refused.

What was this floating temple of opulence? What richly decorated prison lay before her eyes?

In the corner of the room, a tall, ornately dressed bald man watched her from the shadows. 'It is useless to fight,' said the man. 'You must resign yourself to your fate.'

'What fate?'

The man did not answer. With a quick nod he dismissed the guards, who exited through the curtained archway onto the outer deck.

'Who are you?' Kiya growled.

'I am Imhoter,' said the man.

He stepped from the shadows and bowed low. His long robe was as white as Khufu's tomb. He held its wide sleeves together in a priestly manner, concealing his hands. Kiya observed the finely embroidered skin of a leopard, the symbol of a high priest, adorning the robe's thick edging. The only part of his body that that was not covered by cloth was his head, which was so well-shaven it shone like a copper bowl even in the somnolent shadows.

'Where am I?'

'Look around,' said Imhoter. 'Where do you think you might be? Think hard, for the owner of this ship does not fancy a fool.'

Kiya observed the richly decorated room. Feeling the holy man's eyes upon her, she sought clues to the occupant's identity. He must be quite highborn indeed, she thought, to be able to afford such finery. Kiya knew nothing about the Khemetian aristocracy, except that they lived in palaces and villas and floated about the streets of Memphis in litters borne by slaves.

'If I guess incorrectly will you let me go?' she asked.

'An interesting question. Already you show cleverness,' said Imhoter. 'But, nay, I will not let you go.'

Kiya felt as if she were being put to a test that she did not wish to pass. Still, she would not have the priest believing her a fool.

Her eyes scanned the cabin's adornments, searching for clues. On one table she noticed a gold pitcher, displaying a hieroglyphic relief. Kiya could not read hieroglyphs, but she recognised two of the symbols easily enough: a sedge plant and a bee. *The symbols of Upper and Lower Khemet.*

Next to the pitcher, a platter of finely glazed *faience* pottery held a pile of kebabs. Kiya's mouth watered as she admired the succulent cubes of recently cooked mutton and drank in their earthy scent. Since the beginning of the drought only the most landed nobles had been able to afford to consume meat. Kiya spied plates that held other meats—duck and perhaps gazelle. Clearly the owner of the boat possessed land.

Behind her she beheld a beautiful tapestry. It depicted two women: one with the head of a cobra, the other with the head of a vulture. They were the Goddesses Wadjet and Nekhbet—the celestial guardians of Upper and Lower Khemet, the Ladies of the Two Lands. It seemed safe to say that the owner of the boat was part of the Khemetian government, probably quite high up. The King's *vizier,* perhaps? Or some very powerful *nomarch*?

It wasn't until she beheld the small wooden statue of a falcon-headed man that she realised just how high up.

'I am on King Khufu's ship?' Kiya asked, disbelieving.

'That's a good girl,' said the priest. 'In fact you are in King Khufu's living quarters. His sleeping quarters are on another ship. You see, the Great River was too low for the royal barge. I think these smaller vessels serve admirably, though, don't you?'

The priest was speaking to her as if she had been ferried about on ships of gold her entire life. What could she possibly say in response? *Yes, they are quite nice, good priest, though it would be well if the cushions were a bit larger.*

Hem! Never in her life had Kiya beheld a space like this, let alone been allowed into it. She wondered what Tahar would think of this boat and felt her throat tighten.

'This is a very nice vessel, yes,' Kiya said carefully. 'It is certainly worthy of His Royal Highness, King Khufu, Lord of the Two Lands.' She was not sure if she had embellished enough so she added, 'Horus Incarnate, Keeper of Khemet, He of Sedge and Bee, long may He reign.'

The priest nodded reverently, but she thought she could detect a slight smile dancing faintly across his lips. 'I am the King's Advisor and Holy Seer, though I admit that I have not seen *you* in any vision.'

The priest was unusually tall and exuded strangeness, as if he had come from another world, and yet there was something familiar about him.

'Am I a prisoner?' Kiya whispered.

'Far from it,' he said.

She straightened herself and spoke with firmness. 'Well, there must be some mistake. I am not royal. I am not even highborn. Good priest, I do not belong here.'

'Speak no more, silly woman. Of course you belong here. You were chosen by the King himself.'

The priest seemed to be floating across the room towards her.

'The Gods have set you upon a path far more important than whatever path you travelled before,' he explained.

He stopped just inches from where Kiya stood, and she had to tilt her head to see all of him. There he was, looming above her like the spectre of a god.

'In a few short hours you will break bread with the King of Khemet. In this very room.'

What? Kiya felt herself grow dizzy. To balance herself, she grasped the holy man's arm. This couldn't be. She needed to return to Meemoo and her grain. She needed to make camp and a fire. Something to signal to Tahar if he should come for her.

What if Tahar should come for her?

The priest placed his cool, soft hand on her arm. 'Do not fear for your beast or any of your possessions. They are being cared for.'

Kiya gazed up at the holy man's impassive face. This could not be happening. Tahar might still be alive. Even now he might be on his way. If he arrived upon Abu and did not find her, what would he think? Perhaps he would simply give up. Or, worse, he would comb the island in search of her and instead find the tips of soldiers' spears. And when they noticed Tahar's Libu scar? What then? They would surely place him in bonds—that was if they did not simply slay him on sight.

'Whoever he is, Hathor, you must let him go now,' the priest said, reading Kiya's mind. 'The next few hours will be the most important of your life. You must not speak to the Living God unless he speaks to you. You must never turn your back to him—not even if you have been dismissed. I pray that you will *not* be dismissed, however.'

'Dismissed? What do you mean?' Kiya's skin prickled.

'I mean only that you should try to win the King's favour. Many have endeavoured; all have failed. You will likely fail. But let us not speculate. Only the Gods know what is meant to be. That is all I will say.'

A perfectly manicured hand poked out from under his sleeve. He reached for a bell and rang it. Seconds later a small woman stood in the doorway. She wore a plain white tunic and a striking black wig that framed her face and accentuated her large brown eyes. They stared at Kiya in wonder, then quickly looked at the floor.

'This is Neferdula,' explained Imhoter. 'She is a gifted artist whose job it is to paint the face of the King. She will also paint your face.'

The woman bowed.

'Neferdula will groom you for your encounter. She will bathe you and clothe you and anoint you properly. She will also explain how you should comport yourself. You must do as she says. Do you understand?'

Kiya nodded.

'Now I will leave you to begin,' Imhoter said, nodding to Neferdula. 'It takes time to create a goddess—though I must say you have quite a remarkable start.'

Kiya was stunned. A goddess? She was a beggar, a nobody. *A boy.* Was the priest in his right mind?

'Excuse me, good priest, but do you mean that the King wants to break bread with *me*?'

Imhoter lifted an eyebrow. 'He wishes to break bread with Hathor, Goddess of Love and Abundance, Mother of the Flood. Do you understand?'

Kiya flushed. So she was to be an imposter once again. She felt dizzy. She could hide amongst tomb workers and disappear into the streets of Memphis. But to pretend before the Living God…? This was a ruse she could not sustain. She did not even know how to address him. She did not how to move or speak or even breathe in his royal presence.

She found Neferdula's eyes. *Do not fear*, they told Kiya. *I will make you into Hathor*.

'Yes, I understand.'

Kiya felt a rush of gratitude towards Neferdula, followed by a pang of longing for Tahar. What if she did not wish to be made into Hathor? What if she wished to return to a certain oasis, deep in the desert? What if what she really wanted was to strip off all her disguises and curl her body into a certain desert trader's big embrace?

Naked. Playing the role of herself.

'The King will arrive at sunset,' said Imhoter, closing the door to the cabin. 'Try to please him, Hathor. I dare say the future of Khemet is in your hands.'

'But why? How?'

'If you are as clever as you seem, Goddess, then you shall see. You shall see.'

Chapter Twenty-Nine

'Come closer, Goddess,' King Khufu said.

His voice was higher pitched than she would have guessed. It clanged against her ears like copper upon granite.

'Let me see you in the light.'

He was perhaps twice Kiya's age, but unusually well-preserved. His pleated white wrap was tied smartly about his waist, its front knot concealed by a square blue sash. Above the sash small ripples of naked flesh gradually expanded into a solid brown chest. Several golden necklaces lay heavily upon that swath of flesh, including a looped *ankh* cross inlaid with beautiful carnelian stones. His shoulders were broad, and they extended into thick upper arms adorned with bracelets.

Kiya took a deep breath, then stepped out of the shadows. She kept her eyes on the ground, careful not to trip upon the soft linen gown that dragged luxuriantly behind her. Neferdula had taken the garment from her own closet and added embellishments of moonstone and turquoise along the seams.

'It is just a lounging dress,' Neferdula had told Kiya kindly. 'I will not miss it.'

Neferdula's demeanour had changed once she had set upon the task of painting Kiya. With the concentration of an artist Neferdula had dipped her paintbrushes into tiny cups containing the colours of the earth: red, brown, green and gold. Kiya had noticed tiny golden flakes inside the cup of gold.

'Yes, that is real gold,' Neferdula had said flatly, 'so that you may sparkle before the King.'

Neferdula had scolded Kiya several times for not holding her position, and had cursed when one of her painted spirals had come out as oblong instead of round. After many hours of effort, Neferdula had dabbed a sweet-smelling resin upon Kiya's neck. She had held a brass mirror before Kiya and proclaimed simply, 'You are my best work.'

Kiya had not recognised herself in the reflection. The black lines encircling her eyes made them seem both larger and deeper somehow, and her skin exuded its own special light. Her long, luxuriant wig and ruby-red lips completed the vision, which was nothing like how Kiya really looked. She was, Kiya reluctantly admitted, quite beautiful.

As Kiya approached the King now he set his golden goblet aside. His eyes grew wide. 'I did not think it was possible for you to be more beautiful. Neferdula has outdone herself.'

'I am honoured, My King,' Kiya said with assurance, but her hands were shaking and she could not control her breaths. She was in the presence of the Living God. She was not prepared for this. She was not worthy of this.

She dropped to her knees as Neferdula had instructed and bowed her head.

The King rushed to her side and lifted her gently by

the arm. 'That is not necessary, My Goddess. We are alone. We can dispense with ceremony. Besides, I should be the one kneeling before *you*.'

Kiya stared in wonder at the man who held Khemet in the palm of his hand, who had built the most glorious tomb the world had ever known, whose *ka* was so exalted it was said that he whispered to the Gods.

And yet he was just a man.

The King reached for the pitcher and poured Kiya a goblet of wine. 'What is that sweet smell you wear? Lily? Myrrh?'

'Forgive me, My Lord, I do not know.'

'I think it is something exotic,' said the King. 'Or perhaps it is just…you.' He handed her the goblet. 'When the Gods told me to come to Abu I had no idea I would find Hathor Incarnate here. Now I see their plan more clearly than ever before.'

The King took his own goblet and clinked it against hers and they drank.

'Tell me, Hathor, am I pleasing to you?'

Kiya was so surprised by the question that she almost spat the tart liquid upon the floor. *Am I pleasing to you?* Was that what he had asked? Was that what the *Living God* wanted to know? Perhaps Neferdula had cast some strange spell upon Kiya's ears. Or maybe she had inhaled too much incense and the smoke had clouded her mind.

The King studied her, earnestly awaiting her answer.

'I do not know you,' she said at length, 'so I cannot yet say.'

The King raised a single brow, then looked away. She realised suddenly that she had insulted him.

'Apologies, My King, I did not mean what I said—'

'Of course you meant it,' the King said. Then a smile

of delight broke across his cleanly shaven jaw. He took a loaf of bread from a platter and divided it in two, giving one half to Kiya. 'And it is exhilarating to experience such honesty. You do not know me, so how do you know if I please you or not? Ha! It appears that you are as wise as you are beautiful. But, tell me, am I pleasing to your eyes?'

The King filled his chest with air. He looked at her sidelong.

Kiya stared at the King in confusion. Did the Lord of the Two Lands really want to know if she found him... appealing? She took a bite of her bread and chewed, trying to delay. She needed to get this answer right.

He was softer than Tahar, and rounder. His chest muscles were not as well defined, and nor did his stomach end like Tahar's did in that fascinating ripple of strength. Still, the King was solidly built. His wide chest and thick, powerful arms were not unappealing. His eyes had been kohled and his body shaved in the fashion of highborn Khemetian men.

Kiya chose her words carefully. 'You *are* pleasing to my eye. You are both strong and soft.'

'Hie!' the King shouted, laughing. 'Your honesty moves me.'

He finished the bread and swallowed the contents of his wine glass. Then he took Kiya's arms and guided her down onto a large cushion. 'And what think you of my face?' he asked. 'Pray, be specific...'

Kiya studied King Khufu's face as he rested it against the large, soft cushion. 'Your nose is like ancient King Sneferu's Second Pyramid of Stone.'

'How so?'

'It is bent.'

'Hazah!' The King chortled. He grazed his fingers lightly across her arm. 'What else?'

'The shape of your face is as Thoth's—pale and round and full.'

'It is indeed,' he said.

He patted her wig, placing a portion of her long black hair behind her ear. His eyes lingered uncomfortably on the length of her neck.

'Your eyes are narrow, but they shine brightly,' she added.

'Do they?'

He moved his body closer to hers. He was lying so close to her now she began to fear what he might do next.

'And your lips…' Kiya paused. She thought of Tahar's lips. So smart and well-defined. So certain. If she had not been discovered by the King she might be kissing those lips right now.

'What about my lips?' urged the King.

His arm reached around her waist and Kiya caught her breath. *Your lips are pale and lifeless. They are nothing like Tahar's*.

'Your lips are sacred. They confer with the Gods,' she said.

'Hem,' said the King.

Kiya could feel him stiffen.

He pulled his hand from her waist and sat up. 'My lips have not conferred with the Gods for a long while, for if they had the Great River's blessed flood would be flowing across the land.'

Kiya felt her limbs relax. Her words had diverted the King from his path of lust. Imhoter would not be pleased, but Kiya was relieved.

'Aye, the drought is a terrible hardship.'

'Hardship?' The King growled. 'It threatens my reign. My very survival!' He let out a breath. 'I am sorry, dear Hathor. It is just—the drought makes me cross.'

'I can only imagine how you must feel,' Kiya said, her visions of a benevolent king shattering into a million shards. While the people of Khemet starved, King Khufu worried only about his *reign*! She sat up and drew her legs close. 'Such threats should stay where they belong,' she added, 'in tales.'

'Aye,' said the King, lying back on the pillows. He ran his finger along Kiya's arm, making her shiver. 'Do you know *many* tales, Hathor?'

'Yes, My King.'

'Then tell me one of them. Tell me one and ease my weary mind.'

Kiya searched her mind. She had heard many tales, but never before had she actually *told* one. If only she were like her mother, who had always had a tale upon her lips worthy of a king's ears.

In that instant Kiya grasped a truth so profound and shocking that she thought she might just sink through the floor of the King's floating palace. Her mother had been King Sneferu's concubine, and this man was King Sneferu's legitimate son. She had to stop herself from laughing aloud. *I am this man's half-sister.*

Careful not to stare, she stole another glance at His Majesty's face. Though she did not share his bent nose and rounded profile, there was something in the shape of his eyes that matched her own—at least as they had appeared when Neferdula had held the mirror to her painted face.

This man and I share the same father.

Kiya felt her limbs grow cold. What had Imhoter told

her? *He wishes to break bread with Hathor, Goddess of Love and Abundance, Mother of the Flood.* If Kiya was to be half as clever as Imhoter believed, she knew she could not reveal her true identity to the King. The fragility of his pride told her that his disillusionment would quickly turn to wrath. Still, it was clear that he meant to bed her—and she could not allow that to happen either. Royal brothers and sisters often married, but it was well known that they did not share the same bed.

'Well?' the King added impatiently. 'Any tale will do, Goddess. Share your wisdom with me.'

Kiya sat up, remembered her mother's beautiful face, and began. 'I would love to tell you a tale, Your Majesty.' *My Brother.* 'There was and there was not…a man who was visited by a god. And the God told him to make out of his own home a ship, for a great flood was coming…'

As Kiya recounted the old Sumerian tale the King listened closely, and when Kiya came to the end a single tear traced a path down his cheek.

'Many people died in that great flood, did they not?' Khufu asked.

'Aye.'

'The Gods did not help them?'

'Nay—they helped just the man and his wife, to whom they granted immortality. The rest of the people turned to clay.' Kiya paused. Her mother had once told her that the job of a storyteller was to cause pain and then to take it away. She had clearly caused the King pain. How was she to ease his mind? 'My King, I have seen the Great River from above. It is much longer than I could have ever dreamed.'

'Why do you tell me this, Hathor?'

'I tell you this because I believe that we are smaller

than we know. We are temporary. We are…whispers in the grass. The Gods are mighty, but they care little about us.' Kiya blinked back a tear, remembering the moment Tahar had first uttered those words to her. 'Therefore,' she continued, 'we must care about each other.'

The King stared at Kiya in wonder. 'I have never met anyone like you in my life.'

'I only wish to take away your pain, My King. But I have said too much—'

'Nay, you speak your mind, and it is a beautiful mind.' He took her hand in his and pressed his lips to it. 'But I fear I am still in pain. What else can you tell me?'

What else? Her mother would know what to say. Concubines were trained for such moments. Kiya was not a concubine, however, and nor did she ever wish to be. What she wished was to return to shore, where she might wait for Tahar.

She would not coddle the King nor flatter him, therefore. He was her own half-brother, after all. She would simply tell him the truth. 'I can tell you that the flood is coming,' Kiya stated. 'It will be here in a cycle of the moon. It will be late, but it will come.'

The King's eyes lit up, then narrowed. 'You are bold in making such a claim. You may be divine, but there are some things even the Gods cannot know. You overstep.'

'Your Majesty, you may doubt me, but you cannot doubt the locusts, which swarm on the eastern sides of the dunes but do not fly. And you cannot doubt the breath of wind that has lately begun to whisper its way northward in the deepest part of night.' Kiya lifted her wig and pulled out the seed that she had discovered in the sand so many days ago. 'You cannot doubt that the acacia seeds that lay beneath the soil have begun to crack.' She handed the seed to the King. 'Hapi comes.'

The King's mouth dropped open. He lowered his eyes. 'Forgive me, Goddess,' he said. 'It is I who overstep.' He raised himself upon his knees, then bowed to her. He lifted her hand and put his lips to it. 'It is clear to me now that you have been sent by the Gods. You are Hathor, and you have come to bless Khemet and take away its pain. You bring beauty and fertility. You bring the flood.'

The King returned the seed to Kiya's hand and eased her back onto the cushions. She pretended to relax. The King of Khemet, Horus Incarnate, believed her to be a goddess. Was he mad? Perhaps he was simply a man who thought himself a god and believed whatever he liked.

He stroked her wig, then let his hand glide slowly down the length of her back. He pulled her close. 'Tell me, Hathor, do you believe me to be the incarnation of a god?' he asked.

He pushed himself against her and a pang of terror catapulted through Kiya's body. 'My King, I believe… that you are and you are not.'

'My darling,' he said, smiling ruefully. 'You are rarer than the rarest gem and a thousand times more precious.'

He traced her lips with his fingers and she could feel the warmth of his breath.

'And to think I wished only to give you my seed.' He stroked her cheek. 'Hathor, my Goddess, I shall make you my wife.'

Chapter Thirty

Kiya straightened her wig. She balanced herself on a stack of cushions and peered out through the high window at the throng that had gathered at the end of the dock. The royal herald had just announced her: Hathor Incarnate—the King's betrothed.

Sighs and whispers rippled through the crowd as the people of the village of Asyut received the unexpected news. The King was to take a third wife—and not just any wife but the Goddess of Love and Abundance reborn. And she was here on this very day, to greet the people of Asyut and grace them with her beauty and love.

Kiya felt nauseous. The henna designs that decorated the sides of her breasts had begun to run, and she was sweating through her white linen tunic. *The Goddess of Love and Abundance, indeed.*

'Go, Hathor, your people await,' urged Neferdula.

My people?

Kiya could not even hear her own thoughts for the blare of trumpets and the thrum of royal drums signalling her arrival.

'The epitome of beauty and womanhood has graced

the House of Horus,' cried the herald, and it occurred to Kiya that if she delayed any longer he might just promise her arrival would be upon a beam of light.

She imagined it was not King Khufu but Tahar waiting for her on the dock and felt her heart grow light. Then she heard Imhoter's sobering tone.

'Why do you make your King wait?' he called to her from outside the deck house. 'You are to become Queen soon. You must greet the people of Asyut. You must represent the House of Horus and give them hope.'

Imhoter was the last person Kiya wanted to disappoint, though earlier that day she had all but begged him to release her.

'But I am an imposter,' she had explained as Neferdula had lifted a simple linen tunic over Kiya's head. 'I am not Hathor but Kiya—a common name for a common woman.'

But the old priest had raised his hairless brow and spoken sternly. 'Whoever you were before, she is gone. Whatever you wanted before, let it go. You are Hathor now. You are not common.'

'Nay, you are anything but common,' Neferdula had said, and Kiya had seen the small woman's arm muscles flex as she lifted a heavy beaded object resembling a net over Kiya's head.

The colourful beaded net dress had been settled snugly atop Kiya's white tunic, accentuating her curves. The dress had felt unusually heavy, and as Kiya had looked down at the beads she'd noticed that some even glimmered in the candlelight.

Neferdula had stood beside Imhoter for a long while, appraising her work. 'Look at how the gilded beads reflect the golden flecks in her eyes,' she had commented.

Imhoter had nodded solemnly. 'There is royalty in you, Hathor, whatever you say, and godliness too.'

'I fear you are both mistaken,' Kiya had continued, but it had appeared that the two had ceased to hear her.

'You belong to Khemet now,' Imhoter had said before taking his leave. 'You must bring hope to a dying land.'

Now Kiya looked down at her hands. They were dry and cracked, like Khemet itself. Neferdula's many salves and oils could not revive them. Her fingers were thin and knobby, the fingernails short, the palms callused. They were not the sort of hands made to dole out hope.

And now they were trembling.

Kiya spied a lily in a vase upon one of the tables. 'I should like to hold the lily, if I may?'

Neferdula appeared relieved. 'That is a wonderful idea,' she said, quickly retrieving the long white flower. She handed it to Kiya, then gripped Kiya's hand reassuringly. 'Do not be afraid, Goddess. You shall make their hearts light.'

Kiya nodded and smiled gratefully. 'Thank you, dear Neferdula. You have lightened my own heart.' Then she stepped through the door.

If she had not been able to hear the farmers' murmurs she might have believed them to be ghosts. They watched and waited at the end of the dock, wearing their finest wigs.

As instructed, Kiya placed one hand upon the King's outstretched arm and together they walked slowly across the planks towards the shore, with the royal shade bearers flanking them and the colourful beads of her heavy bead net dress clinking softly with her every move.

The river ended before the dock did. The remainder of the tall wooden structure hovered over a vast swath of cracked mud. As she and the King approached the crowd, Kiya could see it was entirely comprised of farmers—ruddy-faced men and women who worked hard every day, coaxing bounty from the earth. They were the people who made Khemet great, and they studied Kiya with sunken eyes. Their thin, listless bodies seemed to sway in the heat. Kiya glanced between the planks at the dry, barren bottomlands, watered only by the tears of these people's suffering.

As Kiya and the King neared, Kiya caught sight of a girl standing at the front of the crowd. The little fledgling could not have seen more than ten cycles of the sun, but her bony limbs and gaunt face made her appear much older.

Kiya bent down and handed the girl her flower. 'A blossom for a blossom,' said Kiya.

The girl's pale face lit up with a smile.

'The flood will come, little one. Do not fear. It is on its way even now.'

The girl reached her hands around Kiya's neck in an embrace. Kiya held her tightly.

'Behold Hathor, Mother of the Flood!' the King said, and the people erupted in cries of exultation.

Kiya could never have imagined that her words could carry such power. Only three months before she had made herself mute, afraid of her own voice. Now it rang out across Khemet like a song of hope.

And that was how it went. The days passed in a blur of joy and anguish. Dusty villages appeared one after the other as they made their way slowly back up the River, northward towards Memphis. The people of Khemet prostrated themselves before Kiya, believing her a goddess. They reached out to touch her fine dresses, which Neferdula produced as if by magic. They placed their heads in Kiya's hands and wept.

She tried to console them. She dried their tears and whispered into their ears. 'Do not despair. Do you see the breeze that tousles the King's flag? That is Hapi, our precious flood. It whispers to us that it is on its way.'

They were Tahar's words that she spoke, and every time they escaped her lips her heart ached. She had misjudged him profoundly. She had believed him selfish when in fact he had given her everything he had. His knowledge, his words, his life.

Every day she allowed Neferdula to paint her face and drape her in full regalia and make her into someone she was not. The breasts she had worked so hard to conceal were now often exposed, their only cover two thin straps and the sacred henna designs that Neferdula painted on them with such care.

Slowly Kiya lost her timidity, and forgave herself for the lie she cultivated. If posing as Hathor could give a little girl with an empty belly a ray of hope, then Kiya would pose. She only wished she could find her own ray of hope—that Tahar was alive somewhere, that he was coming for her, that he hadn't given up.

Every evening the King visited her in her cabin, ebullient with joy. 'They love me again because of you, Hathor,' he would say, caressing her cheek. 'They forgive me because of you.'

'King, there is nothing to forgive. You have always done what you must—just as I do what I must.'

He seemed mesmerised by her words, by her quiet observations of the world. He circled her like a lion, full of flattery, immune to her indifference. Or perhaps it was her very indifference that spurred him on, for there was nothing she could say or do, it seemed, to repel him.

'You are my little radish, ripe and lovely,' he told her, placing golden necklaces about her neck. 'Your honey skin makes my blood run thick.'

Her mother's warning echoed in her mind. Clearly the King meant to possess her body as soon as they were wed, and the thought made Kiya sick with dread. She did not wish to join with her half-brother, no matter how much gold or praise he lavished upon her. Khemetian kings often married their sisters, for they were gods and could do as they liked. But Kiya did not wish to be touched by a god. She wished only to return to that moment when Tahar had taken her in his arms and told her that she was safe.

Mercifully, her coupling with the King could not take place before their marriage. It was the law. A Khemetian king could take a concubine whenever he liked, but to take a holy wife was another matter. The King's body was Khemet's body, and the parentage of his legitimate progeny must be witnessed and ensured. A king's child was only royal if conceived after marriage.

For that reason Imhoter and Neferdula kept vigilant watch over both Kiya and the King. Neferdula stayed on Kiya's designated boat, ensuring that the King's visits were supervised. And whenever Kiya visited the King, Imhoter stood in the shadows, still as a statue, witnessing all.

'You shall bear me a son,' the King said one morning after they had broken their fast.

He stroked Kiya's belly. They lay side by side against the King's cushions, the gently rocking ship lulling the King towards slumber.

'And I shall call the child Khnum Incarnate, Exalted Child of Khnum-Khufu, Mighty Saviour of Khemet.' The King glanced at the corner of the cabin, where Imhoter had tucked himself into the shadows. 'What do you think of that name, Imhoter?'

'It is a fine name, Majesty.'

'Step out of the shadows, eunuch! By the Gods, I feel I am being haunted by a spirit. And tell me the truth. Do you like the name or not?'

Obediently Imhoter stepped forward, and Kiya thought she could discern a flush of red upon the ancient man's cheeks. King Khufu had embarrassed him.

'In truth, I am not fond of it, Majesty.'

'Seth's blood—why? What is wrong with it, eunuch?'

The crimson in Imhoter's cheeks deepened. Kiya longed to silence the King, whose bitingly personal words seemed to have sliced Imhoter's *ka* in two.

'My Lord, the name lacks…subtlety,' said Imhoter.

After the King had fallen asleep, Kiya joined Imhoter above deck. It was still early, but already the north wind had begun to blow. Imhoter watched the boatmen as they stepped down the mast and took their positions at the oars.

'Greetings, good priest,' Kiya said.

'Good morning, Young Goddess,' he said, bowing sombrely, though Kiya thought she could detect a glint in his eyes.

'It appears the wind is not in our favour,' she observed.

'Fortunately the flow of the Great River itself is,' said Imhoter. 'The royal heralds shall arrive in Memphis before the day is done.'

It was customary for the heralds to travel ahead of the King's entourage and announce his arrival in each of the villages. In this case the heralds were also tasked with announcing the King's betrothal.

'Their job is a happy one,' Imhoter said. 'The announcement alone has diverted the people from their suffering. They anxiously await your arrival.'

'What of the King's other queens, Imhoter?' Kiya asked. 'Tell me about them.'

'Meritites and Henutsen were betrothed to the King as children. They are much older than you—powerful women, half-sisters of the King. They get along well, and are content to leave their husband to his concubines. I suspect they will treat you as a daughter. You are fortunate. Not all kings' wives are so amicable.'

'You have served other kings?'

Imhoter pursed his lips. 'Indeed I have. I served Khufu's father, King Sneferu. *His* wives fought like cats—' Imhoter paused, and a smile broke across his face. 'But I speak too freely with you, Young Goddess. You have made me into a gossip.'

'If a gossip, then a holy one,' Kiya said, enjoying the private jest. She felt strangely trusting of the old man—as if she had known him her whole life. His cool, aloof demeanour did not intimidate Kiya as it seemed to do to others, and she delighted in trying to breach his tight-lipped decorum.

'Will you indulge me but one more indecorous question, Imhoter?'

'Clearly I do not have a choice.'

'Did Khufu's father Sneferu heed your advice as Khufu himself does?'

Imhoter spoke carefully. 'He did for a time, and then he did not.'

Kiya spoke softly. 'Forgive me, Imhoter. Did King Sneferu make you a...what you are?'

'I thought you were going to ask only one indecorous question?' he said. Then he laughed sadly. 'It is as you suspect, clever one,' said Imhoter. 'Khufu's father took my manhood.'

'Will you not tell me how it happened?'

'One day I will tell you, but not today. It is a long, sad tale and not for the ears of a wife-to-be.' He looked into Kiya's eyes. 'I will tell you this, though: it is ill-advised to cross a king.'

'Heave to!' the helmsman yelled, and the vessel lunged forward.

'Ah! The men have rested well,' Imhoter observed as the shoreline began to race past them. 'We shall be within the walls of the palace in no more than seven days.'

That soon? It had taken Kiya and Tahar many, many weeks to reach the southern borders of Upper Khemet. Now, with the help of the Great River, they would be ushered back north in a blur of time. To her home—to Memphis. This time, however, she would not arrive half starving at the docks, searching for scraps. Now she would arrive upon the ship of a king, its blue and white flag flying high, bringing her to the palace dock and into the folds of her new life.

And for that she should be happy. Nay, she should be ecstatic. She had fulfilled every Khemetian girl's fondest dream. She had captured the heart of a *king*! And not merely as a concubine; she would soon be elevated to queen. Queen! She would enjoy power and status and endless wealth. No more scratching her existence from the dirty streets. She would dine on mutton and bathe herself in milk and bedeck herself with jewels.

Why, then, did she feel so poor? Why was her most prized possession still the acacia seed she kept hidden beneath her wig? She retrieved it now and fingered its glossy shell. It had worn thin from so much handling. Soon its cottony pith would be all that was left.

And that was as well, for she needed to forget him. She needed to purge his memory from her mind.

Still, every day she found herself wishing she could go back in time. To the oasis pool, to the cave, to the wide-open plain. Anywhere she might find him—his strong, confident hands, his curious smile, his eyes slaying her soul like daggers. He had shown her things she would have never believed real—visions beyond her wildest dreams—and she wished to see them all over again, with him by her side.

But mostly she wished to see his face.

It was such a *good* face. So angular and strong. So certain. And those eyes… She would prefer the lustrous sparkle of those eyes to the sheen of any jewel.

'We are as actors in a feast-day drama, My Young Goddess,' Imhoter said as he stared at the passing shore. 'We must fulfil our roles. Already you have given the people of Khemet the performance of a lifetime. You have uplifted their hearts and filled them with hope. Soon you shall become the greatest Queen Khemet has ever known. The storytellers will sing of you and the scribes will write your story on many scrolls. If only—'

'If only what?'

'May *I* now speak indecorously?' Imhoter asked.

'You may always speak truths to me,' said Kiya.

'If only you are able to fully embrace your role as Queen,' Imhoter said, gripping her in his gaze. 'Whoever he is, you must cast him from your mind.'

'I have no idea of whom you speak,' Kiya said defensively.

Imhoter lifted a perfectly shaved eyebrow until it wrinkled with accusation.

'It seems I can hide nothing from you, Holy One.' Kiya sighed.

'Once again, your cleverness serves you. But are you clever enough to know what you must forget?'

'I am trying to forget him—but it is impossible, I fear.'

Imhoter watched her closely. 'You must try harder. You must be selfless. You must care for the people of Khemet more.'

Kiya noticed that Imhoter had left out the notion of caring for the King himself.

The helmsman shouted another order and the oarsmen slowed. They were nearing a village. Kiya could see ribbons of smoke stretching from a dozen fires in the distance. Along the shore she spotted a group of children. They were trying in vain to keep pace with the royal boats. Kiya waved to them and they jumped and shouted gleefully before tumbling upon the dry ground in exhaustion.

'Is that not enough?' asked Imhoter. 'To bring joy into the hearts of young ones? To embody their aspirations? As Queen, you shall represent what makes this land great. Everything that Khemet is, you shall be.'

If Khemet is great it is its people, not their Queen, who make it so, Kiya thought.

She turned the seed over and over with her fingers. When she was younger she would sometimes take her night's rest upon the soft grasses that fringed the Great River. She would stare up at the sky in wonder, imagining it to be a great mirror of the earth. Its celestial river flowed in a milky cloud, and she was one of the tiny points of light sleeping at its side.

Back then she'd had no idea where the Great River began or ended. Now she had seen it with her own eyes. It was much longer than she could even imagine. She had seen it. *Thanks to him.*

'Might I travel to foreign lands as Queen?'

'A queen of Khemet may travel as much as she likes. She may see the world, if she so chooses.'

'I should like to see the world,' she mused.

The shore rushed past them in a blur of colour, and Kiya imagined herself on a royal expedition. She was combing across the land, seeing wondrous sights. *Searching for Tahar, wishing he were by my side.*

'The Dark Sea, for example. I should like to explore it. And beyond it to the Lands of the Grass.'

Imhoter seemed to read her thoughts. 'I speak to you for your own good, dear Hathor. I see how you resist the King. You are unable to let him into your heart. Know this: a person departed is but a hollow statue, beautiful and unchanging. Over time their features fade and we forget their faults. I suspect that this man you hold on to so tightly with your heart was not perfect. Or did he descend from the realm of the Gods?'

'Nay, he was not perfect.'

What had Tahar's last words been, exactly? *I wish for you to be free from such an evil man.* If it had not been Chief Bandir who had asked for her hand but some kindly Nubian prince would Tahar have still set her free? Or would he have sold her as he'd planned, his conscience mollified by the certainty of her safety?

'You have a choice before you,' said Imhoter. 'Let the man you pine for go and enjoy the life of a queen. Or keep your lost love in your heart and spend your days in misery.'

It seemed that Imhoter understood Kiya better than she understood herself. She was putting her desire for one man—a man she wasn't sure was even alive—above her own destiny.

Had Tahar really loved her as she did him? She could never be sure. The only thing that was certain was that soon she would be elevated to a position that she would retain even in death. *To the level of the Gods.* She owed her life to Khemet now, and to its mighty King. The small prejudices of her heart were insignificant. They were trifles—tiny points of light that became lost in that great, milky river of the sky.

She held out her hand and let the seed drop into the current.

Goodbye, Tahar. I will never forget you.

Chapter Thirty-One

There it was: the third serpent. She had known it was coming, for that was the way of harbingers—whether in storytellers' tales or on priests' papyrus scrolls: they always came in threes. The only difference was that this was not a tale. This was Kiya's wedding day. And the third serpent was not alive. It was made of gold and it sat upon the crown of the man who, in a few short hours, would become her husband.

Kiya concealed herself at the rear of the great audience hall, peering from behind the curtains as the King made his royal entrance. He stepped out onto the long blue carpet and the crowd went silent. The drumbeats began and he kept pace with them—each beat a single footfall. He wore ritual leather sandals upon his feet, and a simple white wrap about his waist. A golden sapphire and turquoise necklace hung about his neck, forming a collar so large he was veritably clad in its brilliant stones.

It was his dazzling crown, however, that seemed to elevate him to the realm of the Gods. Cased in a red helmet, the imposing headpiece was tall and white, with a conical tip that stretched to the heavens. A spiralling red coil protruded from the helmet and a golden cobra—the fabled *ureaus*—reared up from the crown's base.

The imposing gilded serpent invested the King with a latent power that seemed to mesmerise everyone who viewed him. With his crook and flail in hand, the soft, imperfect man who doted on Kiya and marvelled at her every word had been transformed. He was majestic and mysterious, hard and commanding, and every inch a king.

The drummers thrummed their steady beat as His Majesty walked between the pillars. The hundreds who had gathered gasped and whispered as they beheld their resplendent monarch. At length Khufu climbed the dais and stood before his throne, observing his flock.

The royal herald's voice resounded across the immense pillared space. 'Behold Horus, Son of Sneferu, Lord of the Two Lands, King Khufu the Magnificent.'

The King lifted his crook and each of the hundreds of finely dressed guests dropped to their knees in silent obeisance.

'Rise,' the King said, and all the souls returned to standing. A servant replaced the King's crook and flail with a goblet of wine. The King raised the golden chalice in the air with both hands. 'Let us rejoice, for today I shall marry!'

The crowd erupted in cheers. The King drank a deep draught, then took his seat upon the high throne. A long line of well-wishers rapidly assembled upon the royal carpet before him. Their arms overflowed with gifts: garlands of flowers, bowls of spices, small elegant boxes containing jewels.

The ritual presentation of gifts began. The King's assistants announced each gift-giver's name and also the nature of the gift he presented, while the onlookers oohed and aahed. After its formal presentation and description, each gift was placed on a display table for all to behold. There were jars full of honey, barrels of natron, and shards of beautiful stained glass. There were baskets full of Sumerian frankincense so potent that Kiya could smell its earthy scent from where she stood. There was even a trained monkey, who drew applause and laughter when he demonstrated his amazing ability to braid a woman's hair.

The King stroked his long, ceremonial black beard and accepted his subjects' offerings with pompous amusement. One after another the people came, kissing the ground before him, pouring out their adulations, presenting their gifts.

'What a happy day!' they exclaimed. 'For the greatest King of all time is to be married to the Mother of the Flood. The Gods smile upon us all.'

Presently a richly bejewelled man arrived, followed by three plainly dressed young women. 'Your Majesty,' he said, bowing deeply. 'I bring you help for the royal kitchen.'

'You are too generous, Ranofer,' Khufu told the highborn man. 'They will be much appreciated by the cooks.'

Kiya watched with open-mouthed horror as the women were escorted to the table and told to stand where the other gifts were being displayed. Could it be that the King's highborn guests were giving the King *slaves*? As *gifts*?

She felt a gentle hand upon her arm. 'Come, Blessed Hathor,' said Imhoter. 'Spying is unseemly for a queen.'

Kiya followed Imhoter back to the royal robing room, trying to forget what she had just seen. She needed to quiet her emotions, for she was being prepared for her own royal entrance. Still, she couldn't get the three young women out of her mind. *One of those girls could have been me*, she thought.

'Are you clever enough to know what you must forget?' asked Imhoter suddenly, as if he had read her mind.

He had asked the same question of her many weeks ago, on the deck of the King's ship. She knew that he was trying to protect her now, as he had then, to strengthen her for the coming ordeal. Still, she wondered if she could ever forget being married to a man who accepted slaves as gifts. She wondered if she could possibly overlook the fact that she had abandoned all hope of ever finding her true love.

She looked into the old man's kind, wrinkled face. She wanted to make him proud, but feared she never could.

'I am clever enough to know when to stay silent,' she said.

She followed him into the bustling robe room, where a small army of servants hurried about, readying the painting area, waving ostrich feather fans and pouring water into golden goblets.

Kiya stood before her designated seat opposite a tall copper mirror. Presently a servant appeared and patted her sweating brow with cloth. It was the first day of *peret*—the growing season—but *akhet*'s relentless heat lingered still.

Kiya lifted a goblet and took a sip. The water was cool and sweet, but it did nothing for the dryness she felt in her throat.

She longed for Tahar. Many weeks had passed since she'd vowed to forget him, but he haunted her thoughts still. She had tried to smile and embrace her new life, but she could not. It was as if her soul had been suffering a drought, and only Tahar could bring the flood. Even now she imagined him standing beside her, whispering in her ear.

'Do not fear,' he told her. *'The world is large and we are small.'*

'Aye, My Love,' she said back to him. *'Whispers in the grass.'*

She set down the goblet and studied her gown. The fabric was unusual—like nothing she had ever known. It was smooth, like glass, yet soft—extremely soft—like a girl's freshly combed hair. When light shone upon it, it glowed like oil, and when it moved against her skin she felt as if she was stepping into the waters of a tranquil pool.

She touched the unearthly material, as if it might cool her hands.

'Do not touch the dress!' barked Imhoter. He had brought it to her just days before, having procured the fabric from a Lebanese merchant who claimed to have travelled far beyond the Big Green to obtain it. 'Tiny insects spun the threads of this fabric,' explained Imhoter. 'The merchant called it silk.'

'Silk…' Kiya repeated. The word seemed perfectly matched to the fabric it named, for it trickled across her tongue like a stream of water.

Imhoter had paid the man in gold for the material—a goodly number of ingots. 'Trust me,' Imhoter told Kiya. 'When the King and his guests behold you in your gown the illusion will be complete. It will all be worth it.'

Imhoter did not need to reassure her. He was the only person in this strange, highborn world whom she trusted at all, though she could not explain why that was so. Indeed, she trusted him enough to defy custom, for it was traditional for a queen-to-be to wear a simple tunic on her wedding day.

'It is truly a beautiful dress,' she told Imhoter now.

He stood beside her and gazed into the mirror, transfixed. Like other gowns, it had thick straps that ran over her shoulders, covering her breasts, but that was where the similarities ended. With its silver-blue sheen and long, loose train, the dress was like none that had ever been seen in Khemetian court. Kiya appeared covered in liquid, as if she had just stepped from the Great River itself.

She looked beautiful and elegant and, she admitted, not quite human. 'I do not deserve such finery.'

'Of course you deserve it. You are a goddess in full. You have proved that to me.'

'May I confess to you a secret, dearest Imhoter?' Kiya whispered. 'Before I become Queen?'

'Of course, sweet child. Tell it now and let the burden be lifted from your lovely shoulders.'

Kiya leaned close to Imhoter's ear and spoke softly. 'I was born in the royal harem.'

Imhoter stared at Kiya in the mirror, but she could not see what was behind his large, dark eyes.

'You were born to a concubine of Sneferu's, then?' he murmured, and turned to look at her directly.

'Aye, I am a child of the deceased King.'

Imhoter wrinkled his lips in thinly veiled horror. Had she offended him? Had he become so convinced of the divinity with which he had cloaked her that he was insulted by the truth?

'It cannot be…' he said. He was poring over her face as if trying to decipher an ancient scroll.

But of *course* she was a child of the deceased King.

All the children born in the royal harem belonged to the King, did they not? Or what was the purpose of a harem?

Kiya wished to discuss it further, but Neferdula arrived, carrying a large white sheet.

'It is time to paint you and to arrange your wig,' she said sharply. 'Please sit.'

Kiya could read the nervousness on Neferdula's face as she sat and allowed herself to be blanketed by the protective fabric.

Neferdula studied Kiya's face in the mirror's reflection as if studying a blank papyrus. 'Today I shall do my most important work.'

Meanwhile Imhoter had dropped to his knees and was busying himself with the bottom of Kiya's dress. When he finally stood, Kiya discerned a glassy quality to his eyes.

'What cannot be?' she asked him.

His breaths came quickly to his lips. 'It is nothing. An illusion—that is all. For a moment you reminded me of someone I once knew.' Imhoter looked away. He appeared to be choking back tears. 'I will leave you now in Neferdula's capable hands,' he said, bowing deeply. 'I will return when her work is complete.'

'Thank you, Imhoter,' said Kiya. 'For the dress, for your wise counsel, for…everything.'

'You are most welcome, Blessed One. There is no one more deserving than you.'

Kiya bowed her head, humbled by this unassuming man who seemed to blow the invisible winds that kept the ship of Khemet from harm.

Why had he suddenly appeared on the verge of tears? Surely it was the dress.

Kiya had doubted all his elaborate artifices at first, especially when the people of Khemet suffered so gravely from the drought. But now she had begun to see how the pageantry gladdened people's souls, she could no longer believe it completely frivolous. It had only been when they had arrived in Memphis, however, that she had truly understood the import of the elaborate mask Imhoter had asked her to wear.

In the King's absence Menis, the most powerful priest in Memphis, had approached his tenant farmers and promised to waive their rents for ever if they joined him in arms against the King. A host of Menis's farmer-soldiers had been camped at the docks, waiting for Menis's order to attack.

Meanwhile Menis had colluded with the other priests, plotting the King's overthrow. His timing had been auspicious, for most of the King's soldiers had been dispatched to the Red Land in their pointless search for the Libu raiders. The few of Khufu's soldiers who remained in Memphis had been willing to forget their loyalty in exchange for the right amount of grain.

Menis had campaigned amongst the people, doling out his grain and urging them to acknowledge the will of the Gods—whom, he had claimed, had forsaken King Khufu long ago.

'I will bring the flood and restore *maat* to Khemet,' Menis had promised, filling their grain bags with his private stores. 'It is clear that the Gods wish for Menis to become your Holy King!'

There was one thing, however, that Menis had not accounted for in his quiet usurpation. There was something the people of Khemet craved more than grain.

It was love.

Love was stronger than loyalty, stronger than greed. It

was stronger, sometimes, even than hunger—for it was what fed the Khemetians' souls: stories of love, professions of love, promises of love. *Love embodied.*

Imhoter, unlike Menis, understood this craving, and when the royal ships had arrived at the docks of Memphis he had fed it. He had placed the red crown of Hathor upon Kiya's head and set her upon a litter festooned with flowers, right beside the King's own.

'Behold the Goddess of Love,' the herald had sung as she was paraded into the city. 'Hathor, Mother of the Flood, the King's Betrothed. She has come to deliver us from the drought. Rejoice!'

The spectacle had had its desired effect. Menis's minions had laid down their arms and prostrated themselves before Kiya and the King, weeping like babes and begging for mercy. Never again would they allow the promises of an ambitious priest to turn them against what they had always known: King Khufu was divine. They had stared up at him and his Goddess Betrothed in awe. How could they have ever doubted the builder of the Great Pyramid of Stone?

As the entourage had proceeded the remaining King's Guards had remembered their forgotten oaths. They had pledged the grain they'd received from Menis and joined the procession, which had grown and grown as it had proceeded through the city, with Hathor and the King at the helm. The citizens of Memphis had emerged from their smoky hovels to behold the sight. They had stepped through their doorways and bounded to their rooftops to witness the Living God and Goddess and to be blessed.

When the entourage had arrived at the white walls surrounding the royal palace it had grown a hundredfold.

Kiya had stepped from her litter into Imhoter's warm embrace.

'Well done,' he'd whispered in her ear. 'Take this now.' He had handed her a long, polished stick with a forked bottom and a thin, angular handle. 'It is the sacred Was Sceptre. Hathor wields it to keep the forces of Seth at bay.'

The King had taken Kiya by the hand, accepting his own gilded crook from Imhoter, and led Kiya up a steep set of stairs.

They had emerged at the top of the wall and looked out at the citizens of Memphis. 'Behold,' the King had pronounced. 'The Goddess of Love Incarnate!'

The crowd had exploded with cheers.

'My Betrothed!'

Kiya had looked out over the thousands of faces staring up at her and felt her knees grow weak. Some had cheered, others had been weeping, still others had knelt upon the ground, deep in prayer.

'The Mother of the Flood assures us that Hapi comes,' the King had continued, glancing significantly at Kiya. He'd spoken soothingly to his flock, explaining that he understood their weakness in the wake of his absence, and that in his magnanimity he forgave them all.

Or, almost all. There was one man whom he did *not* forgive—Menis himself. With a wave of his crook Khufu had divested Menis of all his lands. Menis's private stores of grain had become the property of the King, and he had ordered them to be distributed to all the people of Khemet. The flood was late, but it *would* come, the King had assured them. In the meantime the grain he gave from Menis's coffers would sustain them.

The people of Memphis had rejoiced. With his betrothed Queen, the King had appeared to them even grander than before. The Gods were clearly favouring him once again, for they had blessed him with both beauty and triumph.

It should have been enough—but not for Khufu. Later that day he had imprisoned Menis in a small cell in the stone-lined basement of the Royal Harem. The cell had been designed for food storage—a cool place for the palace cooks to keep their cheeses and meats. There was a small stream fed by the King's Shallows that ran through it, where caught fish could be held and kept fresh.

Kiya had heard that Menis had stayed there for many days, in the company of those doomed fish. Then, one day, a man had arrived. Not a cook, nor a fisherman, but a physician. Khufu's physician, carrying a physician's instruments.

He had not come to cure the old priest of his ailments, however.

Now Menis stood with the other priests in a semicircle behind Khufu's throne. He was bald and wrinkled, like the others, but his face was a little paler, and there was a slight limp in his gait. The people called the King 'Khufu the Merciful', for they believed their mighty monarch had pardoned the evil usurper and shown compassion. But Kiya knew the truth.

Khufu hadn't pardoned Menis at all. Menis was like Imhoter now—a man but not a man. A eunuch.

Kiya wiped her brow, remembering the very real mercy that Tahar had shown their would-be killers that day upon the plain. *'You gave them all our meat,'* she had accused him, unable to comprehend his kind, selfless act. Now, as she observed Menis's dull, sunken eyes, she understood Tahar's actions perfectly.

The world needed mercy more than it needed strength or cunning. It needed more men like Tahar.

Kiya tried not to move as Neferdula completed the arrangement of her wig, carefully separating the hair into three sections—two that rested against her shoulders and a third that was trained down her exposed back. She topped the arrangement with a diadem made of the same silk fabric that had been used for her dress.

Neferdula moved quickly to the task of powdering Kiya's face. Instinctively Kiya reached up to wipe the small beads of sweat gathering above her eyebrows.

'You must not touch your face, Goddess,' Neferdula scolded. 'You will ruin the effect.'

Neferdula restored Kiya's smudged brow by patting it with an alabaster-soaked cloth. Then she took a long, thin brush in her fingers and dipped it into a pestle containing a thick kohl paste.

Steady as a scribe, Neferdula painted Kiya's eyes, following their curves and extending them into a thick black line that reached to the sides of her temples. From there she moved the brush in short, coiling loops all the way down to Kiya's collarbone. She did the same on the other side of Kiya's face, then stood in front of Kiya and studied her work.

'They are perfect,' she proclaimed.

'They?'

'See for yourself, Goddess,' Neferdula said, then stepped out of the way.

Kiya looked into the mirror and beheld a stranger. Her ochred lips appeared red as blood against her skin's moon-white surface. Thick black lines surrounded her eyes and extended outward to her temples, where they were transformed into two coiling black serpents.

'Serpents…' Kiya uttered, but before she could say anything more Imhoter appeared behind her.

He swallowed audibly. 'The lady of serpents…' he said perplexed. 'My vision has come to pass. It cannot be…'

'What vision? What cannot be?' asked Kiya. She turned to discover Imhoter's face twisted with concern.

'It is nothing, dear Hathor,' he said, gathering himself. 'I—ah—did not know that Neferdula was going to create such a divine display. The serpent is a powerful symbol of death and rebirth. Like a serpent, you have shed your old skin and emerged anew. Neferdula has given the people a powerful and unexpected vision.' He turned to Neferdula. 'Carry on, for it is fated that you do so.'

To complete her vision Neferdula fitted Kiya with two serpent bracelets. Their gilded bodies wrapped thrice around Kiya's arms before ending in bejewelled heads that stared up at her as if ready to strike. Neferdula placed similar golden hoops around Kiya's ankles, then asked Kiya to stand.

'I think we are ready,' Neferdula said.

One of the servants retrieved a large golden necklace from an adjacent table.

'We have waited to adorn you with your necklace because it is quite heavy.' Neferdula pronounced. 'Now, bend.'

Obediently Kiya bent her head, and found herself encircled in an elaborate web of turquoise filigreed with gold.

'Another name for Hathor is the Lady of Turquoise,' Neferdula explained.

The necklace was beautiful, but it weighed on Kiya like an ox's yoke.

Neferdula helped Kiya to her feet. 'Your hands are so

cold, Goddess.' She motioned to a servant to bring wine, which was poured into a goblet and put to Kiya's lips. 'Drink,' Neferdula urged. 'You must try to relax. Soon you shall meet your destiny.'

Kiya drained the contents of the goblet and returned to the edge of the curtains, where she stared out at the finely dressed crowd. Never before had she beheld so many highborns together in one place. The air was thick with their flowery perfume, and Kiya could hear their sharp whispers.

Where is Hathor?

When will she make her entrance?

'May I have more wine?' Kiya asked.

The King had now received almost all the well-wishers: only a few remained in the gifting line. Kiya spied the backs of three men cloaked in soldiers' armour. It appeared that the King was being presented with another twisted kind of wedding gift—this time a captured criminal. The unusually large prisoner was so hunched and defeated it seemed he might collapse where he stood.

Kiya cringed to think what the King might do to the beleaguered man. *What my husband might do to him.* She guzzled another goblet full of wine.

'Careful,' said Neferdula, plucking the goblet from Kiya's fingers. 'We do not want the boat veering into an eddy, now, do we?'

She smiled playfully as she led Kiya to the end of the royal carpet and the beginning of her new life.

Chapter Thirty-Two

A dozen young women marched ahead of Kiya—the King's concubines. They carried baskets full of oleander flowers, which they had been instructed by Imhoter to toss upon the royal carpet as they went. Silently they began their march. Behind the concubines followed the two queens, Meritites and Henutsen, their expressions as vacant as the royal granaries.

Kiya took her first step behind them, hearing the single beat of a drum. She took another step, and another, trying to keep her pace even as she made her way down the never-ending carpet. She had been told to keep her head up, but she could not bring herself to do it. She stared at the ground, picking her way among the blossoms.

Mother, what have I become?

As the entourage approached the throne the flower-bearers veered from their path and found their positions, flanking the carpet. The priests of Memphis stepped forward, and the Queens installed themselves in two of three thrones that had been positioned below the King's. After their marriage Kiya would be expected to take her place in the third throne, but for now she was expected to remain standing, to address the King and make her obeisance.

Now, just steps from the throne, she gathered the courage to lift her head. The King gazed at her from atop his high perch and Kiya felt a pang of fear traverse her heart. *Never cross a king*, Imhoter had told her.

Kiya noticed the three frightened servant girls, still standing just beyond the throne at the gift table, watching her with wary eyes. The royal scribe stood near them, his writing kit in hand, ready to finalise the marriage contract.

Kiya yearned for another glass of wine. Or something stronger. Milk of poppy, perhaps. Or the pinch of a serpent's fangs upon her neck. Anything to free her from the dread that had suddenly flooded into her soul and threatened to drown her.

That was when she saw them. Just beyond the girls. She would have recognised them anywhere. Their blue flames burned into her, melting her heart.

Those eyes.

Those impossibly blue eyes.

They peered out from beneath his heavy brow like secret wells.

It could not be.

Kiya fought to keep her balance.

It was. An overgrown beard concealed the contours of his face, but still she recognised it. It was the face she loved. The face she wanted to run and kiss. The face she wanted to stare at for a thousand years.

Tahar.

The King's coppery voice sliced through her heart.

'Welcome, Blessed Hathor, to the House of Horus,' he said.

She bent to the ground and kissed it three times, as she had been instructed. Her whole body was trembling.

'You may rise.'

'Thank you, my Beloved King,' Kiya said, standing.

There was something else she was obliged to say, but she could not think of it now. She could only glance repeatedly at the ragged man who stood just paces beyond the base of the King's throne. He was stooped, but strong. Battered, but alive. His long hair just concealing the crescent-shaped scar that marked him for death.

'Why do you study the Libu captive, Goddess?' asked the King, turning in irritation. 'Do you know him?'

Her eyes had betrayed her. She diverted her gaze to the floor and prayed that Neferdula had applied the alabaster powder thickly enough to conceal the crimson she was certain rose in her cheeks.

'Yes, Your Majesty,' she responded, but her words were scarcely audible.

I do know this man. He is the man I love.

The King's nostrils flared. '*How* do you know this Libu murderer?'

The crowd whirred.

'Libu scum!' someone yelled.

'Kill him!' another shrieked.

With a brush of his hand Khufu silenced his guests. Then he motioned to the soldiers, who dragged their prisoner before him.

He was now standing so near to Kiya that she had to stop herself from reaching out to touch him. It appeared that his legs had been bound together by rope, so that he could only take the smallest of steps. His hair was matted, and the filthy shreds of a headdress were all he wore about his sinuous body. He was caked with dirt and smelled of sour sweat. He was a giant made small—a god reduced to rags.

'Slave, tell us who your people are,' Khufu commanded.

'I have no people,' said Tahar.

'You bear the Libu scar. You are Libu!' shouted the King.

'Not any more,' Tahar mumbled, shaking his head.

Kiya studied the destruction that had been wrought upon his body. Red gashes criss-crossed his chest and bruises speckled his limbs, as if someone had made a sport of causing him pain. Her heart heaved. She wished to tend to his wounds and cut his bonds and wash the filth from his skin.

'Do you deny that you were part of the raid on my grain tent?' Khufu asked him.

'I do not deny it.'

'How do you know the Goddess Hathor?'

'She was my captive.'

'Your captive?'

The King stroked his long ceremonial beard and Kiya read his thoughts. Right here, right now, Khufu could increase his popularity even more. Before this crowd of highborn witnesses he could condemn the Libu villain and the people would love him for it.

'Is this true, Goddess?' asked the King.

'I was his captive for a time, but then he set me free.'

The King's mouth twisted into a scowl. 'If he captured you then he sinned against Osiris—my heavenly father!'

Kiya wondered how much the God of Death and Rebirth really worried about Tahar. It seemed the King was invoking the Great God's name much as he invoked the Goddess Hathor—for his own purposes and gains.

Now the King lifted his eyes to the crowd. 'This lowly Libu worm captured the future Queen of Khemet!'

The guests hissed with rage.

'This dirty Redlander participated in the raid on the grain tent and surely also on Zoser's tomb!'

More angry howls.

The King's voice crescendoed. 'This strange outsider has sinned against the Gods. For the good of Khemet...' the King paused, savouring the moment '...he must be sacrificed.'

Chapter Thirty-Three

Tahar felt his legs buckle as ferocious cheers rose up from the crowd.

'This man shall pay for the Libu's sins against Khemet,' continued the King, pointing a bejewelled finger menacingly at Tahar.

A sandal flew out of the crowd, hitting Tahar in the face. Another punched into his ribs. A leather belt slapped him across his back. The guards kept Tahar on his feet—gripping him like a prize. He closed his eyes, keeping the image of her at the forefront of his mind as he tried to ignore the pain. How beautiful she was—his Hathor.

The King's guests sneered and shouted.

'Die, Libu vermin!'

'Kill the Libu thief!'

It was as if the Khemetian highborns believed Tahar alone to be the cause of all their hardship. And as their cries grew louder Tahar realised that they might have been the cries of his own Libu tribesmen the night of the raid. And King Khufu might have been Chief Bandir, fomenting the crowd's anger and playing upon the people's prejudices until their only solace was the promise of violence.

Indeed, Tahar had given the King just what he wanted—the chance to sacrifice a human being. Not since the time of Narmer had the Khemetians performed the appalling spectacle. Now, it seemed, it would be part of the King's heroic act.

There were no winners in this perpetual game of power, Tahar thought bitterly, only endless victims. And he, apparently, was to be the next. He had finally found her, the woman he loved, and now he was going to lose her again—along with his own life.

He heard the loud clang of metal upon the ground.

'No!' he heard her yell.

He opened his eyes to discover a large copper goblet caught upside down in her hand. It appeared that she had plucked the metal projectile out of the air, preventing it from landing on his head.

'Holy King,' she shouted breathlessly, 'if you sacrifice this man, then you must sacrifice me as well!' She smashed the goblet upon the ground.

The crowd hushed and the attention of a thousand eyes turned to Hathor's dauntless face.

The King scowled. 'Hathor,' he explained, 'this man has harmed Khemet. He shall be sacrificed to the Great Osiris, God of the Dead and Judge of Spirits. This is justice. Osiris will look upon this man's death and smile.'

'Then, Your Majesty,' Hathor continued, 'I should die too—for I, too, have sinned against Khemet,' she said.

The King stared at her in confusion. 'Hathor, you are not in your right mind.'

'Do not do this, Hathor,' Tahar begged softly.

But there was no stopping her. She was as wonderful and fearless as the desert wind.

'My King, I have never been more sane. If you want justice, you must sacrifice us both—him for the grain tent raid and me for…for labouring upon the Great Pyramid of Stone.'

The King's eyes became tiny slits. 'You are Hathor, Goddess of Life. You could not *possibly* have laboured upon my tomb of death and rebirth.'

Kiya raised her voice above the horrified gasps. 'I disguised myself as a man. I helped pull the carts up the tunnel,' she explained. 'I am not a goddess, Your Highness. I am not Hathor Incarnate. I am… I am just a woman.'

The King glanced at Tahar, his eyes glimmering with rage. The cobra upon his head appeared to grow larger, and Tahar thought he could see the red flicker of its tongue.

'If you worked in the tunnel, then tell me the number of chambers—I challenge you!' the King shouted.

Hathor bowed her head. 'There are three, My King—one large, one small, and one beneath the earth.'

The King's large round face grew as red as the setting sun. 'Woman, you are a traitor, an imposter. You have dishonoured me and my noble house. You have offended the Gods.'

The King's eyes flitted about the great hall. It was as if he were hoping to mollify the humiliation he now suffered before his guests.

'By Horus's tongue,' he said suddenly, 'for how long did you work upon my tomb?'

Kiya paused.

Civilisations came and went. Rivers flowed through the desert. Ancient seas teemed with creatures strange and wonderful. The world was greater and older than anyone knew, and nobody saw the wonder of it. Nobody except him. He had opened her eyes to possibilities beyond the realm of the Gods. He was her spark of light in a dark, suffocating world, and she did not want to live in it without him.

'Two full cycles of the sun, Your Majesty,' she lied, and she knew that it was just the answer the King needed.

'Two years?' the King repeated. 'You laboured on my tomb for *two full years*?'

'Aye, My Lord.'

'Then *you* are the reason for the drought!' The King stood. 'You are not Hathor the Beautiful—you are Hathor the Imposter!' Khufu raved. 'I thought Osiris had sent you to be my wife, but now I understand that he sent you to be sacrificed. For Khemet!'

Stunned, Khufu's guests glanced worriedly among themselves, as if searching for the correct response. Had their splendid monarch just commanded an act of sacrifice? For the good of Khemet?

'Neferdula!' the King shouted. 'Relieve this imposter of her royal finery.'

Slowly, Neferdula emerged from the crowd. Her smudged eyes betrayed the tears she had been shedding in the shadows. When she reached Kiya, she bowed slightly.

'You are still Hathor to me,' she whispered as she lifted off the heavy turquoise necklace. She pulled each of Kiya's serpent bracelets from her arms, her hands trembling. 'I am so sorry.'

'And the wig,' the King added.

Amidst quiet sobs, Neferdula stroked Kiya's beautiful black wig, then pulled it quickly from her head. Kiya felt both relief and shame, and she slumped her shoulders in exhaustion.

'Guards, take them both,' commanded the King.

The dozen King's Guardsmen who had been standing placidly around the hall's perimeter marched forward, surrounding Kiya and Tahar. Kiya felt four different hands on her arms, pulling her in different directions. The men turned and began to drag Kiya and Tahar through the parting crowd, towards the workers' entrance to the hall.

'Hathor the Imposter and this Libu worm will be sacrificed upon the tomb they have desecrated,' said the King. 'We shall spill their treacherous blood upon the Great Pyramid of Stone—a gift to my father in the sky.'

The King opened his arms for all the crowd to see.

'And then we shall finally have an end to our drought.'

Chapter Thirty-Four

Beware the three serpents... her mother had warned her. *The third will succeed...*

Fie—he already had. In only three days Kiya would feel his deadly bite.

In the meantime she waited, imprisoned in the same dank grotto where Menis had met his fate. Outside, two guards kept vigil, allowing just enough candlelight into the chamber for her to see Menis's bloodstains. Kiya positioned herself as far away from the gruesome smudges as she could, trying not to think of the malevolent act that had made it. Still, her thoughts turned to Imhoter.

Long ago, the kind old priest and advisor to the King had endured the same vicious sentence. What sin had the gentle man perpetrated to deserve that penance? Kiya considered the cold-heartedness that would be required to exact such a punishment. Khufu's father had not been above it, and apparently neither was he.

Khufu was no different from any other king. He did whatever it took to get and keep his power. To be his Queen would have meant supporting him in that purpose above all else. It would have meant becoming his slave.

She had seen the blank, lifeless looks in the eyes of his two other Queens. Whatever joy Kiya might have found in helping ordinary Khemetians would have been eaten away over time by her complicity in their manipulation. Everybody was an actor in Khufu's great plan; everyone was expendable. It would have been a miserable life, and she was glad she would soon be free of it. She only wished to see Tahar's face just one last time in this world before she began her journey to the next.

The hours passed like days inside the underground cell. Soon she could no longer tell if it was morning or night. On the far side of the space a small stream traversed a stone channel, where she bent for sips of water. The stream's source was certainly the Great River: she could taste its silty waters as surely as she might taste wine. The water entered and exited the room via a rock-lined tunnel, which was barred at both openings by two trellised metal gates. The gates allowed water to flow freely from its source outside, but thwarted the movement of anything—or anyone—through the tunnel.

There were two large perch hovering in the stream—trapped, just like Kiya. They had likely been caught the previous day by one of the King's fisherman and were being stored for the Festival of Mut's Departure, to take place immediately after Kiya's own departure. As Kiya's hunger grew she considered capturing one of the stout swimmers, but something inside her would not allow her to do it.

Let them meet their doom together.

Her hunger was soon satisfied anyway—and in a most unlikely way. Kiya was sitting against the metal bars of the cell door when she sensed movement above her head.

She looked up to find a delicate, finely manicured hand reaching through the bars. The hand held a heel of bread.

'What is this?' Kiya asked.

'Shh,' whispered a young woman. A candle flickered in her hand, lighting up her face. 'I am the King's concubine, Iset. The guards have allowed me to visit, but just for a few moments. Please—take it.'

Kiya accepted the bread—likely the last she would ever swallow. 'My deepest gratitude,' she said.

'It is my joy.' The young woman handed Kiya a wineskin.

'Wine? I am truly blessed!' Kiya exclaimed, untying the skin. 'I owe you a debt—one that I fear will never be paid.'

Kiya lifted the skin to her lips.

'Stop, Goddess!' Iset cried. 'Do not drink the wine. It is…um…*special*. You may not wish to drink it until you are…ready.'

Slowly Kiya absorbed the young woman's meaning. She tied the leather tie tightly about the neck of the skin. The wine had been poisoned. She had been given the means to take her own life.

'Why do you help me, Iset?'

'There is much talk of you at the palace, Blessed Hathor.'

'I am no longer Hathor. I never was.'

'To me you remain Hathor, and to many others as well—including Imhoter the Seer.'

Imhoter the Seer? It was the first time she had considered the title, though she recalled that he had used it the day he had introduced himself to her.

'Imhoter was my advisor and my friend,' Kiya explained. 'I betrayed him by confronting the King. I have disappointed him beyond measure.'

'I do not think so, Goddess. I think you shine even more brightly in his mind—as you do in mine.'

Kiya was confounded. She had ruined all Imhoter's plans. By unmasking herself she had destroyed his vision of hope for the people of Khemet.

'After you were taken, Imhoter begged the King to spare your life.'

'He did?'

'Aye. But the King would not hear him. He ordered the guards to seize Imhoter. Now the Seer is imprisoned with the Libu captive.'

'They are together? Where?'

Iset moved her mouth close to Kiya's ear. 'They are in the slaves' cells, near the docks. I visited them late last night. The guard let me speak to them over the high wall. Imhoter said that you must be *hungry* for escape.'

Iset gave the heel of bread a significant look.

'That I am,' Kiya said, glancing at the bread. 'Very hungry. But you risk much to bring me this news. Why?'

'You are an inspiration, Hathor.'

'Forgive me. I do not understand.'

'You are a commoner,' whispered Iset, 'and yet you captured the heart of the King. Your story makes people believe that anything is possible. It makes *me* believe...' A tear traced a path down Iset's perfectly painted face.

Kiya reached with her finger and plucked the tear from Iset's cheek. This lovely young woman was a concubine, as Kiya's mother had been—sentenced to a life in the service of a single man. Kiya remembered all those glass vials littering her mother's chamber. Like her mother,

Iset abided in a kind of prison, and would do so for the rest of her life.

'Listen to me now,' said Kiya, 'and I will tell you the secret to capturing the King's heart. It is quite simple.'

'You will? It is?'

'Aye, but first you must know that the King is not special. To all other Khemetians he may be the Living God, but to you he is just a man. As such he is easily conquered.'

'But how?'

Kiya smiled to herself, remembering the long boat ride downriver. 'Do not flatter him without cause or give your gifts freely. Know your own worth and make sure he knows it too. That is how you will win his heart,' Kiya said.

Iset's eyes grew wide with amazement, and Kiya continued.

'You must understand that *you* are the prize, dear Iset. You must know this and believe it in your heart. The King must labour to deserve the affection of the people of Khemet; so he must labour to deserve yours.'

The young woman burst into tears. 'You are indeed a goddess, my dear Hathor,' she said, wiping her eyes. 'Thank you. For ever, thank you.'

She glanced behind her. A guard had silently moved his body inside the arched entrance to the space. He slid Iset a biting look.

'I must go,' Iset said. 'May the Gods protect you.'

As Iset stepped back through the archway Kiya saw her drop an ingot of gold into the guard's hands. Their few minutes of conference had come at a high price.

Go forth and conquer him, thought Kiya. *In time, Khemet will be the better for it.*

For Kiya, however, there was no time to lose. She pulled apart the bread to discover a thick copper rod. The object was not large, but it appeared strong enough to bend metal.

She walked to the site of Menis's bloodstains, and poured the poisoned wine upon it. She would not take her own life. She refused to follow her mother's fate. If she was destined to die then her blood would be on the King's hands, and all of Khemet would know it.

But she was not going to die.

She stuffed the heel of bread into her mouth and let it fill her with strength. *Thank you, Imhoter.* Then she lowered her body into the channel, letting her fine silk gown become soaked to the waist. The agitated fish swished around her as she wedged the thick rod against the wall and pushed hard on the first bar. Slowly it began to bend. She pushed with all her might and soon she had made a gap.

She smiled as the two fish shimmied through the narrow opening and swam away. *Go forth, my piscean lovers, for you are finally free.* In fact the gap she had made was quite narrow, and she was not sure she could squeeze through it. She heard a voice inside the chamber. A guard had entered the outer room and seemed to be calling through the bars, searching for her in her cell. If she stood up now she knew she could return to her cell without consequence, making some excuse about accidentally slipping into the stream. But if she waited any longer the guard would surely spot her inside the stream, attempting her escape. She had to make a choice.

Sucking in her breath, she pushed her body through the small opening. She felt the bent rod press against her skin as she squeezed her body against the tunnel wall. She heard the back of her dress rip.

'Come quickly!' shouted one of the guards. 'She escapes!'

She heard the guard's footfalls at the edge of the stream just as her feet cleared the small opening and she was thrust into the dark tunnel. She propelled herself forward with the current, making no splash. She was a giant perch, a lonely crocodile, a mighty serpent careening silently to freedom.

Then—*whoosh!* She exploded into a large, flat bay surrounded by palms. It was night-time, but Thoth's almost round face hung high in the sky, illuminating her path across the bay to the Great River beyond. Before her a long, sandy beach stretched for many measures. Kiya recognised the lovely, tranquil space as if it were her own home. It was a home she had never been allowed to enter: The King's Shallows.

The dream that she had dreamed so long ago—she was fulfilling it. This was her safe place. There were no crocodiles here, nor anything that could harm her. She bequeathed her jubilant tears to the tranquil waters, stretched out her limbs and began to swim.

She swam without fear or anger. She swam apart from time. There was only the feel of the cool water upon her skin and the knowledge that this was *hers*, all hers. She was a nobody, a street orphan, a woman without a home. But right now, as her body propelled itself across the moon-drenched bay, she belonged to the world and everything in it.

Soon she arrived at the papyrus gate that protected the Shallows from the main course of the Great River. Metal rod in hand, she hacked at a corner of the woven barricade. Again she had to squeeze through. She sucked in a breath and pushed herself through the small hole she had wrought. She could hear the sound of voices arriving at the beach as she slipped invisibly into the Great River.

Now she moved with the current, feeling the cool water flow over her dress. She swam with pure awareness, sensing where the depths changed, where the thick water grasses grew, and where the hippos and crocodiles lurked. She did not falter. Her finely tuned senses had been honed through a lifetime of risk, and they kept her from harm.

The docks were not far from the Shallows, and soon she began to hear the telltale slapping of the river water against their wooden legs. She pulled her dripping body from the depths and made her way to the traders' holding cells on the shore.

Built for the temporary staging of livestock and cargo, the three windowless chambers were housed in a single building with high, mud-brick walls and no roof. Kiya imagined Imhoter and Tahar milling about their small fortified cell during the day as the Sun God blazed down upon them. At night the two men likely shivered with cold as the stars moved mockingly across the sky, marking the hours before their deaths.

Kiya's heart squeezed. After two days the men were probably already mindless with fear and privation.

'Tahar? Imhoter?' Kiya called softly.

She was standing outside the wooden door of the first of the three cells. Thankfully the two guards on duty had not noticed her shadowy figure.

'Is anybody there?' she whispered at the door.

Nothing.

Cautiously she stepped closer to where the guards had made their camp, around the corner of the building.

'Tahar? Imhoter?'

Nothing.

She moved to the final one of the three cells. She was now so close to the guards' camp she could hear the men's muffled voices and see the glow of their small fire.

Suddenly the knot of a rope hit her upon the head. Her heart wept for joy as she silently wrapped the rope about her waist. She braced her feet against the wall of the building and gave it a single tug.

Soon a thin shadow was cresting the wall. *Imhoter.* He moved with quiet stealth, despite his advanced age. He set himself down beside Kiya and embraced her, and Kiya felt her *ka* flood with joy. With a finger to his lips Imhoter took his place next to her, wrapping the rope about his own waist. Together, Kiya and Imhoter braced themselves against the wall, holding fast.

Tahar was next.

Tahar's large figure moved over the top of the wall with catlike grace, then bounded safely to the ground without a sound. In the slight glow given off by the guards' fire Kiya could see that Tahar was naked but for a ragged loincloth tied loosely about his middle.

This was no time to be looking at a man's exposed flesh, Kiya told herself. But what living woman *wouldn't* steal a glance at the towering pillar of strength and masculinity that now stood before Kiya, sucking in the free air? His broad shoulders stood watch over the kingdom of muscle and taut flesh that was his body, and as he adjusted the cloth about his manliest parts Kiya felt her own most womanly parts respond in turn.

Curses—this was not the time for such reveries.

Just then a guard holding a blazing torch came around the corner of the building. 'I'll just be a few minutes, brother,' he was calling back to the other guard. He looked up to discover the three fugitives, then paused, saying nothing. He stepped towards Tahar and gave a reverent bow. 'Go quickly!' he whispered, then abandoned his torch upon the ground and dashed away.

'You heard him,' whispered Imhoter, and soon they were weaving through the quiet outskirts of Memphis, heading west towards the desert.

It had been a miracle that the guard had let them go. As they tiptoed past dwellings and shuffled beside animal pens it occurred to Kiya that by saving them the guard had put his own life in danger. By now the second guard had surely discovered the abandoned torch and dangling rope and was calling for reinforcements. There would be many guards searching for them soon: they had to keep moving.

Tahar ran ahead of Kiya, but he looked back at her often, as if to promise her they would not be caught. Why would a King's Guardsman endanger his own life to save theirs? The man had bowed respectfully to Tahar before disappearing into the night. *Why?* What reverence did he owe a Libu man who had been condemned by the King himself to die?

Soon the shadowy mud brick buildings of Memphis were but a distant blur. Following Imhoter's lead, they turned northward, stopping to take their rest at a small stand of tamarisk trees growing just beyond the river floodplain.

Kiya collapsed into Tahar's arms, which quickly grew wet with her sobs. 'I thought you were dead.'

'I might as well have been,' said Tahar, smoothing her hair and rocking her like a babe.

'Come, dear girl. You must eat,' said Imhoter, producing a small linen package from under his tunic. 'You have a long journey ahead.'

He opened the cloth to reveal a large honey cake.

'But how is it possible that you carry honey cake? Were you not imprisoned these many days, as I was? Are you not starved?' asked Kiya.

'Aye, we were imprisoned,' said Imhoter, 'but the guard whom we saw tonight was our salvation. He kept us fed, brought us water for washing, and allowed the King's concubine to visit us. Just today he supplied us with the rope we used to escape.'

'I do not understand. Why did the guard help you?'

'You did not recognise him, did you?' asked Tahar.

'Nay,' said Kiya. 'Do I know him?'

'You do indeed,' said Tahar, 'for he tried to kill you. But that was long ago—in another life.'

In another life. Tahar's words sent a pang of longing through Kiya's body. In another life she had been neither queen nor captive. In another life she had been standing by this brave, merciful man's side.

Then it came to her. The King's Guardsman—of course! The man was the elder of the two who had attempted to put an arrow in her heart and take Tahar's head as a prize. Tahar had captured both guards that day at the second oasis, then sent them away with enough meat and grain to see themselves home.

'I remember him now. He owed you his life.'

'He owed me nothing,' said Tahar. 'But I gratefully accepted his goodwill, for it meant that I might see you again.'

Kiya's breaths quickened with her hope. Had Tahar yearned for her as she had him?

'I, too, wished to see you again, my dear Hathor,' added Imhoter, 'though I have little time to explain myself now. I have had a vision—an army on the march towards Memphis. Tahar confirms that it is true.'

Tahar nodded. 'Chief Bandir marches from Nubia along the desert route—five thousand strong.'

Kiya closed her eyes in stunned comprehension. 'He captured you then? The day you set me free? As I scaled the Theban peak and beheld the Great River you were drawing him and his men away from my path.'

'By sunrise I was already many hours' journey into the Red Land, but capture me they did.'

Kiya could make out the shadows of Tahar's features, but his eyes remained dark caverns that she could not read. 'Because you were on foot?'

'Aye.'

Kiya's worst nightmare had come to pass. In setting her free, Tahar had doomed himself.

'I was Bandir's prisoner for many weeks,' Tahar continued. 'He tortured me with both fist and flail. When I wasn't being beaten I dug latrines and tended to beasts. I was Bandir's personal slave. But I remembered your courage, Hathor, and it gave me strength. Eventually I managed to escape. But just as soon as I was free of the Libu raiders the Khemetian hunters found me.'

'Where did they find you?' Kiya did not even need to ask. She already knew the answer. 'On the Island of Abu?'

Tahar nodded gravely. He had followed her there, just as she had hoped. He had been searching for her and instead had found the tip of a Khemetian soldier's sword.

The veil of numbness that had overtaken her, the slow mummification of her spirit that had begun the day she had dropped the acacia seed into the river and bade him goodbye, suddenly disappeared. She felt her *ka* spark through her body in a blaze of joy.

'You came for me, then? You sought me out upon Abu?'

'Of course I did.'

Tahar bent and embraced her so tightly that she could scarcely breathe—and that was all right with Kiya, because she didn't need to breathe. Nor did she need to eat or drink or sleep, as long as she had him.

He lifted her body off the ground. 'I thought I had lost you for ever,' he whispered in her ear.

Kiya did not know how long they stayed like that, locked in their embrace. It might have been a minute, or perhaps a dozen minutes. But soon Imhoter's gentle voice split the silence.

'Do you hear it?' he asked them.

'Hear what?' asked Tahar.

The old priest put his ear to the ground. 'Hoofbeats. The army approaches. They will reach the city by daybreak.'

'We must flee,' said Kiya. 'We must find a boat.'

'The Great River fills with raiding parties even now,' explained Imhoter, standing. 'They will come by land and by water to surround the city. You must travel on foot, in darkness.'

'Into the desert?' asked Kiya.

'Nay, I will never be able to find you there,' said Imhoter. 'You must head northward now.'

'You are not coming with us?'

'I cannot, my dear girl. I serve the people of Khemet,

and Memphis is my home. I must return to the palace and warn the King. My warning is the only chance the people of Memphis have against an army of this size. Go now,' Imhoter said, motioning northward. 'Make for the Great Pyramid of Stone. Stay away from people, for there is a bounty upon your heads. Find the workers' entrance and hide yourselves inside. The day after tomorrow I will come for you. I will remove you from Khemet or I will die trying.'

Imhoter gave Kiya a significant look.

'I have something important to tell you, but not now. Now you must go.'

He bowed low, then turned back towards the rooftops of Memphis.

Chapter Thirty-Five

It was not until the Sun God had stretched his long arms above the eastern horizon that they finally reached the base of Khufu's House of Eternity—the Great Pyramid of Stone. They had travelled in silence all through the night, keeping their pace fast and their footfalls light as the Moon God moved across the sky.

'We have returned to where we began,' said Tahar.

The sunrise cast a brilliant glow upon his fine angled jaw. His beard had been shorn, apparently in preparation for sacrifice, but his hair had been left untouched. The ragged locks fell around his face, softening it and reminding her of how absurdly handsome he was.

His body towered over hers. Was it a trick of her mind, or had he grown stronger over time? He was leaner now, and his muscles were more coiled. If she had not known him, she would surely have been cowering beneath his fearsome, looming figure. Since she *did* know him, however, she merely wished to admire him.

He knew nothing of his own beauty, and yet his body was a temple of proportion and strength. His broad chest tapered into a perfect sacred triangle, standing upon its

apex. The elegant shape found its terminus in two fascinating muscles that angled like bows down the sides of
his hips to the mounds of his upper legs. If there was any
imbalance to his figure it was those legs. They were large
and strong beyond any practical use. It was as if a sculp-
tor god had shaped Tahar to perfection, then slapped the
remaining clay upon his legs as an afterthought.

'You are injured,' she told him.

A fresh knife wound, likely received when he'd been
dragged through the crowd of angry wedding guests,
traced a crooked line down his arm.

'It is nothing,' he said. 'Already it ceases to bleed.'

'We shall tend to it properly soon,' Kiya said, and she
could hear the worry behind her words. He nodded, then
looked at the ground. She knew he shared her thoughts.
By now Chief Bandir's army would have arrived at the
gates of Memphis. Many lives were being lost, including, quite possibly, Imhoter's.

Even if Imhoter survived the attack on the palace,
Kiya thought, he would be captured by the raiders. What
then? Knowing Chief Bandir, Imhoter would be tortured
until he disclosed the location of King Khufu's Libu prisoner…and, of course, the location of the famous Hathor,
Bandir's escaped bride.

If the Khemetians did manage to stave off Bandir's
army, Imhoter would still have to face the King. Would
Khufu have mercy on the sacred advisor who had warned
him of the attack, or would the King punish Imhoter for
escaping his incarceration? With Kiya and Tahar disappeared, Kiya suspected that Khufu would have no mercy
on the dear old priest.

Kiya bowed her head. Right now hundreds of men

were dying—and for what? To make a rich man richer? Kiya bristled as she pictured Bandir's roving black eye.

The raiders did not fight for Bandir alone, however. The Libu Chief had merely harnessed the anger they already carried in their hearts. Kiya understood that anger well, for it was born of longing—the longing for a better life. She had felt that longing all her life. Why should the highborns have all and the low-borns have nothing? She had always wondered. And surely the Libu must wonder something quite the same: Why should the Blacklanders have all and the Redlanders have none?

Now, because of Tahar, she understood that she had been asking the wrong question. The world was wide and there was enough for all. There was so much more than just the Red Land and the Black Land. There was the Green Land and the Yellow Land and the Pink Land, and every kind of land stretching into for ever. It was a great big world, with so much in it, and no reason to despair. Kiya only wished she could see it all, with Tahar by her side.

Kiya whispered a cheer as Tahar pushed back the boulder that concealed the workers' entrance. A shaft of light poured into the large, flat space where only three months ago Kiya had gathered every day with her work gang. They stepped inside, and small flecks of dust illuminated by sunlight floated like tiny insects all around them. They did not have candles, and they would need to reseal the entrance soon so they would not attract attention.

'We shall be safe for the length of this day and the night that shall follow,' announced Tahar, and he rolled the large stone back to its place in front of the entrance.

A profound darkness surrounded them. Kiya could hear Tahar's breaths, but she could not find him. 'I have lost you already,' she said, aware that just days ago they had been condemned to die in this very space.

'I am here,' Tahar said, and he pulled her against him.

Ah, the exhilaration of his embrace. She buried her face in his chest and let him hold her until she felt her breaths grow even again. Soon his heart and hers seemed to be beating in the same rhythm. They lay upon the cool ground together and Kiya felt her eyes grow heavy with sleep.

She awoke to the soothing feel of his fingers running through her short hair.

'We have been sleeping for many hours, I think.'

Her head was in his lap.

'I have wanted to do this since the day I captured you,' he said, tracing the length of each of her eyebrows with his fingers.

Kiya felt a dull stab of emotion. 'If you wished to hold me close, then why did you set me free?'

'I told you why—so that I could create a false trail.'

'But could we not have waited and escaped together? Surely we could have lingered with Bandir's army until a better opportunity came. We could have escaped together.'

Tahar's words were measured. 'I could not wait and watch you become Bandir's slave.'

'You mean his wife?'

'It is the same thing, is it not?'

Kiya smiled to herself. 'I have taught you well, then.'

'You have, Goddess,' said Tahar. He stroked Kiya's hair. She had been stripped of her wig and all her jewellery, but her natural hair had grown much. It grazed the bottoms of her earlobes. 'Your hair is so soft,' he said. 'It is like—'

'Wait,' she said. She moved his hand down to touch her gown, sending a thrilling shiver all through her body. 'It is like the fabric of this gown, is it not?'

'Verily it is,' Tahar said, stroking the fabric against her stomach. His voice was thick. 'I have never felt a material so soft.'

'It comes from the Land of the Potters,' Kiya pronounced. 'Far beyond the Big Green. They employ insects to create it—can you believe it? Worms!'

'Worms? How very strange. I should like to see them for myself,' he said.

She wanted to say that she would like to see them, too, with him by her side. But did he feel the same way? His body's response to her remained strong. Even now, as he caressed her hair, she could hear his breaths growing shorter. But it did not answer the question on her mind: Did he wish to continue the journey they had begun?

He had let her go, after all. He had set her free. It had been the act of a good man, a noble man, but also a man who did not see his future with her. It was true that he had returned to Abu, but perhaps it had merely been to ensure her safety. And then there was the darker question she harboured: if a more respectable suitor had bid for her—someone gentler and nobler than Bandir—would Tahar have sold her into marriage after all?

She was not ready to know the answers to these questions. If their paths were destined to diverge, they would. In the meantime she would think of Tahar as her friend— a strange kindred soul—that was all.

They settled themselves against the wall of the dark room, side by side, and talked for many hours. Tahar described his ordeal: how Chief Bandir had captured him and made him run until he'd collapsed; how he'd been bound in shackles and beaten nearly every day; how he'd been made to grovel upon the ground for his dinner. He explained that he had never had to live such a life, the life of a slave, and it had humbled him.

As she listened her eyes filled with tears. She could not believe the pain he had endured. It sounded much worse than the life of any slave. And he'd done it to secure her freedom.

Finally, Kiya gathered her courage. 'Can I ask you two questions, Tahar?'

'You may ask me a thousand questions.'

'If Bandir had not claimed me—if his party had never happened upon us—would you have taken me to Nubia after all?'

They sat together in silence for so long that Kiya couldn't bear it.

'The second question is this,' she continued. 'If you had found me at Abu, what then? Would we have continued on to Nubia? Would you have sold me to a more amicable suitor? A Nubian prince or some such?'

It annoyed her that she could not see his expression. What was going on in his mind? And why did he not answer her?

'It is unnerving to be so enveloped in darkness,' he said, 'when one is so accustomed to light at this time of day.'

'There is nothing we can do, alas.'

'Not nothing,' he said, avoiding her questions.

'What? Do you intend for us to walk up the tunnel?'

'Why not? I have often longed to see the inside of this great structure.'

'But we would march in total darkness. None of the torches will be lit.'

'How many times a day did you say your gang hauled stones up the tunnel?'

'Thrice a day.'

'For how many months?'

'Three.'

'That is many hundreds of journeys. I think you are quite prepared to lead the way.'

Kiya started to protest, then realised that he was right. What were they doing here, squatting in the darkness, when they could look upon all of Memphis and perhaps even discover clues to the outcome of the battle?

'Fine. But you have not answered my questions,' Kiya said, releasing Tahar.

'No, I have not. I will answer them at the top.'

Chapter Thirty-Six

Kiya felt her way along the perimeter of the chamber until she found the concealed rock that guarded the entrance to the tunnel.

'Does not the tunnel begin on the other side of this room?' asked Tahar. 'I noticed an opening when we entered.'

'The tunnel you saw is a decoy. It was designed to stop looters.'

'Let me guess: it leads to the subterranean chamber.'

She could sense him grinning in the dark. 'Yes! How do you know?'

'The Chief came here the day of the raid in search of slaves. He became enraged when he entered the underground chamber and found not a single soul.'

'Ha!' cried Kiya. 'They were certainly hiding behind this rock,' she said, thrusting the large square boulder forward until she felt the cool, familiar air of the inner tunnel caress her face.

Tahar followed her through the opening and helped her return the rock to its place. 'Yet another of my dreams is about to come true,' he said.

They spoke little as they ascended the tunnel. She had so much to tell him—about her discovery on Abu, her trip down the Great River, her experience at the royal palace. But nothing seemed worth saying. Instead, small words of guidance came to her lips.

'In two steps we shall make the turn,' she told him. 'Here is an uneven patch. Watch your footfalls.'

It felt strange to hear the high chime of her voice inside the tunnel. She had been Mute Boy for so long, daring not even a grunt as she helped pull the carts up the long, square spirals. Now her words echoed harshly against the walls, as if intruding on the tomb's sacred silence.

She stopped at an intersection. 'Do you feel a difference in the air here?' she asked.

'Aye, it is slightly cooler than elsewhere,' said Tahar. 'And there seems to be more of it.'

'Our path intersects here with the path to the second burial chamber, where the King's *ushebti* statue will be housed,' she explained. 'They built the path when I was still a girl. It is said that when Khufu was having this part of the tomb built, he allowed only a half-gang of workers to labour here—all of them slaves. The men completed the second and third chambers, then he took them far beyond the Big Green and freed them.'

'He showed mercy,' said Tahar.

'At Imhoter's insistence, I'm sure. I think Khufu wished for their secrets to disappear with them,' mused Kiya.

'You mean their knowledge of the additional two chambers?'

'That is what I believe—though it is impossible to prove the chambers' existence. They have been sealed inside the rock.'

'That is unfortunate,' said Tahar. 'I would have loved to have seen them for myself.'

'One day, many thousands of years from now, perhaps our descendants will find those hidden chambers and all the world will marvel at the riches that surely lie therein,' said Kiya.

They walked on in silence. She had used the phrase 'our descendants' in a general sense. But as it had echoed through the tunnel it had seemed that she spoke of their future children. She felt her cheeks flush, and was grateful Tahar could not see them.

She should have been uttering prayers of contrition, for surely her presence here was offending the Gods. Still, she could not help but wonder if the Gods really cared that much about her, or even the tomb which she ascended so brazenly.

'Watch your step again here,' she told Tahar, and she felt his hand reach for hers.

She took it and guided him slowly forward. She felt his thumb graze the raised mounds at the base of her fingers and paused, remembering when he had last touched her that way.

'I think you can proceed on your own now,' she said, releasing him. She could not allow herself to think of him like that—not until she knew for certain that it was she, in fact, whom he truly wanted. Indeed, she wondered what he could possibly say to alleviate the growing doubt she had begun to feel in her heart.

When they arrived at the top of the Pyramid night was falling. She walked out onto the square, cart-sized platform and looked south to Memphis. She saw no signs of the outcome of the attack—no line of vanquished raiders, no throng of escaping citizens. Nothing.

Tahar joined her, squinting to discern the city so far away. He placed his arms upon the limestone wall that surrounded the platform and leaned outward, as if a few more inches might improve his chances of seeing who had won and who had lost. Finally he stopped trying. It was too dark: they would have to wait until tomorrow.

Kiya breathed deeply, taking in the magnificent view. She could see a great distance even as the cloak of night fell upon the land. There was the Great River, to the east. Beside it she could see the low buildings of the workers' village and the inlet that had been dug to receive the Pyramid's large stones. To the south was the City—she could just make out the white walls of the royal palace. The Red Land stretched endlessly to their west.

Kiya thought she could see the beginning of the glow where the Moon God would soon rise in his splendid fullness. And somewhere beyond to the north lay the Big Green. It was a view made for the Gods.

She looked down the sheer, angled slopes below her, their polished limestone glowing white even in the low light. Dizzy, she stepped backwards and closed her eyes. Few had been allowed to set foot upon this sacred space, and certainly not any of the workers. In time, none would be allowed here. When the King began his journey to the afterlife the holy *benben* would be placed upon this space. The dazzling golden cap would draw Ra's light, creating a pathway to eternity for the King.

The King who was, Kiya remembered, just a man.

'Are you well?' asked Tahar.

'Aye, just a little dizzy. We are so far from the ground.' She stepped forward, peering once again over the ledge. 'Look there. I see a fire.' She pointed south, to the outskirts of Memphis. A tiny speck of light wavered against the horizon, barely visible.

Tahar stood at her side, squinting. 'Ah, I see it.'

'Do you think Bandir succeeded?'

'Nay,' said Tahar. 'Bandir is far too impulsive and Imhoter far too clever.'

'But it is not Imhoter whom Bandir seeks to unseat, it is the King,' said Kiya.

'I suspect that Imhoter is the reason there is a King at all.'

'I suspect that you are right,' Kiya said, smiling sadly. She prayed that Imhoter had prevailed. She imagined him escorting the last of the Libu and Nubian villains through the city gates.

'Now go away and don't come back,' he would tell them kindly.

If only Imhoter's gentle hand were steering the ship of Khemet and not the stone fist of Khufu, who would surely torture any captured invaders and then enslave them. Kiya shivered to think how close she had come to spending the rest of her life at King Khufu's side, at the helm of that evil ship.

Instinctively, she leaned her head against Tahar's arm. She heard him sigh. His fingers sought to entwine with hers and she felt her heart beat faster.

Stop, Kiya. She could not let him do this. She could not allow him to envelop her in his whirlwind of passion and make her once again forget her purpose. Would he have sold her or wouldn't he? She needed to know the answer.

If the answer was yes, then she would not blame him. He was part of the same world she was. He would have done what he had to do to survive, just as she had.

But if the answer was yes she knew that she could never give him her heart.

She pulled her hand away from his and walked to the northwest corner of the platform. She blinked up at the sky. The great milky river above had begun to reveal itself. Kiya breathed in the cool night air.

'If each of us becomes a star when we die,' she said, 'then one day the night will no longer be the night, for the dark sky will be full of light.'

Tahar turned to her. 'What a strange idea. But our bodies do not burst into flame when we die,' he reasoned. 'Instead they return to the earth, and soon even our bones disappear.'

Kiya turned away. She loved his lessons in observation—but she was not interested in one now. She wanted to know what was in his heart. He'd paused, and she felt his eyes upon her.

'But if we do become stars after we die, then you are right,' he admitted. 'We shall light up the night.'

'If we are destined to die, then I wish to die knowing the truth,' Kiya said finally. She had opened the door; she could not stop now. 'And you can die knowing you did not conceal it from me.'

Tahar stepped across the platform and joined her. 'And so I will give you the truth.' He reached out his hand and offered it to her. 'But you must hold my hand while I tell it, or I may just fall over the edge.'

Obligingly Kiya took his hand, and Tahar began. 'I have anguished over your questions,' he said, 'but not for the reasons you might suspect. I have thought about them because it pained me most profoundly to hear them, and it told me that I have failed.'

Kiya felt her hand grow moist inside his.

'I have failed because before I met you I had grown desperate—so desperate that I considered bartering the life of another for my own gain. I was no better than the chieftains and kings who play with people's lives like cones and reels in a game of *senet*.'

Tahar pulled her hand closer to his face, and enveloped it in both of his hands.

'You changed that. You reminded me that you were human and that I was, too. How could I wish to be accepted by others and yet not accept you? How could I wish for peace between Redlanders and Blacklanders and still intend to sell you like a sack of grain? Forgive me for taking so long to understand, dear woman. Nay, I did not intend to trade you. I extended our journey because I could not bear the idea of parting from you. Nubia was a ruse, a lie. It was the most distant destination I could contrive. I could not admit it to myself at first, but slowly I came to realise that I would never have sold you—not to Bandir nor to anyone else. I never wished to part with you. The only reason I did was because you showed me that your life is your own, as mine is my own. You made me understand the value of freedom. You made me a better man.'

He pressed her hand to his lips.

Kiya kept her eyes closed and let his words sink into her heart. They were the words she had yearned to hear, for they confirmed what she had always known: Tahar was a noble man, a good man. In a world gone mad, he was sane. He did not need to use others to achieve his ends. He saw the beauty and the wonder of the world and it was…*enough*.

'But there is another reason I have failed,' he continued. 'I have never told you that I spend every waking moment thinking about you. Even when I am asleep I see you in my dreams. You have assaulted my body and invaded my heart. I no longer wish to be anywhere but by your side. I no longer wish to go anywhere unless you are with me. I no longer wish to find my homeland because I have already found it. It is you. You are my homeland. As long as I am with you I am happy. I am at peace. I am home. I... I love you. I do not even know your name, but I love you.'

Kiya opened her eyes. He was on his knees before her, as if he were praying before a sacred altar. Kiya bent and met him there, her spirit overflowing with love. 'Kiya,' she said. 'That is my name. Just Kiya.'

'Ah,' he said. 'Kiya. That is a beautiful name.'

'I believe that is the first time I've ever said it aloud.'

'Nay, not the first time.'

'What?'

'In the cave—you said it the morning you awoke.'

'Then why did you not call me by my name?'

'I knew you would deny it, and then probably say something about your imaginary family in Abydos.'

She could not see his face, but she knew he smirked.

'It takes a jackal to know a jackal,' he added.

He put her hand to his lips and kissed it, a long, tender kiss.

Stay away from men, Kiya, her mother had warned. *They only mean to possess you, to enslave you.* If only she could explain to her mother how good this man was to her, how kind.

They sat in silence. *What else to say?* There was nothing—unless she were to tell him that she had tried valiantly to banish him from her mind, but to no avail. There he had remained, all those weeks while she had prepared for her betrothal to the King. He had hovered at the edge of her awareness, hacking away at her resolve, destroying all her well-laid plans. There was nothing to say unless to tell him that he had won, that she was still his captive, for he had long ago taken possession of her heart.

'Tahar?'

'What is it, Kiya?'

'I love you, too.'

Forgive me, Mother, but I do. She stared out at the lone fire in the distance. It danced and flickered, a tiny uprising against the increasing darkness.

Let us stay here for ever. It did not matter that Memphis might have fallen, nor that the Great River would not rise. It did not matter that tomorrow, when they rolled the large rock aside once again, they might indeed meet their end. All that mattered was this night.

She found the place where his arm had been cut. She wished she could tend it, as he had done her own injuries that day in the cave. She stood on the tips of her toes and pressed her lips softly against the wound. She looked up and there were those eyes, fierce and luminous even in the darkness. They searched hers, probing for the answer to one last unuttered question.

Chapter Thirty-Seven

Yes, her eyes told him in silent answer.

He encircled her in his arms. He pressed his lips upon the back of her neck and kissed away her doubts. Then she felt the sensation of soft bites upon her shoulders. What was he doing? Whatever it was, she wanted him to do it more. She arched her head back and stared at the sky. There it was again, that great, milky river. It seemed so close, and as Tahar nibbled on her neck it began to flow.

Kiya rocked forward into Tahar's body. He absorbed her weight with a low moan and held her for a long while. Gently he turned her around, to face away from him, then kissed the side of her neck.

'I thought about you every second,' he whispered into her ear. 'I died when I lost you, and when I saw you on the royal terrace that day…your wedding day…' His voice was thick, his breath warm and musky. 'None of it matters now. All that matters is this night.'

Kiya leaned back into his embrace. If his hands had not been holding her by her waist, she was certain she would simply have floated away into the night. His soft lips continued to explore the back of her neck, and his hands set out on a path across her body. They forged a trail down her lower back, lingering upon her buttocks, where they trekked lightly up and down the soft rise. The kisses upon her neck grew deeper, and she felt a growing heat between her legs.

His hands set out again, on a trail to her waist and northward, to her breasts. They found the soft rises of her nipples and remained, grazing across them and causing them to tingle and tighten. Meanwhile his kiss became a gentle suck, as if he were extracting poison.

'Oh, Tahar,' she murmured, and she pushed back against him, lifting her arm behind her and running her hand through his hair. It was as if she were a harp and he was plucking her strings, making her whole body hum.

He pushed himself upward between the cleft of her buttocks, just as he had done that day in the oasis pool. She had imagined that moment a thousand times since then, and every time the memory made her skin itch with desire. Now that he was behind her again it was as if that itch were being scratched. He slid up and down the long fissure of her buttocks and she felt his alarming girth. Anxiety and yearning did a frenetic dance inside her mind, while her body rose up with a fearsome wanting.

They had been separated by circumstances, walls, and the whims of a desperate king. A thin silk dress was all that separated them now. He sucked her breast with greater intensity and her whole body began to ache with yearning. She wanted—needed—to turn around, to move her hands upon him as they moved upon her. She twisted, trying to face him, but his hands returned to her waist, keeping her facing away from him.

'No, no, my little cobra,' he whispered playfully, his tongue plunging into her ear.

He wanted to drive her mad. He wanted to wind her desire so tightly that she begged him for release. But his aims were too ambitious, for already he had become engorged to the point of pain. He had never wanted a woman as he wanted her. It was as if he were being drawn into her by some invisible force that was stronger than any army, more powerful than any king.

He feared to face her...feared what he might do given the opportunity to kiss her succulent red lips. *This is her first time*, he reminded himself, though her movements suggested that she would not be shy. Had she thought about the oasis, as he had? Had she, too, gone over and over those moments of passion in her mind, keeping that intense desire alive in her body like the embers of a nomad's fire?

His hands dived beneath her tunic and he cradled her breasts, possessing them, feeling their lovely weight. How many times had he pictured doing this? Surely as many times as there were stars in the sky. Her skin was so soft and supple beneath his touch. He wanted to feel it—all of it—against his body.

He bent down and grasped the bottom of her dress. She gave no resistance as he lifted it up over her head, revealing her naked backside. He prayed she would not turn around, because he knew that to look at her face under the starlight would make him lose control. He needed to make this special for her. He needed to go slowly.

He unwound his makeshift loincloth and cast it aside. Naked and throbbing with lust, he positioned himself behind her once again. Her bare body melted against his and he claimed it with his hands. They tumbled over all her delicious curves and ridges. It was as if he'd unwrapped a new layer of her, and he wished to explore every last inch.

Keeping his feet planted behind her, he twisted his body around hers and bent low, his lips closing in upon her nipple once again.

'Oh...' she breathed as his mouth tugged in a gentle rhythm, and he felt her body stiffen with want.

They remained entwined like that until low, rhythmic moans began escaping her lips.

He detached himself from her breast and stood tall once again. The heat between their bodies had expanded and their skin had become slick with their sweat. What would it feel like to slide up and down her slippery body? To push himself into her hot, wet entrance from behind? His desire stood throbbing against her backside. There was no cloth between them, nothing to prevent them from becoming one.

He was so close.

All he would have to do...

She could not endure it any longer. There he was— so large and so hot behind her. Hastened by the moisture of her own sweat, his desire slid against the small of her back, as if begging for release. But it was she who was begging, for the searing ecstasy of his lips upon her breast had been too much to bear.

'Please,' she cried. 'Please.'

She stood on her toes. And then he was there, pushing himself inside her from behind.

'Ah...' he groaned into her ear, and a fiery pain ripped through Kiya's body.

It was him, the whole of him, entering her. His hands clasped her waist and he pushed, aided by Kiya's own wetness, up through the painful tightness.

'Oh…please…' Tahar moaned, and then his entirety was inside her and they were one.

The pain was exquisite. Tahar moved slowly up and down, touching the deepest parts of her. The feeling was like nothing she could have imagined. She was so full of him. All of her body seemed to be crying out for the sweet agony he delivered with each thrust. His breaths grew frenzied, his movements more rapid. He nuzzled his face into her hair and seemed to become lost.

Then he froze. Kiya sensed his efforts to gain control of himself. She could feel his throbbing heat. Gently, he pulled himself out of her. Then he turned her around to face him. He grasped her face in his arms and pushed his lips upon hers.

Those lips. They were the lips she craved. The ones that pushed and probed, that funnelled his vast desire into her with such gentleness. But this time his mouth was hotter, wetter. It moved faster and more powerfully against her own. His hands toyed ruthlessly with her nipples while his tongue plunged unapologetically into her mouth.

She felt her entrance begin to throb with renewed longing and the pain melted away. She wanted him back inside her. She wanted to feel him plunge into her once again while he kissed her. She wanted him to possess her completely, to flood her with himself.

She pushed her hips against him.

He felt the push of her hips and the return of her longing. He smiled to himself. Ah, this was going to be sweet. He kissed her hard with his mouth and let his finger slip gently into her.

'Oh…' she breathed.

She was so incredibly wet. He stroked her gently. Softly.

His kisses became softer, too. He withdrew his tongue from her mouth. Then he traced his finger along her lips. He would return to them soon. Now he had other business. He kissed her breasts—a dozen tiny kisses finishing at her nipples—the right then the left.

He kissed down her stomach, arriving at her navel and pillaging it with his tongue. He continued kissing downward until he found himself on his knees, humble before the Goddess.

Her hands tousled his hair. *What are you doing?* they asked.

He caressed her lovely buttocks. *Just you wait,* they told her. He kissed her soft, curly mound, then let his tongue probe deeper. He could hear her suck in a breath. He reassured her, moving his hands across her muscular legs. He moved his tongue slowly up and down her folds. Once. Twice. Her fingers raked across his head. Thrice.

Her body shivered. *Yes, my love,* it seemed to say. She opened her legs slightly, reminding him of that day in the cave. Gods, how he had wanted to feel her fingernails in his hair then. Now he had earned it.

He moved his tongue slowly: he did not want to scare her. Her buttocks flexed. Her stomach moved up and down. Her obvious hunger made him wild with lust. He made his tongue taut and traced the soft contours of her entrance. Then he probed deeper. Her hands planted themselves firmly on his head. He pushed his tongue into her. Her hot wetness enveloped him. Her hands squeezed and her body shivered. She was nearing the edge.

Seth's teeth, so was he. He pulled her down to her knees and their lips met again. They twisted around each other, their bodies sliding against each other, unable to get close enough. They writhed and coiled, stretching to discover every hill and valley, every plain of flesh—like two serpents inextricably entwined, tangled together beyond time.

Tahar rocked backwards, lacing her fingers with his as he lay back upon the ground—*atop the Great Pyramid of Stone*—desperate to feel her above him. He pulled her down until her hands were flat on the ground and her legs were straddling his waist. He could feel her hot, wet entrance. It rubbed against him, teasing him. Would she do what needed to be done? Perhaps he could nudge her.

'I have to tell you a secret,' he said, thrusting his hips upwards.

'What secret?'

'Do you remember the day in the cave? When I extracted the venom from your leg?'

'Yes, of course. That was incredibly kind of you. It was beyond kind. It was—'

'There was no venom to extract,' Tahar said.

'What?'

'I lied. It was an excuse. I wished to get closer to you.'

He watched her shadowy expression in the starlight. It moved from confusion to surprise to indignation and finally to thrill in fascinating, irresistible waves.

Her eyes narrowed. 'You are a wretched demon,' she said, smiling.

'You have no idea how badly I wanted you that day,' he said.

'I must punish you for your treachery.' She positioned him at her entrance and leaned down to kiss him.

And it was the most delicious kiss she'd ever tasted. Feeling the tip of his need hover at her entrance while she entwined her tongue with his sent an ache through her body so sweet it verged on pain. She pushed herself onto him slowly, teasingly, giving and then taking back, until he groaned with yearning. She kissed him again. Then she pushed a little more. More kissing. Finally, she had sheathed him.

He let out a howling groan. Then he placed his hands on her waist and rocked her gently up and down. A strange wave of pleasure began to grow within her. It felt so good, and his gentle encouragement stimulated a haunting need. She felt her whole body begin to curl up into a tight ball of want. They continued to rock, faster and faster, until she felt as if she were careening down the side of the pyramid.

Or maybe they were careening together.

Then—*crash*. She shattered above him. Her body convulsed in waves of pleasure and release. What strange, wonderful feeling was this? A second later he followed her—exploding into a million pieces—and she shivered as he throbbed inside her. She collapsed upon him and they lay together, still joined, breathing heavy breaths. He pulled her onto his chest and they embraced for what seemed like minutes, hours, a lifetime.

Finally Kiya rolled over onto her back. And there was Thoth, in his full, glowing glory. She had not even noticed he had risen. She peered at Tahar as the moon's soft glow washed his handsome face with light. Already she missed their joining. Already she craved his touch.

Together, they stared up at the great globe and the infinity beyond it. Tahar retrieved his headdress and placed it beneath their heads. He lifted her arm and placed a dozen long, lazy kisses upon it. She turned to him and stared into his eyes, breathing in the delicious odour of his breath.

'I don't want this night to end,' she said.

'It never will,' he said. He rolled over on top of her and began kissing her again.

Chapter Thirty-Eight

They were two nomads who had found each other, two solitary serpents who twisted and coiled together until it was unclear where one ended and the other began. There, at the centre of the known world, two beleaguered souls converged and their burden of solitude was lifted.

Soon Thoth sank near the horizon and the stars began to disappear from the sky. Kiya buried her head into the space under Tahar's arm, vowing never to forget how beautifully they had shone.

Ra came in a burst of light, despite how much Kiya wished him away. A memory of that morning of the grain raid rippled through her body, and she half expected to find a viper at her feet. An epiphany struck.

'Tahar, whenever you save my life a serpent precedes you.'

'What do you mean?'

'The day of the raid, a viper appeared on my foot before you captured me.'

'But I captured you. I did not save your life.' Tahar tilted onto his side and gazed at her quizzically.

'You *did* save my life,' Kiya said. 'Or did you not notice the arrows that flew past me just before you lifted me onto Meemoo?'

'Ah, the arrows…I did see those.'

'I was a fool to resist you.'

'Indeed you were. But thanks to my formidable strength, you were not able to.' Tahar flashed Kiya a self-assured grin.

'I believe you saved me even before that moment,' said Kiya.

'How so?'

'You waved your headdress upon the bluff that day, just before the Sun God rose.'

Tahar lifted a brow. 'How did you know that was me?'

'I guessed,' said Kiya, smiling. 'Your warning caused a stir amongst the workers. It scared the viper that had coiled around my ankle.'

Tahar reached his arm down her body and circled her ankle with his hand. 'This ankle?' He dived beneath the headdress and kissed it.

'You saved me a second time after I was bitten by the asp,' Kiya said, enjoying the softness of his lips upon her skin.

'I will own to that without protest,' was Tahar's muffled response. 'And now I am obliged to kiss your inner thigh.'

He moved his lips upon her skin softly, almost imperceptibly, causing her whole body to shiver.

'The third serpent appeared only days ago,' she pronounced.

'It did?' asked Tahar, emerging from under the headdress.

'Aye. It was a golden cobra, rising from the base of

King Khufu's crown on the day of my wedding. Khufu was the third serpent.'

'Khufu *himself* was the serpent?'

'And you saved me from him.'

Tahar shook his head. 'But how did I save you, dear woman, if I am the reason the King condemned you to death?'

'You saved me because if you had not appeared I would have wed the King and my life would have ended.'

Tahar lay back and stared at the sky. 'You would have become a great queen. I dare say your life would have begun.'

'A life of lies and manipulations—a prison of pomp and power. No life worth living.'

Tahar pulled her atop him and placed a dozen soft kisses on each of her fingertips. 'I do not believe in prophesies, but I will admit that in this case your mother may have been right. Three serpents did try to take your life. And the third almost succeeded.'

'Almost,' said Kiya triumphantly, 'but not quite.' She touched her lips to his.

The Sun God moved higher in the sky. They kissed until his rays poured over them and tiny beads of sweat began to form upon their skin.

'We must be on our way soon,' Kiya said. 'If Imhoter made it through the night he will be arriving presently.'

Kiya cringed. *If he had made it.*

She stood and gazed out at the workers' village but could not discern any movement in the harbour or adjacent river. If Imhoter was coming for them he was moving in the shadows, invisible even from above. She fixed her gaze southward, where small rivulets of smoke twisted upwards from Memphis and the palace's strong walls glowed white in the morning light. Neither victor nor vanquished could be seen; the city looked almost serene.

Tahar lay upon his back, gazing up at Kiya's naked body, now drenched in Ra's light. 'If I am to pass into the next world on this day, let this be the last thing I remember.'

Kiya reached out and offered her hand. Today they would discover if Imhoter had survived, and if they would survive, too. And yet Kiya was content. She looked into Tahar's eyes. It had all been worth it.

But they could not delay any longer: they needed to descend. Kiya placed her silk dress over her head while Tahar fashioned his headdress into a taut loincloth around his middle.

'You are so beautiful in that dress,' said Tahar. 'I have never seen anyone more beautiful.'

Kiya felt a tear of gratitude find its path down her cheek. 'You are kind. You have always been so kind to me,' she said.

It was cool and dark inside the tomb once more. To Kiya, the air felt thicker than it had yesterday, the enclosed space more suffocating.

As they began their downward trek her mind raced. What if Imhoter had been taken? What if the Libu and Nubian raiders—or the King himself—had deemed Imhoter too great a threat to allow the holy man to live? Imhoter's demise would surely spell doom for Kiya and Tahar, though as they descended the tunnel, Kiya could only think of Imhoter himself, whom she had grown to love like a father. She could not bear the thought of opening the door of the Pyramid and not seeing his kind, wrinkled face, his mysterious eyes staring back at her.

'It was dark like this where I was imprisoned,' Kiya said absently, trying to calm her worried mind. 'I could not discern whether it was day or night.'

'You were taken to the prison after we parted?' asked Tahar.

'Nay, I was kept in the basement of the Royal Harem— in a storage room guarded by a barred metal door.'

'But how did you escape?'

'Iset, one of the King's concubines, visited me there. At Imhoter's behest, she delivered me a heel of bread.' Kiya thought of the poisoned wine, but did not mention it. 'The bread contained a metal rod. Did Imhoter not tell you of this ploy while you were locked away together?'

'He said only that he held hope for your arrival,' said Tahar.

'The holy man reveals little,' said Kiya, walking slowly downwards. 'He surrounds himself in mystery.'

'That is true. But how did you manage to break out of the room with only a small metal rod?' asked Tahar.

'There is a stream that runs through the cell. It is guarded by small metal bars. I used the rod to bend the bars enough to squeeze through them. I followed the stream until I was released into the King's Shallows.'

'And the Shallows led to the River?'

'Aye, though I had to squeeze through another barrier before I reached it.'

'How did you squeeze?'

'What do you mean, how did I squeeze?' Kiya asked, confused.

'Would you say it was...like a serpent?'

'I suppose...' said Kiya.

They walked on in silence for several moments. Her mother's words filtered into her mind. *Beware the three serpents. Each will try to take your life. The third will succeed, unless you become like.* That was all she had said. It had never occurred to Kiya that that had been all she had meant to say. *Like what?* Kiya had always wondered, but now her mother's last message rang perfectly clear.

Like a serpent.

A serpent was what she had needed to become, and she had. She had squeezed and swum and slunk her way out of the Shallows. Her silken dress shimmering like a second skin, she had slithered onto the docks and stolen her way to the slaves' quarters where Tahar and Imhoter had waited, holding out hope that she could do it, that she could make it.

'That is it. That is the meaning of the prophesy,' she said, and her words echoed in the tunnel like prayers.

'Perhaps some illusions are not false.'

'It was not just an illusion,' said Kiya. 'I did not tell you this, but my mother spoke that prophesy to me the day she died. I was quite young. I scarcely remembered it until the day of the raid.'

Tahar was quiet. After several moments he spoke again. 'It is hard to lose a parent in one's youth. I lost my father as a boy.'

'You did? How?'

'You must tell me first how you lost your mother,' Tahar said lightly. 'Terms of trade.'

Tahar's body was following so closely behind hers that she could feel its warmth. She knew that if she were to stumble upon any stone he would be there to catch her.

'The story may seem to you fantastical,' Kiya warned.

'I will never doubt you again,' said Tahar.

Kiya described her mother's place in the late King's

harem. She explained her mother's special magic, her ability to tell tales, and the love she'd given to Kiya so grandly and fiercely. Kiya recounted the day of the raid on the harem and how she had found herself, at the age of seven, alone and hungry on the streets of Memphis.

'Then you are the daughter of a king,' said Tahar in wonder. 'You are noble.'

'It was my mother who was truly noble, for she refused to be taken alive,' Kiya said proudly, though she knew the statement was not entirely true. In a sense her mother had begun to kill herself long before the raiders had invaded the harem. It had not been milk of goat that had filled the vials from which her mother had drunk so greedily.

What pain had Kiya's mother suffered that she should fall under the spell of the dangerous tonic? What terrible trauma had she endured that she would leave her beloved daughter alone in the world, without putting up so much as a fight? It was a mystery that Kiya feared she would never solve. Besides, she liked this version of her mother—the noble concubine.

'Now tell me of you, Tahar. What of your homeland? Terms of trade.'

As they spiralled ever downward Tahar filled the empty tunnel with his words. He spoke of a land beyond Kiya's imagination—a place of endless plains rich with grasses that nourished goats, sheep and cattle, and strong, passionate people who travelled with their herds. He described a sky so thick with clouds that they blocked Ra's rays, where freezing rain floated down from the sky and blanketed the land in an ashen white cloak.

Tahar described his intrepid father and his cautious mother, and the terrible storm that had left him an orphan at the edge of the desert. He told her of the kindness of the Meshwesh Libu, and the wonder he had felt as he'd discovered the desert for himself.

'The people who live in a place often do not see it,' explained Tahar. 'It is sometimes only the foreigner who can truly grasp its beauty.'

Kiya thought of the endless mounds of amber sand they had traversed. The Big Sandy was desolate and deadly, but to Kiya's eyes it had also been beautiful—an ocean of gentle, undulating waves frozen in time. Tahar was right. If the Big Sandy had seemed a marvel, how might the steppes of Tahar's homeland seem?

'I should like to discover your homeland for myself,' said Kiya.

'I should like to rediscover it with you.'

They had arrived at the end of the tunnel. They passed through the hidden entrance and resettled the secret stone. Together, they kicked their feet in the dust of the flat staging area and studied a splinter of sunlight that had entered via a crack at the entrance. What lay beyond that crack was their salvation…or perhaps their death.

'Whether in this life or the next,' said Tahar, 'let us make the journey together.'

He pulled Kiya into his arms and gave her a long, deep kiss. Then he pushed back the stone.

Chapter Thirty-Nine

'Touched by the Gods,' said a familiar voice, 'both of you.'

A shaft of light poured into the tomb and Imhoter's tall, slim figure took shape amidst the brightness.

'I did not even need to knock.'

Kiya shrieked with joy. She ran into the priest's embrace.

'Did I not teach you anything about decorum, young Hathor?' he asked, taking her into his arms.

She lingered in his embrace for as long as he would allow. He was alive. Imhoter was alive! She had shouted at the Gods, taunted them, even doubted their existence, but in this moment she thanked them with all her heart.

'Well met, dear Imhoter,' said Kiya. 'Very well met indeed.'

The old priest's robe had been ripped. Its ragged edge no longer skirted the ground and its lotus-white folds were marred with stains of filth. Half-moons of sagging skin had appeared beneath his eyes, and he carried his shoulders in a tired slump.

He found a seat upon a boulder near the entrance. 'It was a long night.'

'We feared Chief Bandir had taken the city,' Kiya said.

'He tried,' said Imhoter. 'His army attacked in the night, but the people of Memphis gathered around the perimeter of the wall—women and men alike. Some wielded weapons—spears and arrows and the like. Others used pottery shards and stones. I have never seen the people of Khemet display such unity or such bravery. They fought off the Libu horde valiantly.'

'It was your warning that saved them,' observed Kiya.

'Nay, it was you, dear girl,' Imhoter said, searching Kiya's eyes.

'What do you mean?'

'They fought in your name.'

'What?'

'Hathor the Brave, they call you now.' Imhoter's eyes sparkled.

'I don't understand. The King wants me dead.'

'So do the highborns—but there are so few of them.' He lifted an eyebrow. 'Commoners vastly outnumber highborns—a small fact that Khemetian Kings tend to forget.' Imhoter rubbed his ancient hand over his sweat-stained forehead. 'When word spread that you had escaped, the commoners of Memphis rejoiced. They were astounded by the valour you displayed upon your wedding day. Some say you acted out of honour, but most believe you acted out of…love.' Imhoter stole a glance at Tahar. 'I tend to agree with most.'

Kiya smiled. The mysterious old man had been right all along. It was love that triumphed—whether in the minds of a people or in the depths of a street orphan's heart.

Imhoter stood. 'I bring one last bit of news,' he said, almost offhandedly. 'In the small hours of the morning, as Bandir's army dispersed, the Great River began to rise.'

Kiya felt her knees unlock. She found a seat in the place where Imhoter rested. 'Pray, dear Imhoter, what did you say?'

'The River swells,' Imhoter said, a tiny grin dancing at the edges of his mouth. 'The drought is over.'

'But how can you be certain?'

'I checked the King's river steps this morning. Three steps are already submerged. You were right all along, oh, Mother of the Flood. Hapi is late, but it has finally come,' Imhoter said.

Kiya locked eyes with Tahar. 'It was the man you see before you who predicted it,' Kiya told Imhoter. 'He taught me to read the signs.'

Imhoter regarded Tahar. 'Is that so? Hem, it seems we Blacklanders have much to learn from the people of the Red.'

'And the King? Does he still seek our heads?' asked Kiya.

'The King has been humbled. He has expressed his contrition to me, and realised that he was mistaken to condemn you. Soon he will want you back.' Imhoter glanced out at the dry plain. 'I fear he seeks you already, though he will not find you. Come. Your means of escape awaits.'

They passed through the workers' entrance and the figure of a familiar-looking beast came into view. 'It cannot be!' said Kiya. 'Meemoo?'

'Did I not promise I would take care of your beast?'

said Imhoter. He stroked the horse's long neck. 'And it is as well, for he is the only donkey I have ever met large enough to bear me without complaint.'

'He is not a donkey at all, dear Imhoter,' explained Kiya, kissing Meemoo on the snout. 'He is a horse—a beast from the Land of the Grass.'

'He will do just fine,' said Tahar, stroking Meemoo's long mane. 'Thank you, Imhoter.'

'I am afraid I have been unclear,' said Imhoter. 'This… um…*horse*, as you call him, is not your means of escape. By the looks of him I would guess that he is as old as I am.' Imhoter placed his foot in a stirrup and hoisted himself into the saddle. He held out his hand to Kiya and helped her do the same. 'Come, Tahar,' he said, holding out a helping hand. 'We are to the River.'

Tahar flashed Imhoter a sly grin, then broke into a run. 'Catch me if you can!' he shouted as his long legs carried him towards the Great River.

Without any encouragement Meemoo burst into a trot, and in less than an hour they were standing before a small sailing boat, bobbing in the shallows of the Great River.

'Behold your escape vessel,' announced Imhoter.

The boat was not large. The rectangular cabin that defined its deck was scarcely as big as a goose's coop. Behind it a mast stretched upwards, lifting a small square sail into the air. Before it two sets of oars rested in their positions near the bow, and the prow was carved into the traditional face of a hedgehog.

'It is magnificent,' Tahar said, his eyes filling with tears.

'It is the smallest boat in the King's Fleet,' Imhoter said, winking. 'He will not miss it.'

As they climbed aboard the vessel Kiya observed that it was extremely well made. Short, well-dressed planks had been fitted together expertly to form the sturdy hull, which was further stabilised by the strong cross-planks of the deck.

The cabin itself was made of a combination of wood and tightly woven papyrus, and a small, ornately carved door guarded its entrance.

Imhoter stepped halfway through the door and stretched out his arm to Kiya. 'Come, let me show you something,' he said.

Inside, a richly decorated space similar to the one Kiya had shared with the King was spread before them. Thick, lush carpets covered the floors, and exquisite embroideries adorned the walls. A large, deeply padded bed, abundant with pillows, crowded the far corner.

Tahar stole a conspiratorial glance at Kiya, then addressed the priest.

'I am without words, Holy Imhoter,' he said. 'This is a debt I…we…can never repay.' He pulled Kiya beside him.

'You have already paid it,' said Imhoter. The priest handed the lovers two goblets of water, which they drank heartily. 'It was your ability to read the signs of the flood that helped lift Khemet's despair,' Imhoter continued. 'It was your love that inspired Hathor the Brave. But here is what I wish for you to see.' Imhoter pointed to a large wooden box on the floor. He opened the lid to reveal hundreds of gold ingots—a king's treasure. 'This is for you, my dear,' he said. 'It is my gift to you.'

Kiya stared into the treasure chest, unable to speak. It was enough gold to supply an army.

'It is my life's earnings,' said Imhoter, his brown face all aglow. 'It is all for you, my Kiya.'

Kiya stared at the priest in disbelief. 'I am sorry, I do not understand. And how do you know my true name? Dear Imhoter, I am confused.'

'Hem,' said Imhoter, shaking his head. 'Nay, of course you don't understand—for I have not explained any of it.' He touched his bony chin. 'We have precious little time, but I think I should like to tell you a brief story. Perchance you would like to hear it?' he asked.

'I love stories,' said Kiya.

'That does not surprise me at all,' said Imhoter, easing onto a cushioned bench. 'Have you ever heard the story *How the Date Palm Got Its Dates*?'

'Of course,' said Kiya. 'It was one of my mother's favourites. I haven't heard it in a long while.'

Kiya's mother had told it so often that Kiya had almost grown tired of it. Now, she treasured it more than a hundred sacks of grain.

'Would you enjoy hearing it again? Come, sit beside me.' Imhoter patted the soft seat beside him. 'Indulge an old man.'

Puzzled, Kiya sat upon the bench. Across the cabin, Tahar watched them curiously.

Imhoter traced the leopardskin border of his sleeve. One of the threads had become loose and he twisted it in his fingers nervously. 'Forgive me,' he said. 'It has been a long time since I have told this particular tale. I must be sure to tell it well.'

Imhoter cleared his throat and began.

'There was and there was not, a lion, a leopard and a monkey. The monkey had the most joyful heart. She swung through the trees all day long, laughing and playing. The lion, who was King of the land, admired the monkey, for her endless antics made his own heart lighter. So he took her from the trees and brought her to his den. Without her beloved trees the monkey became sad. Slowly, her laughter faded…

'One day the leopard visited the cave and met the sad monkey. Being a leopard, he also loved to play in the trees. He understood the monkey as the lion could not. That night, while the lion slept, he helped the monkey escape. All night the leopard and the monkey played together in the trees. They fanned themselves with giant leaves and leaped between the branches. They plucked little brown fruits and made beautiful garlands. At the end of the night they hung the biggest garland from the loveliest tree as a symbol of their joy and love.

'The next morning they awoke to the lion's angry roar. He had discovered the leopard and the monkey sleeping in the trees. The lion shook the trees until they both came tumbling out. He bit off the leopard's ear and brought the monkey back to his den, where he tied a rope around her leg. There she lived in sorrow for the rest of her life. But she never forgot the leopard, nor the beautiful necklace they made together. It hangs in the date palm still. And that is how the date palm got its dates.'

Kiya turned to Imhoter. Her eyes swam in a bath of tears. 'I am the necklace. And you…you are my father.'

Imhoter stared at Kiya and his eyes glowed with an inner light. 'You are clever. You understand the story.'

'But—but why did you never tell me?

'I was not certain until very recently.'

Kiya felt dizzy, as if the whole boat had begun to spin. 'When?'

'On your wedding day, when you told me that you

had been born in the royal harem. You are unusually tall, you see, and King Sneferu was quite short. So was your mother.' Imhoter stood to his full height, bumping his head upon the ceiling of the cabin. 'I am also tall—do you see?' He smiled. 'But it wasn't until you stood up to the King that I was completely sure. As I watched you tell him to take your life I did not see you, but your mother. She made a similar plea to the deceased King long ago, for she had betrayed him.'

'By falling in love with you.'

'Aye.'

'And he punished you for it,' Kiya said. *By making you a eunuch.*

'Yes.'

'And Khufu will never let you forget that you betrayed his father.'

'Yes.'

'I thought that I had disappointed you beyond measure,' said Kiya. She took Imhoter's hands in hers.

'On the contrary, my dear, you made me as proud as a father could ever be.'

Imhoter squeezed Kiya's hands and she could see his lips trembling. She stood. She stared into his eyes and saw that they were *her* eyes. Dark, with golden flecks of light.

'Father,' she said, and fell into his arms.

Her heart was overflowing and she began to sob. She was not a parentless street orphan, nor the starving Mute Boy, nor a captive queen. She was not even King Khufu's half-sister, as she had always believed herself to be. She was not royal at all, in fact. Nay, she was better than that—she was the child of a truly good man.

'I tried to find you,' Imhoter said. 'After the raid on the harem. I looked for years. I begged the Gods...'

'So much time and I was right at your feet,' Kiya said. 'On the streets of Memphis.'

Imhoter faced her. 'Daughter, can you ever forgive me?'

Kiya let the word sink into her soul. *Daughter*. It was like music. *Daughter*. Like the soft rustle of date palm leaves tickled by the breeze. *Daughter*.

'Father, there is nothing to forgive.'

Imhoter's eyes were wells of tears. 'Now I may journey to the next world, for I am happier than I have ever been or ever shall be,' he said.

'Will you not come with us?' Kiya asked suddenly. 'Please, join us, Father. We shall see amazing things. We shall measure the size of the world.'

Imhoter gave Kiya a sad smile. 'But there are only two sets of oars, my dear.'

'You have given us all your wealth. Why not come with us? Flee this tempestuous realm and find peace at sea...with us.'

Imhoter shook his head. 'What gives a king's life more value than a farmer's, or even a beggar's?' he asked wistfully. 'Your mother asked me that question long ago, and at the time I could not give her a satisfactory answer. Now I know that the answer is nothing. Nothing makes anyone's life more valuable than another. I must continue to serve the people of Khemet.' He gave Kiya a deep bow. 'Besides, I am too old for journeys.'

Imhoter turned towards the small doorway.

'You must see the world, daughter, then return to Khemet and tell me what you have seen. You know where

I will be.' Imhoter blinked back tears as he embraced Kiya and kissed her on the head.

Kiya followed Imhoter through the cabin door and helped him over the rails and into the shallow water. Imhoter stared down at his legs.

'The water was below my knees when we boarded only an hour ago. Now it is above them!' he exclaimed. He clapped his hands together like a child, then lifted the mooring stake and tossed it onto the deck. 'Go now—you must escape the King's reach.'

Moments later Imhoter was sitting high atop Meemoo, standing at the shore of the river. The horse whinnied loudly as Imhoter shouted his goodbyes. 'Safe travels, blessed ones!' he called, waving his long arm. 'May your sails and your bellies always be full!'

Kiya blew him a kiss. She watched and waved until his body became a tiny, distant blur.

Or was that the blur of her tears?

Tahar put his hands around her shoulders. 'Are you all right?' he asked softly.

'Aye. Just glad for the time I had with him.'

'I know that feeling,' Tahar said. He sat down beside her. 'We shall return to Khemet one day.'

'With many tales to tell?' Kiya said, brightening.

'Many tales indeed!' Tahar said.

He kissed her cheek and stood. His chest might have been the sail itself, filled not with wind but with happiness. He walked about the deck with his arms folded, surveying every inch of the expertly crafted vessel. *This will serve us well*, his expression seemed to say.

Kiya could feel the force of the Great River's current carrying them northward, towards the Big Green. After a few moments she saw Tahar's figure atop the roof of the cabin. He let down the sails, then returned to the deck and took his position at the oars.

'The breeze is from the north now,' he said. 'It does not help us, so I shall.' And he began to row.

'Are you going to take us to the lands beyond the Big Green, then?' Kiya asked.

'My mother may yet live,' said Tahar. 'I should very much like you to meet her.'

'As would I,' Kiya said, admiring Tahar's strong limbs as they bent and flexed with purpose.

She was full of love for this humble, beautiful man.

And perhaps, she admitted, a bit of lust too.

She gazed out at the silky water for a long time and her lids grew heavy. She wandered into the cabin, removed her dress, and dived under the bed's fresh linens.

Her whole body relaxed and she lay there for what seemed like hours, dreaming dreams of the past and of the future. At length, she opened her eyes. A date was being placed into her mouth.

'You spoke my name while you slept,' said Tahar. 'I thought you were calling for me.'

'Did I? I am sorry I caused you to abandon your oars.' Kiya chewed, savouring the date's rich flavour.

'The oars will not miss me.' Tahar popped a date into his own mouth. 'I think it is safe to let the Great River take us now. No more labouring necessary—at least above the deck.'

He flashed her a mischievous grin. Kiya's eyes skimmed across his body and she felt a pang of longing shoot through her stomach. She buried her face in the pillows.

'It is too late to play shy, My Love,' Tahar said.

When she opened her eyes once again she saw that he had removed his loincloth.

'Your face is red,' said Tahar, lying down beside her. 'You must be angry with me because I finished all the dates.'

Kiya shook her head and smiled. He knew full well that it was the breathtaking sight of his naked masculinity that had made her blush.

'Do not fear, my dear, for I have set several lines and will soon have a nice fat fish for you.' He wrapped his arms around her.

'Of that I have no doubt,' said Kiya, finally able to speak.

'First I must take my rest,' he said, but his large hands were doing anything but resting. Soon he was atop her, slowly kissing her breasts. 'This is the best rest I think I have ever had,' he said, sucking and blowing in turn.

Delicate shivers danced across Kiya's body. Before she knew it he was tracing the length of her stomach with his tongue.

'I think it is the same for me,' said Kiya, giggling in ecstasy as he arrived at her womanly mound. 'It is a lovely rest.'

She had lived many years without knowledge of the amorous arts. Now it seemed she had discovered their chief artist.

Tahar returned to her lips, which he traced carefully with his finger. 'I love these lips,' he said.

Kiya smiled. 'Tahar, do you believe that we have been favoured by the Gods?' she asked. 'Do you think they steer our course?'

'I do not think so. I do not think the world is controlled by the Gods.'

'Then who do you think controls the world?'

Tahar's eyes flashed. 'Isn't it obvious, My Love?' he asked. '*You* do.'

Then he dived under the sheets and begged Kiya for her first command.

* * * * *

*If you enjoyed this story
check out Greta Gilbert's historical novella
MASTERED BY HER SLAVE*

SPECIAL EXCERPT FROM

(H) HARLEQUIN®
    ™

ℋISTORICAL

We are proud to present Georgie Lee's stunning
contribution to **THE GOVERNESS TALES**, a series of
four sweeping romances with fairy-tale endings,
by Georgie Lee, Laura Martin, Liz Tyner
and Janice Preston!

Read on for a sneak preview of
THE CINDERELLA GOVERNESS
by **Georgie Lee**, the first book in
Harlequin Historical's enticing new quartet
THE GOVERNESS TALES.

Joanna fell into his comforting embrace and the
temptation in his kiss. Her heart pounded with the risk and
the thrill of his body against hers. She rested her hands
on his chest and his strong pulse beneath her fingertips
reminded her she was young and alive and all her dreams
might still come true. A shiver coursed through her as he
traced her lips with his tongue, his breath one with hers
as he held her close. He tasted like the drink of strong
port she'd sneaked once at a soirée for the school patrons,
rich, sharp and forbidden. She savored him as she had the
liquor, each illicit taste making her crave more.

She slid her hands up over the sturdy curve of his
chest, past the white cravat and collar surrounding his
neck. With small circles she traced the smoothness of
the skin before raising her fingers to slide them into his

hair. In the circle of his arms was a belonging she'd never experienced before. Despite her being hidden away and ignored, he'd seen her for who she was and he wanted her. It almost made every risk she was taking with him worth it.

A faint darkness crept in beneath her bliss, like a mist along the ground at dusk. He had little to lose with this liaison while she might sacrifice everything for a fleeting bit of happiness. She clung to it like she did his biceps, his muscles hard beneath her grip, trying to forget reality, duty and consequences. Beyond the strength of his kiss, the tightness of his fingers against her back, nothing else had changed, not his situation or hers.

She withdrew her fingers from his hair and broke from his lips, but not his embrace. He eased his arms from around her waist, but left his hands to linger on the narrowness of it. Every argument against their being together nearly died on her tongue as she held his fierce gaze. The dreams of being with him that she'd entertained in the middle of the night felt more real than anything she'd experienced at Huntford Place. Her heart urged her to embrace whatever was happening between them and perhaps gain everything she'd ever desired.

Don't miss
THE CINDERELLA GOVERNESS by Georgie Lee,
available September 2016 wherever
Harlequin® Historical books and ebooks are sold.

www.Harlequin.com

Turn your love of reading into
rewards you'll love with

Harlequin My Rewards

**Join for FREE today at
www.HarlequinMyRewards.com**

Earn **FREE BOOKS** of your choice.

Experience **EXCLUSIVE OFFERS** and contests.

Enjoy **BOOK RECOMMENDATIONS**
selected just for you.

PLUS! Sign up now
and get **500** points
right away!

Earn **FREE REWARDS**
Join Today!
HarlequinMyRewards.com

MYR16R

HARLEQUIN®

A *Romance* FOR EVERY MOOD™

JUST CAN'T GET ENOUGH?

Join our social communities
and talk to us online.

You will have access to the latest
news on upcoming titles and special
promotions, but most importantly,
you can talk to other fans about your
favorite Harlequin reads.

Harlequin.com/Community

Facebook.com/HarlequinBooks

Twitter.com/HarlequinBooks

Pinterest.com/HarlequinBooks

THE WORLD IS BETTER WITH

Romance

Harlequin has everything from contemporary, passionate and heartwarming to suspenseful and inspirational stories.

Whatever your mood, we have a romance just for you!

Connect with us to find your next great read, special offers and more.

f /HarlequinBooks

🐦 @HarlequinBooks

www.HarlequinBlog.com

www.Harlequin.com/Newsletters

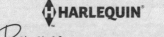

H HARLEQUIN®

A *Romance* FOR EVERY MOOD™

www.Harlequin.com

REQUEST YOUR
FREE BOOKS!

❤ HARLEQUIN®

❦ISTORICAL

Where love is timeless

2 FREE NOVELS PLUS 2 **FREE GIFTS!**

YES! Please send me 2 FREE Harlequin® Historical novels and my 2 FREE gifts (gifts are worth about $10). After receiving them, if I don't wish to receive any more books, I can return the shipping statement marked "cancel." If I don't cancel, I will receive 6 brand-new novels every month and be billed just $5.69 per book in the U.S. or $5.99 per book in Canada. That's a savings of at least 12% off the cover price! It's quite a bargain! Shipping and handling is just 50¢ per book in the U.S. and 75¢ per book in Canada.* I understand that accepting the 2 free books and gifts places me under no obligation to buy anything. I can always return a shipment and cancel at any time. Even if I never buy another book, the two free books and gifts are mine to keep forever.

246/349 HDN GH2Z

Name _____ (PLEASE PRINT)

Address _____ Apt. #

City _____ State/Prov. _____ Zip/Postal Code

Signature (if under 18, a parent or guardian must sign)

Mail to the **Reader Service:**
IN U.S.A.: P.O. Box 1867, Buffalo, NY 14240-1867
IN CANADA: P.O. Box 609, Fort Erie, Ontario L2A 5X3

Want to try two free books from another line?
Call 1-800-873-8635 or visit www.ReaderService.com.

* Terms and prices subject to change without notice. Prices do not include applicable taxes. Sales tax applicable in N.Y. Canadian residents will be charged applicable taxes. Offer not valid in Quebec. This offer is limited to one order per household. Not valid for current subscribers to Harlequin Historical books. All orders subject to credit approval. Credit or debit balances in a customer's account(s) may be offset by any other outstanding balance owed by or to the customer. Please allow 4 to 6 weeks for delivery. Offer available while quantities last.

Your Privacy—The Reader Service is committed to protecting your privacy. Our Privacy Policy is available online at www.ReaderService.com or upon request from the Reader Service.

We make a portion of our mailing list available to reputable third parties that offer products we believe may interest you. If you prefer that we not exchange your name with third parties, or if you wish to clarify or modify your communication preferences, please visit us at www.ReaderService.com/consumerschoice or write to us at Reader Service Preference Service, P.O. Box 9062, Buffalo, NY 14240-9062. Include your complete name and address.

HHI5